March 12 1993

BEFORE
AND
AFTER

Katherine Govier

For Eleanor & Eric
– so hospitable, such
a beautiful day. Thank you

Katherine

VIKING
Published by the Penguin Group
Penguin Books Canada Ltd, 2801 John Street, Markham, Ontario, Canada
L3R 1B4
Penguin Books Ltd, 27 Wrights Lane, London W8 5TZ, England
Viking Penguin Inc., 40 West 23rd Street, New York, New York 10010, USA
Penguin Books Australia Ltd, Ringwood, Victoria, Australia
Penguin Books (NZ) Ltd, 182-190 Wairau Road, Auckland 10, New Zealand
Penguin Books Ltd, Registered Offices: Harmondsworth, Middlesex, England

First published 1989
1   3   5   7   9   10   8   6   4   2

Printed and bound in the United States of America

"The King of Siam" first appeared in *Encounter* magazine;
"Toronto/New York" in *Saturday Night;* "Domain" in *Descant,* in slightly
altered form.

CANADIAN CATALOGUING IN PUBLICATION DATA

Govier, Katherine, 1948-
    Before and After

ISBN 0-670-82429-1

I. Title.

PS8563.085B44 1989   C813'.54   C88-094754-3
PR9199.3.G68B44 1989

BEFORE
AND
AFTER

Contents

The King of Siam

The King of Siam

Jane is in Paris when the news comes: her mother is dead in
the apple orchard in the Okanagan, where she and Jane's
father have retired, supposedly at peace. And Jane
remembers her mother dancing. Not with her father, Saturday night in the living-room, after a discussion about how
much hip she could use in the rhumba. He would be leading, driving her with both shoulders as one would a wheel-
barrow. "That much, no more," he ruled. Her slim hip
poked out; he put it back in its place, a stern man with a
measuring eye.

"Here I go with my best foot backward," her mother
would say, waggishly, because the man always led, and his
forward steps made her step out behind.

No, that is not what she remembers, but her mother dancing, alone, weekday mornings, letting loose, elbows pumping, her mouth a soundless smile. She looks like Mary
Martin. The words she sings are Mary's: "I'm gonna wash
that man right outa my hair . . . ." The record spins in the
dusty-bright air.

The house glares; the cloudless sky and the flat, snow-whitened lawns and streets bounce sunbeams through the picture windows. The beams explode geometrically again and again on motes of dust in the dry inside air, creating a painful brightness in all directions. Alone with the smallest child when the others have gone to school, her mother walks around in the forced-air heat with narrowed eyes, sometimes shading her brows with a forearm. The beige curtains are closed, to filter the light which could take two shades out of the upholstery in one season.

The house is a lightbox, her mother has two dimensions, like a paper doll glued onto sticks. The records are old ones in small jackets, the songs simple, like rhymes.

"Oh what a beautiful morning, oh what a beautiful day, I've got a wonderful feeling, everything's going my way."

Every morning it is the same. They have things to do. They will just put on a record while they work. They listen a few minutes and pretend to dust or sort tea-towels but inevitably are seduced. First, certain pieces of furniture have to be moved, his stuffed footstool and the glass-topped coffee-table with the three cones for legs. Then the choice — *Brigadoon? Carousel? The King and I?* They take off their shoes.

They are dancing. Not with each other, no, they move off into separate orbits, there in the veiled brilliance of the living room. Socks on the pink-beige carpet give shocks if they touch each other or the velvet chair. Bits of them arc through the hall mirror, and also in the glass of the picture frames. Cheap clichés these movements, but wildly sincere. The arched eyebrows, hands on knees, bug eyes for the benefit of the audience beyond the curtains fluttering over the forced-air vent. The faces out of which such words can come:

"I'm gonna wash that man right outa my hair, and send him on his way!"

Or the supple, breathy swaying, mouth slightly open:

"Some enchanted evening, you may see a stranger, you may see a stranger, across a crowded room . . ."

The room where such events can happen is somewhere else. But somewhere else is a place, a place you can get to, if you just keep going, going

until

it is not Jane, but just her mother dancing, Jane watching. Her mother fabulous and strong, her mother tough and funny. And Jane knows a kind of peace, almost holy. Her mother, the light, the music.

We are talking about the fifties, in the West. A growing city with a university, an industry; a small box house on a too wide street, her father working out of town on the oil rigs. The Oil Capital of Canada! Gateway to the North! But outside its boundaries, nowhere. West, but not coast, flattish, but not prairie, that was farther south. The American term "Midwest," conjuring visions of cornfields, did not apply. They call it parkland, but there were no parks, only a place where they sometimes went to see a herd of captive buffalo, brought back from near-extinction. During the gold rush, expeditions embarked from here for the Yukon; some lost their way; in all one hundred and twenty-eight people perished.

And there was the river, muscular, army-green, so wide it would lead Jane, years later, to scorn the Seine as puny. The North Saskatchewan's deep valley cut an S through the city, curling below Lolly Bacon, the treacherous toboggan hill, running straight under the High Level Bridge (One of the Seven Wonders of the World!) and looping the hill where stood the giant blue-roofed railway hotel. Then it straightened out to pass the refinery — when lit at night its scaffolds, arms and towers a fairy castle — and swept east, toward everything else.

In summer the family walked alongside the river, on a narrow path by the Outdoors Club, watching out for quicksand. In winter her father and the boys skied, on long light planks with leather lace-up boots. Jane stood by the back door looking after them down the walk. On either side the heaps of snow were piled over her head; she was too small to go out. Later, she went along, but she was clumsy and fell, and they were impatient.

Winter lasted from October to May. They were farther north than any other city of size except Moscow. In the depth of winter, the sun didn't come up until nine, and it was setting by four. Strange, then, it was not the dark she remembered, but the light. Winter days were dazzling: a clear sky and diamond sun on the packed dry snow, snowblindness as common as frostbite. And her mother dancing.

The rigs went south and so did they. Her mother's eyes went down, her back began to stoop. Something was wrong. Her mother seemed the victim of some terrible disease, consumed by things she wanted to be, or do, and couldn't. She never danced alone, only with him, her father, and it was not dancing any more, it was just obedience. He worked in an office by then.

By the time her father comes home, her mother is trussed with an apron, hands sticky with flour and water, facing into the corner where the sink is. It is a fascinating corner; the mouse is said to live in the back of the cupboard. Jane feels kin to that mouse: she was a mouse in her dance recital, and her father calls her Mouse. There are windows above the sink, looking into the backyard, at the flowering crab-apple tree which the waxwings visit in winter. Probably Jane is at the table drawing, invisible behind the door when her father pushes it open.

"Hi, honey."

He comes up behind and slaps her bottom. Her mother stiffens, turning her face toward him for the kiss, but keeping the chin down.

"My hands," she says, excusing herself. He opens the cupboard doors, taking a glass down with a hard clink, banging the door shut again, opening and shutting the refrigerator noisily. His movements are square, angry. He is already on his way back to the den, where he will sit and read the paper "in peace." Halfway down the hall his voice is louder.

"Kids out again?"

Her mother turns, whispers. "Go see your father. Talk to him."

She rises, looking down at her colouring book. The only thing that makes this bearable is that they are working together, mother and daughter. She knows she is an offering to forestall a perhaps inevitable wrath.

"Dad?"

"Is that you, Mouse?"

Still standing outside the door, not moving until requested to.

"Come in."

She pushes open the door. His feet are closest to her, on the footstool in socks; wide, almost square feet, with toes that arch and curl as if by their own inclination. He is behind these feet leaning back in the armchair; the paper is folded in his lap. He has put down the paper. Now she must prove herself worthy of his attention.

She is invited up close, to sit on his lap. He gives her a rough hug; she ducks his face because of the scratchy whiskers. His head is like a bullet, his neck thick and pocked. Everything about him is strange and threatening. She is perched there when another faint tap comes on the door. Her mother, without the apron, with clean hands. There is a discreet change in his voice, and he sits up. ''I have work to do, girls.'' They both slip out.

He doesn't want music on, music disturbs him at this hour. As dinner cooks Jane studies the record album. Anna and the King of Siam in sunset colours, before the flock of little round-faced children with blue-black hair.

''Shall we dance, On a bright cloud of music shall we fly? Shall we dance, shall we then say goodnight and mean goodbye?''

Anna was a beautiful, gentle woman who went to a strange land to look after the children. They were the King's children, not hers. The King was bald and mean, with blazing eyes and a very straight back, like Jane's father. He had unpredictable rages, he even put people to death if they displeased him. He was primitive, a brute. But Anna fell in love. Jane cannot understand what Anna sees in the King. And why did Anna go there in the first place? Reading closely, Jane discovers that Anna had another love, her true love, who died. Perhaps this was the case with her mother.

At five-thirty her father calls out his door about dinner — is it almost ready, or does someone want to get him another Scotch? Jane is sent to retrieve his glass. He has seated himself, by this time, at his desk and is working with a pencil and a ruler on large sheets of squared paper which roll up at the corners. She takes the glass to her mother, who pours more Scotch in it. By the time she reaches his door it happens. He cannot find the gum eraser.

''Nona! Nona!'' he roars.

Now Jane is in the hall outside his door, and can see them both. In the kitchen her mother's head, ever ready for alarm, rises up like some deer's hearing distant gunfire. She pushes in the drawer where she is counting out table-napkins. Jane hates the panicky, hobbled sound of her mother's heels.

''What is it, dear?'' sweetly, anxious.

"Who's been in this drawer? I told you not to let the kids at my things. Now I can't find my eraser."

"I don't think they have been. I've told them so many times."

Jane shrinks in the background. Has she taken the eraser? The accusation is so strong she thinks she must have.

His drawer slams.

"Oh, what's the point?" (bitterly, bitterly) "I can't get anything done around here."

After eating in silence, he pushes back his chair and announces that he has to go back to the office. Jane and her mother do the dishes together. After, her mother finds the eraser in the drawer, under a pile of envelopes. She reads to Jane, *The House at Pooh Corner*, before bed and she laughs, very hard, about Tigger falling out of the tree.

Jane lies awake in bed. Eventually her father comes home. His voice is still loud, and cross. Her mother murmurs, placating. They go to bed, in the room next to Jane. Jane doesn't want to hear the noises, so she sings to herself.

"Or perchance, when the *last leetle star* has leaved the sky, shall we still be together, with our arms around each other, and shall you be my new romance?"

Later the family found little to recommend these cities, little to remember. They moved to British Columbia, and her mother became more bitter, more crippled. Jane went away without regret. She didn't like ties, didn't want a man, never thought about it. She studied art, as her mother wished her to, and went to Paris. But she didn't paint. As she often said, she had nothing to paint. She worked, when she felt like it, writing features for Canadian newspapers. Her pieces always had some Canadian angle, that was how she sold them.

The day she learns that her mother has killed herself, not

just died, passively, but died actively, by her own hand, all
in the new blossoms of spring, Jane has lined up an interview with an artist. It is her father who telephones. Her
father is sorry, he has been sorry for years, but he does not
say so. And Jane, who thought she had forgiven him, is filled
with hate. All she can think of is his impatience, the way he
beat her mother down, the way her mother shrank. She puts
down the telephone. Then, because Jane is alone and has
nothing better to do, she goes to the interview.

The artist lives in the sixteenth district. Jane travels by
Métro, getting off at the stop he named, turns up narrower
streets than those she's passed through, and finds his door
with a tiny gold nameplate. He greets Jane sternly, and
turns his back. In the sitting room he brings a trolley, serves
tea, and madeleines (à la Proust! he points out in a way not
convivial but instructive). The artist is prairie Canadian,
and very good; Jane wept in the gallery looking at his pic-
tures. He shows her more. They are painted in egg tempera
and are of people in empty rooms, of light from two windows
hitting a corner, or sunglasses reflecting a flat horizon. She
says she is from Edmonton. He was recently there.

"A terrible place full of awful people! And they all look
just like you!"

The madeleines are crumbly and taste like dust. She men-
tions a few names.

"Oh yes! I saw him! He looks like he just came in from
bashing baby seals. And the students! So lazy! All they ever
asked me about was money. How much they could make as
artists. Mind you, they were better than the faculty. These
people, they were so lost, so ignorant. A dreadful, dreadful
place."

Something causes her to be polite, eager to please. She
doesn't dare make her usual joke, that the North Saskatchewan is wider than the Seine.

"The only nice person in the whole city was a taxi-driver. He drove me along the river valley," says the artist.

"It's beautiful, isn't it?"

He glares and presses his lips together. "You don't know Paris if you think that any other city is beautiful."

Jane trips, stumbles from the staircase onto the sidewalk, turns this way and that in the crowded streets. The Métro stop is not where it was. She discovers another. She stares down at the rails in the tunnel. She reassesses the man's paintings. They are unreasonable, relentless, unforgiving. There is a clinical coldness to them; but they have taught her something. They have made her see in terrible relief. The city is split into layers, levels one on top of each other. Gaps and improbabilities occur.

For instance, there on the dull shine of the train rail, a creature is moving. It has a familiar down-tilted, pear-shaped body and scaly tail. The rat looks her in the eye. It stands up on its hind legs as if to declare itself. Jane has never actually seen a rat before. There is a special program for rat control in Alberta, successful to an extraordinary degree.

Jane screams, clamping her hand on her mouth. She begins to tremble. She is falling apart, and on foreign soil. The train pulls into the station and the doors sigh open, with pressure. She enters the car with others. Parisians are so rude, they take the outside seat as if to dare you to climb over their knees to get to the other chair. She does. There is a boy sitting across from her. He has dirty, long hair and a huge Adam's apple. He leans forward in his chair, sensing weakness.

"You speak English?"

She stares straight ahead.

"Mademoiselle, you speak English."

She does not answer.

"Français?"

She keeps staring, hoping to be taken for a deaf mute.

"Mademoiselle, you are American."

That trips her into shaking her head.

"Not American; German, perhaps?"

The other passengers find this amusing. The young man slurs and leans, perhaps he is on drugs, he doesn't seem to be drunk. He puts his hand on her knee. He keeps asking her where she is from, he lists half the countries in Europe, but he really thinks she is English-speaking, and returns compulsively to "America, America." She shrinks in her seat. She is afraid to push him away, to push his hand off her knee; she thinks then he might leap on her.

The man who would not move over is watching. He cocks an eye as if to say, "Why are you putting up with this? Why don't you fight back?" Women smirk. No one in the crowd will help her. They are waiting for her to speak. She cannot speak. Why should she expect them to defend her, if she can't defend herself? The only thing she can do is run away. The next time the train stops she springs over the man in the seat and out the door. People are laughing behind her. The hollow station magnifies her shame.

Jane walks, runs, sweating, through streets that are completely strange, not the Paris she knows. The faces around her are black; words from shopfront conversations fall around her ears like pebbles. The boy on the train has laid a curse on her: she understands no known language, she comes from nowhere. She carries on like this for a while, crying, while passersby look at her incuriously or not at all. When the tears are reduced to hiccups and shudders, she realizes that she is hungry and gathers her courage to enter a little restaurant. There at last, coffee before her, she becomes calm. She sits for a long time.

The man at a table by the window looks like the philosopher-king whose picture Jane has seen in the newspaper. He is very dark, with a beard, and a long, bony nose, long, narrow eyes. She looks past him at the street and recognizes a certain hare-lip newspaper vendor: there is the passage she calls Avenue des Crottes; around from that must be Square Saint-Sulpice. She has made her way back somehow to "her" Paris. She smiles at her empty cup. She lifts her eyes. He is gazing at her.

They leave the café together. He corrects her French as they climb five floors to his room. As if he cares, as if he has been asking, she tells him she is from Canada. He is disappointed. He is crazy about things American, "bask*ets*," which turn out to be track shoes, and Broadway music. *West Side Story. South Pacific.* He has all the records. And a bottle of wine.

The sun is going down pale peach beyond the gummy grey windows. She realizes that the light is wrong, there is a film on everything, the dirty air, the dusty desk top. There must be light. He plays records one after another. *Camelot, My Fair Lady.* Then, *The King and I.* She begins to sing the words. He knows them too, but not what they mean, he tests them in his mouth like unfamiliar candies. He rubs her nipples, hard, and they undress. His body is long and narrow and dark, with a rectangle of hair like a flag on his chest. When they make love, he is making love to America, but she doesn't care.

After, she gets up to dance, putting on his shirt. The philosopher — she doesn't even know his name, but somehow he is making all this possible — focuses a reading light on her. Tears slide over her cheeks, down her throat. By then she is stoned enough to forget about the rat and the terrible boy on the Métro, and the upbeat story she will have to write about the frightening artist — but not about her wasted, horribly dead mother, who has now turned into an ache running from the base of her rib on the left side right into her neck.

But Jane does not stop, she keeps on and she has all the moves, the snap wrists, the jammed-out hip, open mouth and fake innocent eyes; she is all those saucy heroines of the musicals. She is Nona, in the fifties, Nona in her lip-sync revolt.

"Oh, Mother, Mother, Mother," she cries. It is all right to do it; the French understand these things. Didn't de Beauvoir write that Sartre himself cried out for his mother in sleep? She cries and she lets loose and she keeps going

until

it visits her again, that feeling of having no edges, nothing to defend, nothing to fear, that only-one-word-for-it peace from when she was four, or five, in the living-room, watching her mother dance. And this peace is the gift, not the emptiness, not the ticket to leave. There was love, before the end. And Jane too may find it. She may even find it with the King of Siam.

Toronto/New York

Toronto/New York

"I think I'll take the white one," says Althea, eyeing her two coats, which hang by the door. It is a cold January night in Edmonton, Alberta. The white one is fake leather, fashionable at the moment with its epaulettes, but without warmth. The other is a classic navy cavalry twill, heavy and drab.

Judy does not look up from her knitting. The night before Althea leaves for New York she and her roommate are having supper — a plate of instant brownies and coffee — in their basement rooms. The rooms are dark and overheated; there is a tiger-striped aura from the wicker lampshade on the side table. In the corner the gas fireplace is a purple flame over luminous orange imitation coals.

"Take the blue. They have winter in New York too," says Judy.

But Althea puts on the white one and postures in the cheap full-length mirror the girls have hung on the wall.

"With my black over-the-knee boots."

After one more long look she gives up on her image and

turns to her friend. "They do have winter in New York but it's not nearly so cold as here. Ronald says."

In a minute Judy goes on, still without looking up. "You'll be walking and standing around outside a lot, won't you? Sightseeing?" Her knitting-needles click rapidly and without pause as Judy treats the subject of Althea's coat. The faster she knits, the slower she talks. One of Judy's attractive characteristics is that she seems to have all the time in the world to consider such matters as coats for others. But Althea is unimpressed. She has discovered Judy's secret: Judy is always knitting. Knitters concentrate on knitting, which relegates talk to the thin top layer of the mind. Therefore, in conversation, they favour subjects of little consequence spread over a great deal of time.

Judy is knitting an afghan for a friend who has moved to a new apartment. It hardly takes anything for Judy to knit you an afghan, less and less, Althea has noted. It used to be you had to have a baby or at least get married. Now you just need to admire one of the orange, purple and brown throws on the sofa and chairs in this subterranean sitting-room and Judy will offer; she and her needles will be off. She does this despite the fact that she is in her final year of a degree in Honours computer science and she is getting married in three months and has four bridesmaids' dresses to make — one of them for Althea — along with job interviews to attend and exams coming up.

"I wouldn't exactly call it sightseeing," protests Althea, irritated by the clicking needles and the distance they give Judy from the conversation. Besides, Althea will be no ordinary tourist in New York. She will visit Ronald, who is taking a master's degree in business administration at Columbia University. Although she has never been in the city she feels she has a presence there; she has been invited with a view to taking up residence.

"Well, whatever," says Judy easily.

Althea takes off the white coat and puts it back on the hook. She walks to the bookshelf and turns on the radio. The announcer says that it is twenty-four degrees below zero, Fahrenheit. Then she puts on the Doors' record, "Light my Fire." Althea turns it up.

"Mrs Ambrose is home," says Judy.

Althea turns it down again.

The basement apartment — a sitting-room, a damp and dingy bathroom, a small kitchen tacked onto the back of the furnace room, and a bedroom — is underneath a bungalow owned by a widowed schoolteacher who lives with her dog Mellow. It is on the far edge of the student district, a long walk from campus, especially in the squeaking cold of the long Edmonton winter. But it was Judy's apartment first and Judy is an energetic, sensible, long-legged woman from Lac La Biche who doesn't mind being a little out of the way. Althea moved in later, able to pay for these experimental digs with her allowance. Both Judy and Althea go to Althea's parents' house for Sunday dinners.

Judy came down to Edmonton four years ago, in 1966, to do household economics. In the first week of classes she had what she herself describes as a moment of clairvoyance, and switched into computer science. Althea has pressed her on what this moment revealed and all Judy has said is, "I realized that things were changing." Most likely, Althea thinks, Judy saw nothing much, only felt a dim necessity or sensed a possibility and moved toward it.

Because the future is surely as dark, as long and unknowable as the night that crowds the basement windows. It will still be pitch-dark at eight o'clock tomorrow morning when she and Judy leave for class in wool tights and high snowboots and fur hats which tie under the chin and matching fur mittens. The sun will not yet be up. At four o'clock they would meet again in front of SUB caf' to come home, once more in the dark. Except that tomorrow will be different; tomorrow Althea will be on her way to the airport.

Althea drops into the chair opposite Judy and picks up her cup of cool coffee. She examines her roommate's pert, down-tilted face with curiosity. Will Judy let Reid, her fiancé, sleep over while she, Althea, is away? Developments on the sitting room sofa have surely reached a breaking point. Althea thinks it would be the kind thing to do. Mrs Ambrose upstairs would never notice and Reid would appreciate it. Althea knows that Judy takes birth-control pills (there are not many secrets between roommates in a basement flat). Judy takes these pills, she has explained, to regulate her periods. All unmarried women who take birth-control pills in Edmonton in 1970 take them to regulate their periods.

But Althea thinks this is an excuse, and Althea is in a position to know. Every night for the past four months she has shared a double bed with Judy. Sometimes in the night the other woman tosses her head and cries — "No, Reid, no!" Nothing is ever said at any other time about what Reid is trying to do that must be so strenuously resisted. Tonight Althea would like to talk to Judy about this but she sees from the composed look around her friend's eyes and the minute movings of her lips that it is out of the question. Judy is too brisk, too businesslike, too sweet. They can only talk about practical things.

"Is Ronald picking you up at the airport?" says Judy.

"I have to call him from the East Side Terminal," Althea says, breezily, as if she knew what the East Side Terminal was. She is not sure about Ronald's New York; she has never been east of Winnipeg. She is not sure about Ronald, either. He is the first of Althea's boyfriends to be approved of by her father. It is a strange fact that although Althea is

not a rebellious girl and never was, she picks unsuitable
boyfriends. Most of the others have been ski bums and folk
singers. The master's degree in business administration is
not in itself enough to incur Althea's father's approval. In
fact, Althea's father thinks that MBAs are no substitute for a
year or two of scrubbing out oil barrels and then working
yourself up the ladder, but then Ronald didn't ask Althea's
father's opinion before he went to New York, did he?

Ronald went to New York because he thought it was the
place to be. Ronald was the first in their crowd to play
Aretha Franklin's "Respect," and he talked about *Hair!* as
if he had seen it. These are factors in his favour from
Althea's point of view, if not from her father's. To the latter,
the facts that Ronald's father is also in the oil business, that
the young man is well mannered and no taller than himself
are more significant. Furthermore, Ronald is there on the
horizon when something is needed. Althea's father has
stated publicly his belief that nice girls get married when
they finish university.

Not that what he thinks matters much to Althea at twenty-
one. The only advantage in his approval is that he pays for
that of which he approves. He is paying for the trip east.
East is an idea with Althea, a magnetic pull, much the way
west was to her grandfather. She has the idea that life comes
to the East first. Althea has done some acting and she hopes
for a future in television or radio.

As a nod to these vague ambitions, Althea will stop over in
Toronto on her trip, where a series of interviews has been set
up at the Canadian Broadcasting Corporation (by her
father's intervention; he knows someone). Then she is going
on to New York where she will spend the week with Ronald.
The unchaperoned visit is unusual in this time and place but
then Althea is lucky. Her family is progressive in certain
ways. Her parents believe women ought to have training,

and in some circumstances (husband not objecting, children still to come) jobs. Althea goes one better. She believes emphatically in a career that will consume her. As well, at least one parent believes that sexual compatibility is important in marriage, and ought therefore to be tested out beforehand. Althea believes that sex too, when discovered, ought to consume her.

Althea stares resentfully at Judy's composed face, which she suspects conceals much. Judy and Reid are to be married; Judy is on the pill. Althea is off with her parents' blessing for a week with her boyfriend who is bound to invite her, to expect her, even, to sleep with him, and she is not on the pill. Through no malicious intent, but out of a kind of liberal reticence, the progressiveness of Althea's parents has not extended to supporting prevention of pregnancy, only to giving opportunity for pregnancy to occur.

Althea worries. She does not want to become pregnant. Now or ever. It would be the end of her life, the end of everything she wants. She made an effort to get pills; she went to the campus doctor who, like everyone else in town, knew her family. She claimed to be engaged.

"So when is the wedding?" said this doctor, peering over his tortoiseshell glasses. A long way off, she mumbled, and perhaps it was not necessary to start on pills so soon? Indeed it wasn't, said the doctor, and Althea bolted. She later explained, to an unkempt guy called Michael in her drama class who was the only person she could talk to these days, that it was because she hated having to lie. But that was not the reason. She has lied relatively easily about other things in her time. Perhaps she didn't want the pill after all.

"We should go to bed," says Judy. She comes to the end of a row, winds up the strand of wool over the ball, folds her knitting, and sticks the needles into the ball. She stands up.

"You're right," says Althea. Her suitcase is packed. The

coat is the last thing, and she has decided on white. She stands up too. Judy turns down the fire.

The bungalow sinks in the clear, inky vat of night. Outside, the temperature is thirty below zero and the wind is lifting dry snow into horses' tails and flinging them up against the stucco walls. It sucks and huffs intermittently. Judy and Althea lie sleeping one and a half feet apart, hands braced to keep themselves from rolling to the centre of the sloping mattress, into each other. All is still.

Then it happens. Thumps repeat at the ground-level window over the bed. In seconds one of these thumps becomes a loud slam, a rattle and clamour. A ferocious blast of frigid wind enters, and then a wet, cold, heavy thing with claws lands on Althea's stomach, scratching and yelping.

Both girls scream and sit up. It is dark, the thing attacking them is dark, it snarls and scrambles and shakes wet on them and they don't know what has happened until Judy recognizes the dog and shouts, "Mellow! For Chrissakes!" and heaves him off the bed. Then she rises in her billowing flannelette nightgown and closes the window, which is not broken but has only been forced open.

Althea lies back gasping. She is without Judy's competence at moments like this.

"Mrs Ambrose must have left him out," mumbles Judy.

She hustles the dog out the bedroom door and into the furnace room. Then she returns and dives back into bed. The room has been cleansed with the blast of air and feels like outdoors. Judy grasps the three comforters and turns over on her side, away from Althea.

Mellow whines in the furnace room and scratches on the door.

Althea's heart pounds.

Judy lies very still and pretends to sleep.

Althea realizes that Judy was doing it again, before the wet dog landed on them. Judy was saying, "No, Reid, no," in her sleep. Now she can't help herself. She must ask.

"Are you going to let Reid stay over while I'm gone?"

"No," says Judy. But it is a different "no" from what it might have been. It is "no" with an acknowledgment that she has been considering it, not "no" pretending ignorance, which is what Althea would have got if she asked the question in the daytime.

Then Judy says, "Are you going to sleep with Ronald?"

"The pressure's on," says Althea. And then because she has started, because she has said one thing, the rest of what she's feeling comes out. "I'm just not prepared for this." She stops. Real life in all its complexity has woken her from a trance. "Nothing we know is going to help us now," she says. "Nothing is going to turn out the way we think."

"I guess I'm still asleep," says Judy, denying responsibility for the conversation.

This is what happened on Althea's trip east.

She left the campus at four o'clock with Michael from her drama class. They had a few drinks at the Riviera Hotel and necked in the car before he drove her to the airport. On the flight she had two glasses of wine and two hours' sleep. When she arrived in Toronto it was morning and she had to report for her interviews. Dabbing on some blush in the airport washroom, Althea realized that she had not given enough thought to what was going to happen in Toronto. She had been thinking about New York. New York was love and sex and possibly marriage. But New York was later. Toronto was her career, and Toronto was now.

They were all men Althea had to see at the CBC in Toronto, all but one. The first had a wide face and greased hair and hands that sifted over the surface of his desk as if there were papers to sort, when there weren't. He talked about the role of public television, its task in educating the public, the excitement in its live dramatic productions. He didn't ask Althea about herself or offer her a job. She realized, leaving his office, that she had rather expected him to offer her a job.

In the next office the man had a fleshy hand. He asked her what she thought of television. She answered him using a number of the concepts she had picked up in the previous conversation. She thought it was a good conversation until she noticed that he had stopped asking anything and folded his hands.

"Well, thank you for coming in," he said. "Perhaps we'll see more of you when you come to Toronto."

Presently Althea found herself in a room with a famous announcer. She had by then moved down from television to radio, from a glassy new building to an old one, dark brick with metal fire-escapes. His voice was familiar and kind, she remembers her mother laughing at his jokes while driving her to piano lessons.

"What's it like out there?" he asked. "What do they think of us in Toronto?"

She wouldn't say because it wouldn't be polite. "They think it's grey in Toronto," she said. She looked out the window. It was grey. "But it must be green in summer. The trees are big."

"Do you know what I'd do if I were you?" said this kindly man, rising and taking her hand in his and walking her to that window. "See that pub over there?"

Across the street was an old mansion with a red and gold sign hanging from the porch: "The Red Lion."

"I'd go over there and have a drink and meet some of the young people. Get yourself a tape recorder. They'll help you get started."

Althea looked over at the pub and thought how she'd like

to do that. Get out of her white coat and knee-high boots
(dress for New York: love, sex, possibly marriage) and into
some jeans and a sweater (dress for Toronto: career). To
heck with Ronald and New York.

"Where do you have to go next?" he said.

Next was the sole woman on the list. Althea showed him
the name on her piece of paper. He steered her around a corner and down a corridor and into a room where half a dozen
desks were, and as many people talking on the phones.

"That's her there."

May Hewitt was a small woman with short, straight
mouse-coloured hair and several large moles around her un-
coloured lips. Her ashtray was full of twisted butts. She
peered at Althea around a puff of smoke. "So what have you
got for me?"

Althea was startled to think that she had to have anything;
she had imagined it was enough to *be* something, to be
Althea. But in the back of her mind she'd been framing an
answer to the nice man's question about what it was like
"out there". In the first place it hadn't been "out there"
until two hours ago. It had simply been the place where she
lived. In the second place —

"Louis Riel is having a revival," she said, surprising
herself. "People who thought he was a traitor are changing
their minds. Out there," she added.

May Hewitt's eyes slipped down Althea's body and then
back up to her eyes, an unsympathetic assessment, Althea
felt, shrinking. She was not serious-looking, she was not
substantial enough. "I'd like to hear about that," said May
Hewitt, however. "Why don't you make me a tape and send
it in? There's a place left in the summer-student program
and if I like it, you can have a job."

Despite May Hewitt, however, in Althea's final interview
the personnel manager for the corporation asked her if she

could type. Women, he said, began as secretaries and worked their way up. Althea was humiliated to discover her eyes begin to burn and her throat to clutch and her shoulders to rise and fall.

"I'm very tired," said Althea. "I flew all night." She did not say, could not say, that she didn't know how to type. She was made for better things, or so she and her parents thought when typing was an option on the high-school course. (She didn't know how to make a tape for radio either, a fact that was hitting her hard at this moment as well.)

What she thought, as the tears began at the idea of her having to type, was "this is unfair". "This is unfair to Althea, B.A., Double Honours in drama and philosophy." She knew he would not ask it of a boy, even with a general B.A. However she was unable to extend this idea of "unfair to Althea" to the generic observation "unfair to women." It was too early for such an idea with Althea, although it had been aired in certain quarters. One year from now, even six months from now, the generic expression would be available, and the vocabulary with which to make it. And the story of what the personnel manager said to Althea would be part of her repertoire of famous stories. But for now all that was waiting in the wings, and Althea had only such comfort as was offered by the manager.

"The things I deal with," he sighed, getting Kleenex from his drawer. "I had a woman in here yesterday with terminal cancer."

Althea wiped her tears.

When she stepped out onto the front steps of the building it had begun to snow. Her white leatherette coat grew stiff in the cold.

The East Side Terminal was large and draughty; people

flowed into it from one door and out of it through the opposite one. Althea stood by the telephone, conspicuous in
her white coat, which she was now prepared to admit was a
mistake. Ronald's telephone number was busy. She called
every four minutes. Half an hour later it was still busy. How
long could she stand here before the white-slave traders
heard another new girl had hit town, and drew up in a long
yellow car to drag her away?

One more call and Althea gave up on the phone. She went
out the door with everyone else, flagged a cab and gave
Ronald's address. It was really not so difficult. As she
dropped her bag in the foyer he burst through the inner
door, fussing.

"Where have you been? I've been worried sick!" he said.
Ronald was wiry and tense with blond hair and a reddish
moustache which drooped, giving his face a mournful look.
He handled her with haste, a little roughly, taking off her
coat, kissing her on the mouth.

"Your telephone is *busy!*"

"Oh," said Ronald carelessly. He touched her here and
there, looking at her from various angles as one would a
long-awaited parcel. "It's impossible to call across town at
rush hour. I forgot."

Two roommates hovered in a dark-beamed room, drinking American beer, talking through their noses. Ronald
showed her off, first to these friends, then to others, in a
restaurant where they ate things Althea had only read
about — bagels, lentil soup, knishes. Althea wore Ronald's
burgundy ski jacket and her own jeans and walked all over
Manhattan. He took her to Wall Street, the Statue of Liberty,
and various eating places, always stressing how famous they
were. She made sure they walked themselves out every day,
arriving in bed at night as tired as possible. But if he gave
her one of his rough, tense hugs and then went further, she

felt she had to go along. She could not refuse to make love to him while he was spending all this money.

On the basis of no experience Althea had gained an impression that one was drawn to making love by well-nigh irresistible urges, that once yielded to those urges culminated in a fountain of pleasure, the payoff for the risk involved. She assumed Ronald to be an expert. After all, there had been that girl who followed him to Edmonton from California, camping out in his backyard. To the local way of thinking this could mean only one thing: they had been sleeping together and the girl had become unbalanced. Althea was rather charmed by this bit of Ronald's history and on the strength of it expected tutelage. But in that bare, book-strewn room above Harlem she began to see things differently.

Ronald enjoyed her lack of knowledge, her shyness, even her resistance. He made love to her on his own, without her participation. He made no effort to change the way it went. After he finished, when she was sore and a little angry, Ronald would recite the splendours of New York and paint in golden hues the life she would have when she came to join him. She never once responded to his suggestion. None the less, on the last afternoon of her trip, an undaunted Ronald walked her past Tiffany's.

Tiffany's shop windows were draped in crimson satin. On waves and ripples of the red sea stood plaster hands and fingers reaching up, waving, decked out with jewels. Althea could see they were dangerous, sirens' claws, set to drag her down.

"This is *the* famous place to buy the ring," he said.

"What ring?"

He walked her inside. Althea stood well back from the diamond case.

"Ronald!" she said. "You can't afford a ring!" She remembered the fights he'd had with his father over his fees for Columbia. And his red TR4, parked in Edmonton. Ronald was in debt.

"I'm going to get a big job when I graduate," he whispered, taking her elbow. "Just let's *look*."

Althea pointed out the ones she liked, plain and simple with one big stone instead of a lot of little ones. She hoped they cost less. She allowed her finger to be sized. It was an uncomfortable experience. She knew that she and Ronald were not what the discreetly smirking salesman thought, that they were a lie, a pair of impostors. She was awfully glad it was only Tiffany's in New York and not Birks in Edmonton where this happened. In Tiffany's no one knew them and it didn't really count.

The last night Ronald took Althea to see the New York City Ballet. The theatre was tall and cylindrical like the inside of a kaleidoscope; they sat in a single row of seats way up and looked straight down on the stage. The dancers' limbs opened and closed, stretching out in shapes, then folding back to a dot. They lifted their faces for Althea to see.

One dancer entranced Althea; she was a new member of the corps, fine-boned and pliant, with the exquisite quality of becoming. The mature dancers lost their appeal to Althea and she strained forward over the rail to devour every move that her favourite made. When the lights came up, she checked the program: Gelsey Kirkland, seventeen years old.

Afterward, standing in a daze at the side of the theatre, Althea saw her. She wore a long dark trench coat. She had enormous eyes and pale hair in a bun at the nape of her neck.

"It's her," she breathed to Ronald.

"Who?"

"The one in blue? The young one?"

Ronald didn't remember. He was pulling her toward some famous bar for a drink.

"Didn't you notice? She's magical."

Ronald hesitated.

"I mean she's absolutely — out of the ordinary."

Ronald didn't seem to get the point. Gelsey Kirkland got on a bus. Althea became instantly depressed.

Ronald just nodded. He was happy Althea liked something in New York. Perhaps it meant she would come here to live with him. "To me she's nothing but a pretty little ballerina," he said easily.

In the famous bar Althea picked a fight. She told Ronald that she didn't like her drink. She said it didn't matter how famous something was if you didn't know what it was famous for. If you didn't know who they'd been before, what did it matter to you if famous people were sitting in front of you? Or rich people? Or powerful ones, or whatever it was that so attracted Ronald in New York. She didn't like the city, she claimed (or him for being there, he understood). The bar was nothing to her but another way of staying out late. She wanted to go home. And poor Ronald took her there, his head hanging, and all the while he never knew that what Althea thought to herself as they stood on the platform to get their train up to Morningside Heights was that she could never, ever spend her life with a man who thought Gelsey Kirkland was just a pretty little ballerina.

Now a whole month has passed since Althea came home from New York. She and Judy are kneeling on the tacky carpet in their basement with the thin paper of dress patterns spread out over yards of white voile marked with tiny sprigs of flowers. Judy's wedding is only six weeks away.

The telephone rings.

Judy answers. "It's Ronald," she mouths. Althea takes the pins out of her mouth and crawls over to face what she knows will be wrath. Althea left New York on a dark and

rainy morning and she hasn't written, or called, even
though Valentine's Day has gone by, and Ronald's
birthday.

"Hello, Ronald," she says, soberly.

Ronald bursts into a stream of accusations. Why hasn't
she written? After their wonderful week together, after he
spent all that money on her, where does she get off just
disappearing without a word?

Althea says that it hasn't worked out between them. Then
she says that she doesn't know how she will ever see him
again anyway since she has the offer of a summer job in
Toronto. And when that doesn't work she says that she is
dating a guy from her drama class.

Judy hunches over her cutting, her lips pointed. She
thinks Althea may be throwing away her big chance in life.
Even if she isn't, she is being unkind, which is perhaps more
serious. But she says nothing when Althea quietly puts the
telephone receiver down again. Then Althea crawls back
over and continues spreading the thin crumply pattern
paper over the cloth to prepare to cut out the fourth
bridesmaid's dress. And that is the end of Ronald, except
that perhaps a month later Althea receives a letter, only
slightly bitter in tone, in which he says he is sure she will
have an interesting career.

Poor Althea. Her father assumes that Ronald has jilted
her. She attends Judy's wedding with Michael the drama
student, and his beard and long hair upset people's parents.
Judy moves out to a second floor walk-up apartment by the
shopping centre with Reid and their electric bun-warmers
and coffee sets and chafing dishes and bed linen. Through
May and June Althea stays on in Mrs Ambrose's basement
trying to finish a late paper on *The Duchess of Malfi*. She
doesn't even try to make the tape on Louis Riel; she has
been defeated. She imagines May Hewitt to have come to

the conclusion that Althea is a frivolous girl who thinks too much about clothes and boys, and Althea feels incapable of altering this conclusion.

Mrs Ambrose goes to the lake and leaves the dog Mellow in Althea's care. The two of them go for walks. Althea doesn't like Mellow; she hasn't forgiven him for bursting through the window in the middle of the night and scaring her half to death. From that moment she has been aware of how hopelessly unprepared she is for love, for sex, for work, for life.

In her worst moments she envies Judy, although she knows that Judy has sold out on her moment of clairvoyance. She is setting out into the past with Reid, and not into the future. Althea has become obsessed with the future, looming in the East.

She is glad to have escaped the landslide of afghans and bridesmaids' dresses. She knows she will be moving away soon, that a long time from now she will be doing interesting things, important things, she will have a desk to go to, she will not have to behave as other people expect simply because they pay for things. The question she cannot answer is how to get herself into that time, by what door to exit this time (and place) and enter the next. Once she finds the door, and goes through it, life will be dangerous, and wonderful. It will be what she makes herself and therefore, to the part of Althea that obeyed and believed and loved the world of her childhood, never wholly convincing.

The New Thing I'm About To Do

The New Thing I'm About To Do

The summer I graduated, I was yanked home from the comparative sophistication of a co-op house in Edmonton to my parents' home in suburban Calgary. What I wanted was to go to San Francisco to do mescaline and go to love-ins. What I got, through an act of self-mortification intended to demonstrate independence, was a job as a chambermaid at the University of Calgary student residences.

Every residence room — nine feet by twelve, with a single bed and a desk — was the same and had to be cleaned in the same way. It was boring and I didn't like doing it, but worse than that I wasn't any good at it. As my partner, a plump Portuguese immigrant with dark hairs on her upper lip, had noted, I wasn't careful, I wasn't fast, and I didn't have an eye for dust. She sat down beside me at lunch, with her bitter odour of sweat. She told me she was a good mother and she made sure her children went to school in clean clothes but she would die before she had another baby. She'd gone to see the priest but the priest said it was a sin. So she made sure she never lay with her husband any more. He hurt her anyway, she said, by putting all his weight on her. "He doesn't even get up on his elbows."

I must have looked shocked.

"How old you are?" she said, and hearing, laughed. "In Portugal, old maid."

Maria was OK, I didn't mind her. But it was humiliating to be lousy at something so dumb as cleaning. Besides, by the end of the day, I felt as if the bones in my feet had pushed right through my flesh to grind on the tile floors. After one week I said so much for independence and swore I wouldn't go back. Maybe my Dad would get me a job. And he did, through Professor DeMar, who lived across the street from the house I grew up in.

Professor DeMar was over six feet tall, blond and ruddy; he came from South Africa. I used to babysit his daughters. Libby at eight was as large as I had been at fifteen and terrifyingly self-confident. "I don't know what I'm going to be," she said on one occasion, "it's hard to decide because I'm so awfully good at so many things." She did decide finally to go back to South Africa and become a policewoman, but that is another story and happened long after her father met my father in the middle of the street one June evening and in a neighbourly sort of way asked what I was doing for the summer.

I can see them now, on Carding Close in Carmingay Heights, the empty crescent of flat-roofed stucco homes, the mound of a green prairie hill behind them, the sun departing from the west leaving its last light on the backs of the birch leaves. It was a thin place and my father was a thin man; DeMar outweighed him, burly and furred and given a heroic dimension, to me at least, by rumours of political resistance in his homeland.

My father coughed (I imagine) in his precise way, and in his uncomplaining voice complained that I had got a job cleaning the residences but that I had quit. Perhaps he even repeated the reasons I gave him. "All I get to work with is these *women*. They're all married, and they just go on about getting pregnant and varicose veins." He would smile as he said it, annoyed but nonetheless proud of my scorn.

I told my father about the married business because I knew it would work on him. My father had it in mind to save me from the life of a woman. This obsession of his went back to the fact that my mother had taken up with him before she finished school. At that time my father was a high-school English teacher, in fact he had been *her* high-school English teacher. He'd moved up now, into administration, but he was still a teacher at heart. I figured this was more the cause of her wanting to get out (I mean who wants to be married to her teacher for more than a term or two?) than the banal occupations of housewives in our city, but I couldn't disabuse him of the notion that Mum's problem was lack of intellectual activity.

In part because of his mission to save me from becoming my mother, and also perhaps from more complicated reactions to my maturity, my father forbade me make-up and nylons and dates long past my time. It had been a struggle to get away from home to go to university at eighteen. Now that I was twenty-one and he finally had to allow that I was "approaching adulthood," as he put it, he devoted his efforts to encouraging me to use my mind rather than marry some "oaf," always the term for the hypothetical young man. I was supposed to be literary. The idea was that I would be some kind of writer, perhaps a poet, or at least write advertising copy for the Chamber of Commerce.

My father may have imparted some of this to Professor DeMar. He had great respect for the professor without knowing him well, because he was involved in higher academic studies. Immediately Professor DeMar said he was looking for a researcher for his newly funded book project, and promptly offered me a job, which my father just as promptly accepted on my behalf.

He came into the kitchen with the news of my employment.

"Now, hold everything," I said, gripping tight to my Coke bottle. I found the development a little intimidating. I didn't want another failure. "I can't do this job. I'm not qualified." My mother with her usual cheer asserted that my qualifications were most compelling. I had bombed out as a chambermaid, thus becoming available, and I needed the money because they were going to start charging me rent.

I left the house the next Monday at eight-thirty in the morning, one half hour after Maria picked up our cleaning trolley. For an instant as I stepped off the campus bus the hollow rumble of trolley wheels down mile-long hallways seemed to sound in my ears. Then, full of gratitude, I went off to my intellectual assignment at the University Science complex, dressed in a forest-green shirt dress with white polka dots.

The Science complex was a massive grey hulk made of something called stressed concrete. The only windows looked into a courtyard like those tucked inside medieval castles, with benches and a fountain but no sun. It seemed to be designed to block out the world, enclose a space and start over inside. In the surrounding four sections there were staircases and elevators, grey pebbled stone walls, many acres of purple industrial carpet, and a staggering number of classrooms and offices. I waited on the third floor in the hall beyond the Dean's office for Dr DeMar and his partner Dr Gupta.

As I stood outside a door with "DeMar" on it, all kinds of men went by — Africans, East Indians, Europeans, pale Slavic-looking people, Chinese. Only a few nodded. One daring fellow, an Egyptian I thought, smiled widely, remarked, "Waiting for DeMar?" and kept walking, shaking his head. Awed by this display of internationalism and purpose, I stood half an hour until Professor DeMar arrived. He took me along the hall to a cupboard-sized room with a cabinet, a table and chair and a couple of card files. He seemed enormous in the room and I could see immediately that I would be working on my own. He explained what he wanted, gave me his library credentials, slapped the doorframe twice, and went out.

Left to sort out my instructions, I soon grasped that my task was simple. It was to survey the technical literature on our subject, to xerox pertinent articles, to copy out précis of pertinent articles onto file cards, and then to file both article and card in the cabinet. When a précis was not given I was to read the article and write one myself. I was to accomplish this literature search in English and in French. I knew nothing about science and my French was limited to reading *La Princesse de Clèves*, but Professor DeMar said this would be no impediment.

DeMar had started the system, and it looked as if it would be easy to carry on. Copies of the periodical guides were on my desk. I was to keep track of my hours myself, and to be paid the sum of four dollars an hour. It was all very well considered and not difficult for someone having, as Dr DeMar had put it, "my talents." I had a good idea where this reputation for having secretarial or perhaps even literary talent came from, and naturally I did not ask.

Summers in south-central Alberta are short, dry and sunny. The campus was on the western edge of town looking out to where the jagged white ridges of the Rocky Mountains cracked out of the foothills in the near west. It was new and under construction, dusty and treeless, but there was a lemon purity to the light and a geometric beauty in the lines and angles of the buildings scattered over the grounds.

I soon loved my job. My little cabinet was dark and cool. When I closed the door the oblong of glass above the handle offered only a narrow view of the hall; no one could see in without pressing his face against the glass. My comings and goings were known only to me. I stayed a little in the room each morning and then I walked out to the library. After being in the dark cloister, I found it spectacular to walk down the slope, across the open grass in splashing, generous sunlight, and up to the library door.

Smiling on my mission, I would enter the library through the turnstile, turning right into Current Periodicals. There were few users, that summer of 1970; only the odd ghostly graduate student drifted between the partitions. I came to know the librarians, the canteen operator, the gardeners; I was the young lady researching Dr DeMar's book whom they were all pleased to help. I was something special, perhaps because at that time the only women my age in Science were the secretaries.

I like the secretaries. In particular, I liked the secretary to Dr DeMar. Carol had short waving light-brown hair, impossibly blue eyes and high natural pink in her lips and cheeks. She was near my age, twenty-two, but I had never known anyone like her. She existed across several gulfs: she came from a small town, she was married, she had not gone to university. In high school in Okotoks she had fallen in love with Tim, and soon after married him and came to Calgary. They lived in a duplex on 24th Street while waiting to buy their first house. She had worked in Science for four years.

Carol had a great fund of information that I could use, and she was generous with it. At lunch-time we went outside the castle walls to the grassy slope facing south and propped ourselves against the great hulk of concrete with our eyes

shut. Owing to the regularity of Carol's lunching habits I got
my best-ever sun-tan that summer. One of the first things
Carol taught me was that you were supposed to refer to the
professors behind their backs by last name only.

"So what has DeMar got you doing?" she asked.

I had a little trouble with this, raised as I had been with
great respect for academic achievement.

"Researching a book he's writing with Dr Gupta."

"Oh, Gupta," she said, rolling her eyes.

"What about him?"

"You'll see." She held this knowledge away from me, her
eyes full of the joke of Gupta which I was not to know.

I hardly said anything during our conversations at first.
But Carol instructed in the way of superior women over the
ages: she held me above herself, making her suggestions for
my improvement seem like flattery. I was a brain because I
had gone to university. She had heard I wrote poetry which
was odd but admirable. I enjoyed the aura this granted me,
and concealed within it my fascination with her skills. She
dealt easily with paranoid graduate students, irate ad-
ministrators, and panicked foreign students who could not
read their letters from immigration. She smoothed over con-
frontations and made it seem as if she were doing nothing.
At moments I wondered what I had been doing in university
those four years, as Carol had by nature all that was needed
for any job.

We never had an intellectual conversation. It was all
about ways and means. If I were to analyse her conversation
it would perhaps reduce to narcissism under the guise of self-
deprecation, strategies to manipulate, and modest sexual
avidity, all this without changing the innocent face with its
dark lips and high colour, the pure devilish blue of her eyes.
But this would not at all allow for its charms.

What did Carol talk about, then? "You have glamorous

dreams,'' was one of the first things she said to me. (I told
her about going to San Francisco perhaps.) It was an observation, without judgment or envy, easily followed by, ''The
hair on your legs ought to be shaved.'' She expressed herself
carefully and candidly. She was calm, content, and without
conceit. One thing I particularly admired was how she could
confide without losing dignity. She talked about birth control, and how her husband objected to various methods. She
thought she would soon get pregnant, although she dreaded
what it would do to her figure. In fact, her conversation was
not entirely different from Maria's, which, in hindsight, had
been electrifying.

We sat in the sun and I listened to Carol's lyrical voice going on about how Tim took her camping and she'd been so
hungry she ate too much breakfast and had to cut down on
lunches this week. Occasionally I looked across the quad at
the residences and thought of Maria *et aliae*, scrubbing out
bathtubs. The cleaning team only had forty-five minutes for
lunch and never spent it outside, probably because they
didn't want to be seen in their uniforms, too large and of
ghastly blue. Then I would look down at my ankle bones,
nicely browned and pointing together in a graceful curve
below my muscled calves, and think, simultaneously, how it
was true I ought to shave my legs and how nice it was to
have a job where I could use my brain.

The one curious thing about this job was that no one seemed
to care much if I did it or not. Every week or so Dr DeMar
would meet my father in the street and express great
pleasure in my progress. I had to content myself with this. I
did not believe, in fact, that either he or Dr Gupta, whom I
had not even clapped eyes on, ever consulted the files I was
building. They were happy enough to look at my tabulation
of hours and write a cheque every two weeks, to know that

this grant of money awarded for their book was being spent, little by little, in readying a fertile field for whenever they should decide to till it. So far it was my book.

My book was about the Athabasca tar sands. I never studied geology and had only the vaguest notion that it had to do with rocks. We never discussed science at home. Who did, except perhaps the frightening Libby DeMar who might invite one over to see her ammonites? We didn't actually discuss anything at home; my father corrected grammar, my mother negated all comments. "If this was the Middle Ages I'd practically be a grandmother," I might say, by way of trying to get permission to go camping overnight in Banff with my girlfriends.

"If this *were*, and I'd have *been*," said my father.

"Good chance you'd be dead, grandmother or not," my mother would say. "Do you know what the life expectancy was? How many women died in childbirth?"

There were a lot of things I didn't know. I was certainly ignorant of science, and a feeling of ignorance was easy to mistake for hatred. But slowly, through my reading and précis-writing, my ignorance became interest. A book needs to be loved, I had read somewhere, and since no one else was loving this one, I loved it.

The Athabasca tar sands were acreages of treacherous, sucking quicksand occurring in the wilderness north of Edmonton, underneath which was hidden a giant lake of oil. This much I knew already. During my childhood there were periodic flutters of excitement in the public consciousness about "tapping" these sands, but no one knew exactly what that entailed, and anyway something always happened to prevent it. If I had been asked I'd have said you tapped it like a maple tree, by banging in a nail, or a tube, and the stuff would begin to flow.

Within a week of beginning my job I knew this idea,

though generally correct, to be a pitiful underestimation of what was there, and what was required to get it out. The tar sands quite simply contained the largest deposit of oil in the world. They were the key to Canada's and Alberta's future prosperity, and the greatest challenge to technology on the planet.

Imagine my excitement to discover, to the north in that trackless top-heavy square on the map of Alberta, this vast treasurehouse. There was romance to rival the Great Wall of China, mystery as in the jungles of the Amazon, possibly even the streets of Haight Ashbury. Mile after countless mile of muskeg and spruce covered a substance part sand, part oil. It bubbled under the mud, it bulged out of the cutbanks alongside the river, sometimes hard as glass, sometimes running like sap. It was changeable, almost alive; a stick poked in found it hard, in the cold, and softer in hot weather. Like all proper treasure it was guarded by impassable country, frigid in the winter and mushy in summer, policed by black-flies and mosquitoes in tornado-sized swarms. The black gold was not beautiful — it smelled bad and had a peculiar yellow cast.

Not that I ever saw the tar sands. There were not even any photographs in my papers. The authors I collected did not apply themselves to physical description; to do so would be beneath them. Instead there were cross-sectional diagrams of geological time, stacks of curved lines representing billions or millions of years, and gaps between them filled in with a skein of black dots to represent the deposits of oil sand. There were diagrams of the chemical composition of the tar sands; a particle of sand surrounded by an envelope of water connected to other water-coated grains by a film of bitumen, or oil. These were the ways in which we were to know them.

I flew over the surface of the material much as the visitor

to the tar-sands area was advised to fly over the muskeg, because walking in the wet heavy earth and compost mixture was too difficult. Way up there I became enamoured of the clouds of language — ponderous, technical, cumbersome language but somehow thick, exotic, thorough, precise, *real* in a way that Carding Close and Carmingay Heights were not. Words like viscous, porous, impregnable, like hydro-cracking and thermal packing, fine deliberate verbs like saturate, extract, correlate. I did not know what they meant; the sound of them and the look were enough.

"The oil is found in pinnacle reefs which are amenable to vertical flooding, and allow the avoidance of gravity override."

It was a landscape of word strokes, a cerebral painting of suggestive activities and processes, filled with movement. As I xeroxed article after article from magazines with names like *Chemical Weekly* and *Fluid Flow Fortnightly* on subjects such as fractionating towers and delayed coking operations, I began to feel that although the nineteen-sixties had passed us Albertans by, there was potential for drama in this place, under the crust.

Up until then I had seen no deeper into the earth than the repetitive and insecure grid of recently-laid subdivisions, the easy goals at its ends: Motel Village, Westwood Mall, the Trans-Canada Highway. My movements over these sur-faces seemed to be a kind of somnabulism. My feet touched down but knew only asphalt, concrete, or the impossible green of much-watered lawns. Meanwhile the soil and bedrock beneath these deceptive coatings undulated with natural riches whose secrets were known only to geologists.

"The Paleozoic section begins with coarse and arkosic Granite Wash type sands in the Precambrian erosional lows. They become finer, better sorted, and more quartzitic higher in section. These sands drape . . ."

Now the land ceased to be this flat covering I looked down on and became a rich layering, existing in cross-section in my imagination, a walk-on museum. I could mark my place in the geological ages, not in railway crossings and clover-leafs. Dr DeMar had not advised me to search the history of the oil sands; indeed the authors were interested only in exploitation, a word which was to scientists at that time utterly free of negative connotation. But I wanted to know where it all began, where the oil sands came from. So at this point in my research I walked upstairs from Periodicals into Geology. There I discovered more mystery.

No one knew for sure where the oil sands came from. But they did know that four hundred million years ago, in the Devonian age, Alberta was covered by a sea containing many coral reefs. By that fact alone my isolated province, which had seemed to have only the most tenuous connection to the older civilizations, became part of the globe. The twisted and fossil-filled rocks left by the Devonian seas were near relations to those in Devon, England. In their waters lived and died the little seagoing organisms which on decomposition may have become oil. Scientists who held to this theory thought that the oil formed by their death migrated upward through cracks in the layers of earth subsequently laid above it to where it was found — in relatively recent Cretaceous deposits of only seventy million years of age.

The only difficulty with this theory was that absolutely no trace of any oil remained in the Devonian strata. Because of this lack of evidence other scientists favoured the view that the oil was formed in the Cretaceous era, when again the area had been covered by a warm, shallow sea. Cretaceous, I discovered, came from the Latin "creta," meaning chalk, and referred to the best-known cretaceous layer in the world, the white cliffs of Dover.

Cretaceous Alberta was what we would now call

"filmic". It featured many flowering plants, and strange moss-bound conifers. At one point the Rocky Mountains suddenly broke through the earth's crust and pushed up to their spectacular height. Stirred up by all this activity, the seas moved back and forth, depositing sand all over the province. The last of the great reptiles slithered and bounded in the woods. Sand dunes began to build, locking water into warm shallow pools, and trees grew around them. As they died, these trees collapsed into the pools; their decomposition produced the gases needed to create oil.

"The oil sand formation is of Lower Cretaceous age and lies unconformably on a floor of Upper Devonian limestone . . . . These sands drape over the crests of the Precambrian highs or onlap against their flanks . . ."

But this theory was not altogether satisfactory either. Still other scientists thought that the oil was formed somewhere in the unknown north and had migrated through the rock strata in a southward direction, coming to rest in the Athabasca region.

I was pleased that there was no answer to the question of origin. The tar sands were an example of mysterious beneficence, perhaps a supernatural occurrence. The better for me to enjoy its striking portraiture in prose. *Onlap against their flanks!* Who could not feel the sensual music of this language? And *lying unconformably.* I tried to imagine. Not uncomforTably, but unconforMably. Without fitting, I thought, or at least without being the same. I closed my eyes to picture the oil sands and the limestone lying together. I saw more cross-sectional drawings of layers under the soil, curved lines one above the other, like a woman's body lying on top of a man's.

There were other distractions. The sanguine, smiling Egyptian graduate student now lingered in the hall shaking his head and saying, "Beautiful, beautiful." And a Hungarian freedom fighter who had escaped to Canada twelve years before took to dropping by my little office to tell me of his exploits. These men became part of the building, part of being in Science for the summer. But one day I had spied, in the far end of the periodicals room, a giant brown-bearded individual taking out a Ph.D. thesis from the interlibrary loan counter. The librarians told me he was a draft-dodger named John. He was writing a thesis on some aspect of the Bible; no one knew exactly what because most of the items he ordered were titled in German.

"The Upper Devonian reef chain subcrops at the downdip edge of the oil accumulation. Possible traps may be present at breaks . . ."

As I raised my eyes from the oddly stirring geological descriptions they fell on John the bear-man. He looked dominant but caged, solitary in his glass carrel. His great stillness rendered him dangerous and approachable at the same time. I watched him till he looked up, then I looked down.

"Possible traps may be present at breaks in the reef chain . . ."

I had to read that particular paper three times over to get even the shreds of meaning I was accustomed to getting. At the end I looked up and saw John leaving the room. Without thinking twice, I folded my papers and followed him out of the library, across the square, and into the dark halls of the English Department where he entered the last door in the row, next to the fire-escape.

I waited a moment, and then continued past his open doorway using all my will-power to stop myself from looking in.

I took to walking along that hallway every day, imagining I appeared casual, on my way to somewhere. John's door

was always open. Of course he must have known what I was
up to: there was no one around the department that summer, I doubt if footsteps sounded there more than twice a
week. The first time I said hello my legs and my voice were
trembling. He raised great sombre weary eyes to mine and
mumbled a greeting. That American accent! The sadness in
his voice! I promised myself I'd go back the next day, to stop
and talk to him.

It seemed to me the men (and they were all men) who wrote
these paeans to a mineral deposit were of a particular stamp.
I saw them, if not in pith helmets, then in soft-brimmed cotton hats, khaki pants stuffed into high green rubber boots,
army surplus jackets, pockets stuffed with tools. Grown-up
boy scouts with mosquito-netting over their weathered faces,
made strong by a deep inner fund of practical knowledge
and positive thought. Logical and ordinarily reserved, they
eschewed description other than the technical, but somehow
their zeal came through the prose. The only time any of
them was given to poetic leaps was when called upon to
describe the largeness, the potential of the oil sands. A common technique was to imagine a vast engineering project to
convey their enormousness.

Here was a man who wrote that there was enough oil sand
to pave a four-lane superhighway to the moon, *complete with
approaches and exit ramps.* Who wants a highway to the moon?
is the obvious response, but the skill of the author sidestepped
this question by bringing up the matter of ramps and approaches. Exits to where? Approaches from what? The
details gave this speculative project reality, made it seem
feasible, even imminent.

Here was another, writing that if the oil were separated
out the sand remaining would create a desert larger than the
Sahara. It was to be construed not as a problem, but as yet

another marvel. One writer confided that if we built a twenty-storey wall around New Brunswick we could fill the space within to the top with left over sand. Would the residents of New Brunswick not object? The impression of power was such that clearly they would be churlish to do so.

It was the kind of power men liked best, too, I recognized, the power which was only real when rescued from its natural habitat, power needing human unleashing. Its mystery too was of the preferred sort, to men, mystery which could be penetrated, mystery with gold at the end. Because the oil in the tar sands was useless in its natural form. The trinity of oil, sand and water had to be broken, and could be broken only by science. Thus "separation" was the goal. In tar-sands literature, "separation" took on mystic overtones.

When we were able to solve this small problem of separation, Alberta and Canada would be self-sufficient, rich beyond belief, and the envy of the rest of the world. But, more than that, a victory for man would be taken out of those twisted layers of rock, that sink of time. But victory is not the right word, because that implies the defeat of nature. Implicit in these authors' work was the happy belief that nature must give in willingly to the power of reason, and natural substances would move to the higher plane of utility, as spirits rose to meet their destiny.

Geologists were missionaries; their zeal was to "extract," to "develop," to "separate." Their religion was religion's absence; they saw themselves as open-minded seekers after knowledge. The present was the key to the past, and not the reverse. They faced down amateurs and their guesswork, which had brought disrepute on the fledgling science. They had established their precepts. Effect came from cause. Dead ends were discarded. Progress must be made.

This reasoning was not unfamiliar. Soon its buoyancy resounded in me as something known and half forgotten, a set of myths native to this continent and still in the air, but strangely missing from my education. A geologist dug down to build up. His analysis was productive. All the thinking I'd been raised on was reductive. Somehow Freud had defeated us all. I lived with the depressing diagnoses of my English and psychology professors, the reductive explanations of mysterious behaviour as symptoms of sickness. "He was tied to his mother's apron strings" — of Hamlet. Even great successes were interpreted this way: a man who built a business empire was greedy, when someone became Chairman of the Board we said: "He never could do anything by himself."

But geologists, I saw, reasoned on a higher level. They saw history not as the result of flaws and mishaps, but as a designed process of becoming. My parents and educators, neither dogmatic nor faithful, lacked this very element of certainty. How much better the geologist who was always fighting the irrational, who saw what the world was, and investigated the relationship of its parts. He did not despair or fear. These tar sands were our inheritance, but through a slip of the wand they had been presented in unusable form. It was for man to find a way. All things were possible. The world was a laboratory.

On perhaps my tenth walk past, I stopped outside John's office. His head was down on his desk, hidden in his arms.

"Hi," I said brazenly.

He did not move.

What luck! Perhaps he was sick, and I could help him. "You OK?" I breathed, and stepped over the doorsill. I was panting slightly. He raised his head, shook his reddish hair out of his eyes.

"Uh hu—h?" he drawled.

"You've been — um — sleeping?"

He leaned back, heaving a giant breath and letting his enormous arms rise up behind him in a stretch. "I worked all night."

So it was true what the librarians said, he slept in his office. He certainly looked as if he slept in his office. He was rumpled and unfresh. I thought that even from this distance I could smell his breath. "Just checking, you know, if you'd passed out or what," I said, backing up. His sheer physicality filled up the dusty little room.

He rocked with a laugh that was half a roar. I felt my face flush, and dodged out of sight. As I hurried down the hallway he called after me.

"Hey what's your name?"

"Tomi," I shouted back.

I studied the most boring papers I could find at the library.

"If the theory of a tectonic arch is accepted, then shoreline fringing facies should be expected."

But John's head rose in my mind above the untidy stacks of lined foolscap on which he wrote in large black circles and blots, over and over. He had a protruding forehead and heavy red eyebrows. I thought him immeasurably deep, and kind. I cursed myself for running away after I'd spoken to him and accomplished the hardest bit. I longed for him to talk to me, even for a few minutes.

". . . in addition, interfingering sand laminations are present as far west as the Pine Rapids outcrops."

Interfingering sand laminations. It was all too much.

I met Carol for lunch. We stretched out on the south-facing slope outside the Science complex and, without overdoing it, I betrayed a little interest in John.

"There's a guy," I said. And finished up the story. "I made a complete ass of myself. I can't ever face him again."

"Why don't you ask him to go for a walk?" she said. How ambitious she was, how sure! A walk had never entered my mind. All I dared imagine was a ten-minute coffee break.

"Would you?"

"No," said Carol. "But you're different."

I was flattered by her belief in me, but I said nothing. Carol told me she was now certain she would get pregnant. Perhaps it had even happened the night before.

"He started pulling off my nightgown in bed last night," she said, "and I said I just had to get up and put in the diaphragm, but he just kissed my mouth shut and I never made it out of bed . . ."

After lunch my distraction was complete. I repaired to the fainting couch which was still found in the ladies' rest-room outside the Dean's office. I knew one day temptation would make me brave, and I would go visit John in his office, talk to him, maybe even convince him to come out in the sun for a break.

Since their mysterious origin the tar sands had lain for millions of years under Alberta, performing no useful function. Sometime in the recent past of the last two thousand years, passing Indians had begun to use the sticky tar to patch their canoes, as smudge to throw on their fires because it discouraged mosquitoes. No one thought of doing more with it until the white fur traders came into the North-West. Having observed that these newcomers found uses for many products of the wild, a speculative Cree trapper named Wa Pa Su scooped out a handful of gooey tar sands and carried it east to York Factory, where he showed it to Henry Kelsey.

In another time and place Wa Pa Su might have been a Getty or a Howard Hughes. As it was, Kelsey took a good look at the stuff and jotted a few notes in his journal as to where it was said to be found, and Wa Pa Su went home unrewarded. When Peter Pond crossed the Methy Portage from Lac la Loche into the Clearwater River he saw rich black stuff oozing from the banks, called it bitumen, and assumed it was of great value. Wintering over on Lake Athabasca, he mapped the country he considered his own. He drafted three versions, one for the British, one for the American Congress, and one for the Empress of Russia. Each map emphasized the ease of access of these riches to the chosen market. But for the moment he found no takers, in fact, his letter to the Empress of Russia received no answer at all: perhaps it was lost in the mail.

Successive explorers added their observations of the springs of mineral pitch. Sometimes it was thin and oozing, sometimes so thick small birds were trapped in it. By 1870 fur traders were cutting off lumps with knives and boiling it to make tar. I noted these facts on my filing cards with great interest. Now miners began to come, with one scheme after another.

Already, however, they could perceive the problem: how to get the tar out of the ground and, once it was out of the ground, how to get rid of the sand and the water. They tried flooding, they tried drilling with diamonds, they lifted the stuff in buckets. They heated it to make it flow, cooled it to make it stiff, they spun it like sugar in cylinders. They were investors, inventors, cranks, loners. They were panhandlers with a scientific bent, entrepreneurs with vision. There was a group of New York policemen, fired with enthusiasm by a touring scientist, who thought they'd make their fortune until they found that Athabasca muskeg was tougher to get through than the deepest darkest alleys of the Bowery.

My favourite was the German Count Alfred von Hammerstein, who let his cable tool rig loose in the river's Grand Rapids and "all hands" (how many hands he had was not noted) went down with it. The count himself swam ashore and walked back for a second rig.

I couldn't talk to Carol about the Count; somehow her unflappability combined with her exaggerated respect for my brain did not inspire discussion on intellectual matters. I sat with her in the noontime sun, imagining a more stimulating companion. It was as if I were storing up before moving on, absorbing her worldliness, her ways of getting what she wanted. Before long I would use her advice and the confidence she gave me to strike out beyond her limited world. It was a less than admirable way of progressing, and one I have noticed in myself and others many times since.

"Have you taken him a cup of coffee yet?" she suggested, with her unnerving tapline into my hidden thoughts.

That same afternoon I marched out to the Arts Building basement, bought a cup of the black silty water sold in the machine, and took it to John's door. Again when I saw him I had that sense of a huge backed-up, held-off power. It made him desperately attractive. He lifted his head when I came in without pleasure or irritation.

"This calls for a break," he said, stretching again. He always had a rumpled, sleepy look. He got up from the desk, and we went out into the sunshine. We sat down on the lawn in the hot yellow afternoon. It was my dream come true. He asked me what work I was doing. I told him about Wa Pa Su on the twelfth of June 1719, carrying his lump of the pitch that oozed out of the banks of the river in the unknown farwest country to the white men.

"Can't you just see him in his canoe?" I said. "He probably wrapped it in some birch-bark. Or a skin. He carried it in his pack a thousand miles. It was like Inca gold, you see, riches beyond riches. It made the fur trade look like a game of marbles. And they missed it! You had to be an alchemist to understand the potential. Hardly anyone did. Does,'' I said.

We talked about how hard it was to get the oil out, how each grain of sand was coated with water, and the oil clung to the water. I told him that the oil was useless until it was separated from the sand and the water, until it was on its own, explosive, burnable. We discussed how tantalizing it was to those who saw it oozing from the river banks, so easy to reach, how it broke the spirit of those who tried to retrieve it and refine it.

John the dodger was fascinated, I could tell. He was from away, and had never heard of the tar sands. He could see what it stood for, all it needed was a certain gleam in his eye, a nod here and there in my tale, for me to see that he knew, he knew what it all meant. But after a while I stopped myself with an effort, and asked about his work. He explained that he was examining what happened to the Bible as it went through different translations. I remember his voice, how it rumbled like a dirt road with loose gravel beneath big wheels. Was it that day or another when he recited for me?

"Remember ye not the former things, neither consider things of old. Behold, I will do a new thing. Now it shall spring forth. Shall ye not know it?"

"That's the King James version,'' he said. We were propped on the slope on our elbows, feet stretching down the hill. I let the sun settle over the skin of my face and the front of my bare shins.

"But listen to this. Here's the New England Bible. Tell me what you think has happened.'' And his head went back, and his eyes shut, and the voice rolled out into the sun and dry air.

"Cease to dwell on days gone by, and to brood over past history.

Here and now I will do a new thing; this moment it will break from the bud. Can you not perceive it?'

He made it sound so marvellous I felt I was hearing it from God, at least a prophet. There I was, linking minds with him, as I had longed to do. It had a devastating affect. I scrambled for something worth while to say other than, "Take me in your arms and kiss me."

"The music has gone out of it," I said. "I miss the poetic form of the King James, those reversals, you know, like 'remember ye not'. But there is a new image all the same. The flower image, the bud. That's rather nice."

Hoping he approved, I opened my eyes a slit, but did not dare look at him. Instead what came into my line of vision was Carol, there on the other side of the hill, decorously stepping down the path toward her bus stop. It must be four o'clock. She always left exactly on the dot. I prayed she wouldn't wave. It was Friday. I had a fantasy that John and I would stay on that hill until it was impossible to be parted. He would ask me for a beer, we'd drink it and lose control, something of that sort would happen. We would spend the whole weekend together.

"Hmmmm," he said. "Not bad. OK, try this, the Jerusalem Bible: *No need to recall the past. No need to think about what* —"

"I don't like that one at all," I said.

He laughed again, and said he'd better get back to work.

Monday there was a note on my desk. It was only one word long.

"Nitrogen???" it read. And was signed, Gupta.

Perhaps I was falling behind my employers' movement on the project. I searched the periodical indexes, xeroxed articles on nitrogen. I found one entitled "Multiple contact

phase behaviour in the displacement of crude oil with
nitrogen and enriched nitrogen.''

"Nitrogen has some disadvantages," I read, "including
the cost of separating [it] from the produced hydrocarbon
gases, and nitrogen asphyxia.''

Asphyxia. Death by suffocation. Something of the fervour
had entered me, because I listed merely this as an inconvenience.

I took lunch with John every day. Our conversations
evolved from the intellectual to the personal. (I used a little
of Carol for that.) He told me his troubles, and became
touchingly dependent on me, like a large dog. All the same,
our age difference never went away. He was at least thirty, I
thought, and conscious of it. He was scrupulously well
behaved; to my great regret, in all my visits he never made a
single sexual overture. He listened to my tales of tar as if he
cared. Perhaps they meant something entirely different to
him from what they did to me.

"Separation," I went on. "The search is for the perfect
means to divide the useful from the useless. To refine.''

"The wheat from the chaff.''

"But that's so easy. This is far, far more difficult.
Because, you see, the two parts are one, together they com-
pose a new substance. Its properties are of the two acting in
concert.''

I never knew exactly whether he approved of separation.
He was a tease. He invoked Freud, he invoked Reich. He
taunted me with Thoreau and Emerson. "Everything in
nature is made of the power of nature," he said.
"Everything is made of one hidden stuff." I thought he was
wonderful, all the more wonderful because of the damage
that had been done to him.

Because I believed John had been, like Jake in *The Sun
Also Rises*, injured in the war. Not *in* the war, exactly, but *by*

the war, and not physically, but psychologically. In refusing to act, he had renounced the masculine outlet. He was unmanned. He told me he was married to the daughter of a southern general, and his wife and his father-in-law thought he was a coward because he wouldn't go to Vietnam. She moved back to her parents' home, taking the four-year-old daughter. John would have stayed in Tennessee and gone to jail, except that it would further humiliate her. So he vanished in the middle of one night, and went north through New York State where through complex manoeuvres at Niagara Falls he got across to Canada.

Suspended here in Calgary, he read and reread biblical passages, slept in his office, talked to me. I didn't know what else he did; I suppose I began to think he was my property. I sat beside the Arts Building now, and looked over at the hill beside the Engineering complex at lunch. There sat Carol and another secretary, talking their talk. I just knew what they must be saying, in language close to home, plain and unambitious.

"He told me last night my fanny was getting big."

"I've got to get to the drugstore and buy some cuticle remover. My nails are a mess."

"We ran out of eggs so I had to make tuna."

I felt like the inhabitant of a small town who has moved to the city. I saw Carol and this other young woman sit, I saw them eat neatly, with their faces turned slightly to the side so that not even their lunch-mate could see them chew. I saw them dust the crumbs from their lap and fold up the little squares of Saran Wrap and put them into the brown-paper bags. And I saw them stand, brush the blades of grass off the crumpled backs of their skirts, fluff their hair, and head back into the building.

Summer was now halfway over. I still loved my job, the

coming and going from the library, the growing file of papers, what I had learned, and talking about it with John. But I had exhausted the historical parts. I had come to the economic and technical part of my research. The extractors were close to having their way. I now had to record very contemporary, very practical problems. There were no more graceful cross-sections of the geological ages, but rather depressing diagrams of separation cells, froth settlers and conditioning drums. There were no more highways to the moon, only estimates of the number of billion barrels recoverable. There were no more geologists in their high wellington boots and khaki jackets.

The extractors had tried just about everything: washing, dynamiting, flooding, heating, cooling. At one point there were plans to explode a nuclear bomb under the earth to start the oil flowing. All of these were or would have been successful, in the end, in producing pure crude oil. Beautiful, usable, clean oil. The tragic flaw of this oil was that it was too expensive. Procedures for removing tar sand from its strata and purifying it were so elaborate that the oil thus obtained was worth its weight in gold. Or nearly.

Pure science would have called the extraction a success. But these operations violated the very basic principles of the geologists and engineers who invented them. Separation was possible. But it was not practical. At least not yet. The Grail was now not just separation, but *affordable* separation. As before, there were many assurances that science could find the means. But science was not the entire story. There were disturbing intimations that the price of oil had to do with international politics, with wars and alliances and far-off religious fanatics. The purity of the pursuit was lost, and with it much of my sympathy for the searchers.

On the second-last Monday in August, Dr DeMar came in while I was working. He was edgy and took up too much space. I had longed to discuss my findings with him and now I found him obtrusive. I was possessive about the files, rolling my swivel chair onto his toe when he loomed over the card-file boxes. Under Pond he found Peter, and not some Arthur J. for whom he was looking, who had written something on hydrogen desulphurizers. Dr Gupta, he told me, had been in on the weekend again and couldn't find anything on upgrading.

"Dr Gupta!" I said. "I've never even met Dr Gupta!" In the cramped little room I became enraged at the absent Dr Gupta. I started going through my cards but all I could find under U were a few papers on water flooding which should have been under W. Dr DeMar panicked when he saw the tears in my eyes and promptly left the room.

Without waiting until lunch, I ran off to John. He was hunched over his desk as always, and I burst in the door talking. These professors had left me on my own all summer and now they weren't happy with what I'd done! How was I supposed to know all the key words to look up when I wasn't even a geologist in the first place? What did they expect? If they'd just read the things I had put in, it would do them a lot of good, too. Too late I noticed that John looked awful. His eyes were small and red, and his voice didn't roll out, it seemed to halt at the edge of his lip.

"Tomi, I can't talk right now," he said.

"Are you sick?" I looked hard into his face; the skin seemed thicker and less mobile than before, he seemed buried behind his face. I wanted him back, I needed his sympathy.

"I'm not sick," he said dangerously, "just get out."

But I acted the child to him: I wanted his sympathy and I wanted it right then.

"John!" I wailed. "Did you hear what I said? They're not happy with me. I've done it all wrong!"

John stood up. He didn't look sleepy any more. He raised his fist and brought it down in the middle of his desk, hard. His voice was huge.

"Did you hear what I said? I got a letter this morning. She wants a divorce."

I choked on my cry for help. It had come out so easily, but it would be a long time before anyone heard another. My throat and my chest ached holding it in. I felt the muscles in my cheeks manufacturing a smile. I saw John there behind his desk, a giant, and so miserable. I found a voice. It was meant to be a Carol voice, but she would never have made such a blunder.

"Well, that was probably inevitable," I said. "After all, you can't go back, can you?"

I thought to myself I was being kind but I wasn't, of course. I was afraid of losing him, afraid he would, after all, go back to Tennessee and jail. What I wanted to say was, "If you have to go, take me with you." But that would have made no sense at all. Instead I gave him his own quotation back.

"Remember ye not the former things, neither consider things of old. Behold, I will do a new thing —"

His face flamed over the beard. Spit flew out between the hairs of his moustache.

"What do you know, you wretched little virgin? You're nothing, nothing. You don't understand a goddamn thing!"

And he pushed himself around the side of his desk and strode out, leaving me alone in his office. I stood there for a moment, my eyes ripe with tears I would never cry. I was good enough to listen to his troubles, wasn't I? I was good enough to be his friend all summer. If I was a virgin it was his fault as much as mine.

The next day I did not go to have lunch with him. I longed to rest my wounded pride with Carol, to bask and talk of nothing at all, to hear about her birth-control problems and the way the chairman loaded her desk with work. But I had neglected her shamelessly and now she had a new friend. I stayed in my little room, summarizing articles on the latest pilot projects in the tar sands. They were written by officials of oil companies and gave oddly petulant summations of their experience.

"The weather, varying from 90 degrees F in the summer to -55 degrees F in the winter presents operating problems which are almost insurmountable.

". . . Muskeg can only be removed during January and February when the -30 degree F temperatures freeze it so it is easily handled . . . .

"During cold periods the tar sand remains at a steady 40 degrees F and the water surrounding it remains unfrozen. On contact with cold equipment this water promptly freezes, building layer upon layer of ice on the equipment. . . .

"In wet weather the material is transformed into a pulpy mess and deepens until all transportation bogs down completely. In summer the tar sand sticks to anything it contacts in a most tenacious manner . . . ."

I took a certain pleasure in summarizing their troubles.

On the third day Carol and her friend walked by my door before noon. I heard them. They were talking about slicing an onion without tears.

"Once through, and then turn it around. Slice it again, not all the way through. Then turn it around again, so it's all still intact —"

"I just need to look at an onion and I cry. I don't know if this will work for me."

"No, really. Just don't let it fall apart."

They were gone.

I looked down at my work and I had one moment of the purest bitterness. I was unappreciated by the professors, unappreciated by John. My authors were whining, and possibly would never succeed in what they had set out to do. I had lost the one true friend I had.

The next day Carol came and put her face up to the glass oblong, and tapped lightly. I looked up, I know it must have been eagerly, then jumped to my feet and opened the door.

"How are you doing?" she said. "Is the book going to get done this year?"

That was another thing. I realized my professors might never write the thing. I looked at my two drawers of file cards.

"If not it won't be for lack of research material," I said, adopting exactly the sarcastic tone toward the professors that she did.

She smiled. Her little pointed lips parted and the dewy white teeth over which she worked so diligently showed.

"How's Tim?" I said in return.

"We went camping this weekend," she said. Her skin was so fresh, her eyes so clear, she was so kind, she herself a natural wonder. "I ate bacon and eggs both mornings," she said. "I can't believe how fat I feel."

We went for lunch on the lawn and I saw John come out on his own and take his place and nobody said anything about how I had changed sides, not me, not Carol, and not him, for he had no one to say it to. I thought, if I ever get to talk to him again I'm going to tell him that I don't know if the greatest resource in the world will ever be tapped. Separation was a beautiful ideal, perhaps an impossibility. All this power would remain in the ground, impure, natural, unsuitable for higher uses. Perhaps we didn't want separation, utilization, transmutation after all. We wanted to try, and never succeed.

Then in one marvellous gesture my friend raised his slow heavy arm in a wave and I waved back at him in the sunlight across the expanse of dry grass.

Domain

Domain

Donald's bulk dropped into the stern of the Peterborough, boosting his pale wife and child above him on their slat in the bow. The old motor started on the third pull, and dug into the dark water. He experimented with the arm, yanking it in, pushing it out. The wake, a white caterpillar, worked its way backwards on the surface.

"Luck to ya," called Roy as the low wooden skiff crossed the smooth expanse of water enclosed by the T-docks, and hit the slight chop of the bay. Donald's arm was forward, pointing through the gap. His mouth was going.

"Look at that, lecturing already." Roy turned to serve a big new inboard. He bet Donald had himself a pack of trouble with that propane fridge. And the pump! The motor on that pump at the professor's house hadn't been touched in years.

"That one of the Grange boys?" came the voice from the cabin. "Hasn't that place been empty?"

" 'Cept for renters in the cottage," said Roy. "But Donald's brought his wife up to show her, a last visit, like. Hulce is selling the place, we hear."

A silver head with yachting cap emerged, and the spry boater in a white polo shirt and faded bathing trunks jumped onto the dock. "More Germans? They going to make another hundred-unit hotel up there?"

"I dunno," said Roy, who knew better than to get into arguments with cottagers about development. They all wanted their spot on the rock, their dishwasher and satellite dish. Then they became conservationists. He was glad the old Hulce place was going at last; new owners meant more business.

"Hope not," said the inboard owner, signing his gas chit. "That place has a lot of history."

"You might say," said Roy. To his mind, every place had about the same amount of history. Some people were inclined to make more of it than others, that was all. But he wasn't going to pursue the issue. He'd had enough of history, with Donald Grange's arrival.

He'd shown up this morning, striding downhill from the parking lot complaining at the top of his lungs about how you used to be able to see Angel Island but now the deck of the marina store blocked it. Roy took his time getting the boat around for him. He'd only taken it out of storage and put it in the water on Monday; today was Friday. It really needed a week.

"Can't guarantee what shape it's in," he said. "You gotta give me more warning."

But Grange was unaffected by the reprimand. In fact when Roy leaned over to put the nozzle into the old red gas can, he stood up close, sweating, bending Roy's ear about how, before the highway, the religious folk who ran the marina used to bring up the gas by barge. Calling Roy the "new owner" although he'd brought his family here ten years ago and rescued the marina and the tiny settlement from the peculiar gloom that had suffused it in the days of the Jesus set.

What bugged Roy, it wasn't even as if Donald Grange was an old-timer. His dad came up here with Professor Hulce who owned the place; Donald had only been a guest and a little boy at that. You'd wonder he even remembered the things he said he remembered.

As the boat pulled away Roy stood there holding the gas hose and looking at Grange's wife hunched in that pale pink sweater and shook his head. She was scared to death.

By now the boat was halfway to the gap and the wind was going right through Dora's sweater. She held her hair back from her eyes, trying to see where Donald was pointing.

"We get out of this bay, see, cross the open water, go around those first two islands, and take the east channel. We're heading toward the very northern end of the whole system."

"Right," she said. Donald had an atlas in his head; he could look at what was in front of him and squash it flat, onto a page. It was one of the many things she admired about him. Although Dora had looked at the map in advance, she had no idea where these waterways led, which way was open water. What she saw in front of her was a maze of cold turquoise channels and rounded, tree-covered islands. The trees came right down to the edge of the water, which might have been why the light everywhere was queasy green.

His firm, fat hand on the tiller, Donald guided the boat into an extended curve to the right. Another huge vista of water opened up.

"Look, there, straight between those high cliffs. For just a minute you'll be able to see the roof of the house. Then it'll be gone. After that, till we get to the dock, it'll be completely hidden in trees."

Dora couldn't see the roof and couldn't understand why Donald should be so happy that it was lost in trees. Thatcher climbed up onto the bow to look harder. They had passed huge boathouses with three garage doors at water level, and window boxes of geraniums. There were white-painted wooden chairs lined up on docks, and the sails of wind-surfers dried on the rocks. They went by a glassy A-frame with a wind sock and a light plane parked in front. Then the cottages changed. They grew smaller and their paint was not so bright. There were no more boathouses. They came to a log cabin on a point, which looked as if it was from the past century. Across from it there was a farmhouse with a field running down to the shore. They turned there, and ahead was nothing, just a long erratic curve of shoreline with a series of narrow bays like a tracing of the four fingers of a hand. It was late afternoon. The sun lit the flat rocks where Donald was heading.

"This is it! Carscadden Bay!" said Donald. "Can you believe the water beneath us is three hundred and fifty feet deep?"

"Thatcher!" said Dora. "Get down from there! Did you hear what Daddy said?"

"Shut up, Dora," said Donald. "You'd think you'd never been out of Rexdale. You'd think you never even saw a lake."

Dora shrank. She had never seen a lake, not like this. There were rocks everywhere, jagged huge things up on end, jutting way out of the water, piled along the banks as if left there by a giant bulldozer. She knew what it was from school, and more recently from Donald's descriptions. Canadian Shield. Rocks scraped bare by retreating glaciers in the last ice age. Just thinking of it gave her a chill. It was dizzying, crossing over water like this in a boat; it was like going on a tightrope over an enormous pit. Alongside her seat the dull green water was secretive, not lit through, sheer, like the lakes of her imagination.

Dora's parents had never taken their family to cottages. They'd hardly had vacations, in fact. But when Dora told her mother where they were going her grandpa had overheard. He'd lived all his life on a farm north of Parry Sound and was a new member of the household in Rexdale, deaf, stone-faced. His lips moved continually, as if he were reciting a favourite song. That was funny, because Grandpa was a Methodist; he'd never sung outside of church in his life. But he'd caught the name, dragged a voice up his wobbling neck.

"Lake Joe," he said. "I used to fish there. Lost my meerschaum pipe in Lake Joe. It fell over the side and I looked after it and it just went down, down, down."

Dora's mother rolled her eyes, but Dora knew what her grandfather meant. For a few seconds you saw it going and then it was gone and you knew you couldn't ever get it back. He meant it was irrevocable, dropping something in deep water.

The waves were rising; the boat was cutting them at an angle, slap, slap, slap. The hull banged on the surface of the water. They'd gone beyond all the other cottages now. Thatcher's face was into the wind, his red hair full of air. His skin was wiped, white, as if all his freckles had blown off. The boat was bucking hard. Dora had a sudden image of the heavy hull of the boat coming down on her son's head.

"Thatcher! You heard me," she said. "If you fall off we'll run right over you."

"It always gets rougher here!" Donald had to yell, over the wind and the motor and the splashing. "See how the wind comes straight across the wide end of the lake? The chop builds up, you can never be too careful."

Dora clung to the seat, and to Thatcher.

"One time," Donald shouted. He wanted to teach his family the arts of survival at Carscadden, tell them the stories of the dangerous trips in, the narrow escapes. The wind took his words. He cut the motor to reduce the noise.

"One time," he said, more quietly, "one time the whole family, six of us in this same boat, were coming, and Dad flooded the motor, this same motor. Nothing has been replaced. That's a principle of Carscadden. You don't replace anything." He laughed gently, as at the regulations of an exclusive club which were indefensible, but to which he still adhered.

"Anyway it was pouring and Dad couldn't get the motor going. For some reason he got me to stand and hold the metal choke down against the post. Can you imagine? Me, the youngest, feet in the water, hands soaking wet? I stood there, must've been smaller than Thatcher even, for hours it seemed. Finally it caught. When we got to the house Mum gave Dad hell. I could've got a shock. I could've been electrocuted."

His wife and son said nothing. Donald was tasting the old soreness, how hard his Dad had been on him. When they got to the house his mother had rubbed him in a blanket for a long time. Poor old Mum, he thought; and twisted the handle of the tiller so that the motor roared again. He could see the place now, the bare tongue of rock with the lower cottage exposed on it, and beside it the giant spruce and the rising cliff. The main house was invisible in the trees. He could see the main dock though, cut in a curve to fit against the rock it ran from, and weathered to the same grey.

That dock was a beautiful thing. One of the old guys from the Jesus set — the colony had a name, but no one ever used it, they always just said the Jesus set — had designed it. He'd arrived in the middle of July in a black jacket buttoned to the neck, didn't know how to swim even, though he'd lived on the lake all his life. But he had known the water. He'd stood there and drawn the thing, crib and all, at just the right angle to withstand the force of the waves and the opposite pull of the melting ice in spring.

His Dad and Hulce had helped build it. He remembered his Dad saying that the thing would be there long after he, and maybe Donald too, was gone.

Admiring the big dock, Donald realized with a shock that the Hulces' big boat was tied up at it. There was a flag up on the pole too. Hulce never came any more; he must have renters in the cottage.

He went a few hundred feet farther into the bay. There was a second, smaller dock for the main house, which Tom Hulce and his father had built on their own, after the Jesus set split up and its leader ran off to Florida with the community coffers, leaving behind a series of faded ''Jesus Saves'' signs in the bush. He'd have to use it 'though he'd never liked it. He slowed the boat, curved out around the little dock and then cut back in an arc toward the shore and back alongside it, letting the back end of the boat swing toward the boards, trying not to catch his own wake, but keeping the motor high enough to combat the waves. He judged it wrong. He was going to overshoot; he couldn't reach the edge of the dock.

He cut the motor. In the sudden silence his voice was harsh.

''Jump, Dora. Now! Take the rope in your hands and jump up onto the dock!''

Dora stood up all at once, as if in stirrups, her pale thin legs bucking with the movement of the boat. She got the rope in her hand, she got her foot up on the seat, but she didn't jump. The gap of water widened. Soon it would be too late.

''Now!'' he shouted. ''Jump!''

She collapsed on the seat. "I can't."

The dock was out of reach. Cursing, Donald pulled the motor again and made another circle.

"Gee Dora, you're such a natural boat person."

Her shoulder blades poked out of the pink Banlon sweater more, and her head dropped a little lower. Thatcher sat very still, looking over the side at the water.

"I'll drive it then," she said. "You jump."

"You can't drive it!"

They circled alongside the dock more slowly this time, the oncoming waves making the boat buck, soaking Thatcher. Holding the rope, Dora was poised as if to jump to a half-desired death. At the last minute she drew back.

"Hey," she said, "there's no top on this dock."

Donald stood up. The crib was still there, but the deck of the dock was missing, it was all pointed rocks and little pools of water. There were no boards left at all; they must've been pulled away by the ice. Hulce and his dad didn't do so well, did they? He cut the motor again and pulled the boat to a stop with his hand. Dora stood there uncertainly hanging on to the rope.

"Do you want me to jump now?"

Dora was useless.

Donald and Dora sat with cups of herbal tea, resting, finally, on the vast screen porch. Donald stared across the water in a brooding way; he was sore because of the renters, because they'd had to unload on the uneven wet rocks on the bad dock. He was also angry because Thatcher had taken a flashlight to bed. The rule was no electricity at Carscadden, but it was dark in the top of the house and Dora wouldn't let him take a kerosene lamp for fear he might burn down the house.

"See, in the old days, that main dock was for everybody.

It was a camp here. They fished off our ledge and we docked on their side and walked over the little bridge. Back over there,'' he said.

Dora didn't look around. She hadn't said much at all since they'd had to carry their suitcases and bags of bed linen and boxes of food up the rocks. The path Donald remembered, where you rolled the shopping cart, was mud-slick and full of holes. The cart, when they found it, had no wheels so they'd had to haul their stuff up by hand, clinging to the rail fence. Dora was panting and her legs were covered with mud when she finally reached the house, standing high, green and forlorn a couple of hundred feet above the water.

It was not a cottage but a real house, with plaster on the walls, two-storey, gabled, with the wide screened porch running three-quarters of the way around it. It had been standing there so long it had become a part of the woods; it was the same colour as the woods, its shingles like bark, its screens grey with spider webs, its green paint speckled like dry moss on the faded boards. On one front corner, a twisted spruce had become involved with the supports. It curved up from under the porch, and the porch roof held up two of its long branches.

"What a horrid tree," she said. "Let's cut it down."

Donald looked shocked. "Dad used that tree to illustrate symbiosis," he said.

The inside was dark and smelled of stale gas. Pine furniture was piled in the centre of the main room. The floor was covered in a thin yellow dust which made everyone sneeze. They'd had to clean the mouse turds off the kitchen counters before they could even put anything down. Then Donald spent an hour lying on his stomach on the kitchen floor lighting the pilot under the propane refrigerator.

Dora found the bedding where he said it would be,

mothballed in garbage bags in the pine boxes. While she made up the beds Donald took Thatcher down to show him how to start the motor for the pump. They hadn't been able to get it going yet. So she had to clean with buckets of water from the lake, and listen all the while to Donald crowing about how nothing had changed.

If Dora had had the courage to act betrayed, she would have done so now. This was her holiday. There was bound to be too much work to the place, and even work wouldn't improve it, nothing short of a landslide could do that. She was even more disappointed because Donald had been telling her stories about Carscadden ever since they'd met. The magical summer place had been part of his aura.

They met when Donald came to Dora's high school on Careers Day. A student at Branwell Technical College, he stood behind a table distributing pamphlets and telling kids they'd get good jobs if they signed up for a work-training course, as he had. Donald exalted manual labour, real labour, the results of which could be seen, relied upon. He had gone to university but had dropped out to become a roofer. The reasons for this were complicated and had to do with the fact that his brothers and sisters were professionals with whom he couldn't or wouldn't compete. His decision was not unrelated, either, to his father's academic decline into a sixties cliché, but these were realities of which Dora had not been aware until too late.

For as a result of her conversation with Donald and despite the fact that she was a good academic student in grade eleven, Dora dropped out of high school and signed up for a nurse's aide course which cost a thousand dollars and set her up for a lifetime of changing bedpans. She had recently begun to express dissatisfaction to Donald, who diagnosed her problem as psychological, and began paying for her self-actualization course.

Sulking, Dora watched the sun make a wide orange road straight from their porch to the far side of the bay.

"You'd think you could walk on it," said Donald companionably.

Dora jumped.

"I should light the lamps." He was conspicuously cheerful as the sun dropped inch by inch. And he got one of the row of a dozen lamps, filled with kerosene he'd brought. He set it on the table between them.

"It's not bright enough. You can't read by that," said Dora.

"We don't read at night at Carscadden."

"What do we do then?" she said, suspiciously.

"Play Scrabble. Charades."

She looked at him. He seemed to be addressing others.

"All right, so charades would be hard, with two," he admitted. "We can talk. Or think. Watch the lake."

"There's quite a few trees in the way."

"Yeah," he said.

"It would be nice to cut them down, one or two," she said, idly. His tea mug stopped halfway to his mouth.

"Cut them?"

"So you could see."

"Then we'd be exposed, to the lake."

"Nobody goes by, anyway," said Dora, who hadn't seen a living soul since leaving Roy's marina.

"Wait till the third week of July, the water will be jumping with boats."

"That long?"

Donald's patience ran out.

"Dora," he said, putting down his cup and turning his deepset, glinting eyes on hers. They warned of cruelties to come. "Dora, try to understand. You don't come to a place like this to see people. You come to discover your resources. If you have any."

Dora smiled. That was more like it. Equally reassured, Donald turned back to the lake and lapsed into scornful recollection.

"Dad and Hulce wouldn't believe the development on this lake. Shit, did you see that dumbwaiter going up the rocks, by the German's place?"

The night was silent, not a sound issuing from the deep forest or the water. Then a loon cried. Dora opened her mouth. Donald silenced her with a raised finger. Another loon responded. Donald pointed behind him.

"The loons have moved inland," he said. "Did I tell you we've got our own private lake, in behind us? No one but us ever goes there. The mosquitoes are so bad you can't get in there except with nets all over you even on a very windy day."

"Oh," said Dora.

She wished he hadn't told her that. The huge woods were bad enough, but a lake nobody ever saw? What did it do all the time, just lie there absorbing trees and animals and anything that fell into it? Growing algae and green slime? The very idea of its existing there all these years with no human being ever present was terrifying.

"That's wealth, you see," said Donald energetically, educating her now. "That's what Hulce got out of this whole thing. Not just the house and the cottage, they're nice, but they're corruptible, you see. All that nonsense from down the lake will come up here eventually. No, the real wealth is that, behind. An untouched lake no one can get to but you. A lost lake you never look at."

"I s'pose," said Dora, who absolutely disagreed. "It's wealth but you can't do anything with it. If you even touch it, then you've changed it, then it's just like anything else."

At the lower cottage, Chip and Mandy sat in their screened porch gazing at the water. The sun was sliding behind the hills at the far end of the bay; in minutes the coral tips would be gone from the waves. It had been another perfect day.

And not a cloud to suggest a drop in standards for tomorrow. It seemed a sin to be so happy.

"That gas lamp has gone out at the house," Chip said. "And the boat's still there." He rarely lit the propane lamps himself; on the bare rock they had sunlight from seven in the morning until after nine at night.

"They're staying overnight, then," said Mandy.

"Wonder who they are."

Something like this had been said now half a dozen times since they'd seen the Peterborough tied to a rock where the wrecked crib stuck out from the shore. It was the third year Chip and Mandy had holidayed here, always with the whole place to themselves. Each time the weather had been hot, still, clear. It was an atavistic vacation, sun, food, sleep. No television, newspapers, films, or parties. A break they desperately needed, or so they both agreed. She had known this year would be different, with a baby. That was why they had brought Jen.

It was Jen who saw the boat arrive that afternoon, and the couple and their little boy carrying up dozens of grocery bags.

"People!" she had cried.

Her employers were crestfallen, but Jen was pleased to have neighbours. She was English. She couldn't quite accept that this was Muskoka, the Muskoka she'd heard about; she hoped, perhaps, that this shack was a way station, and they were going to move on.

"Let's hope it's not the new owners," Mandy said quietly.

"Can't be. The deal doesn't close until September."

"Then it's some of the professors' old friends on a last visit."

"It had to happen," said Chip with a gust of breath, and reached for the wine bottle. He had always said that the mile of lakefront with acres of forest behind, spectacular cliffs,

three bays and a beach were worth a fortune, and would not
sit neglected indefinitely. It had only been Chip's chance ac-
quaintance with Tom Hulce over a real-estate deal that gave
them the chance to sit like kings presiding over two miles of
empty lake. Still, they felt miffed by this impending sale, as
if they should have been consulted.

"If they're staying we'll have to invite them for a drink."

"Let's think about it. There's no rush."

"True," said Mandy.

When it got too dark to see, they went to bed.

It had become imperative for Mandy to get down to the
rocks in the morning, first thing, even before the marina
boat delivering the papers crossed the far side of the lake. It
was a form of claiming, being the first to see it all remade by
night. Once, she'd stepped out of the half-hidden cottage onto the rock face carrying the breakfast tray, with Timmie
riding on her shoulders, and right in front of her was a
fisherman in a boat. It was a shock, for him as much as for
her. She became conscious instantly of how they looked to
him: an aboriginal mother and child, sufficient on this rock,
with their dainty ritual. And that vision of herself and her
son almost made up for his being there.

Today she had the tray in one hand and Timmie slung
like a towel over her shoulder. As always the sun hit the
rocks beside the dock first, a warm bright crescent on which
to sit. She settled the tray and balanced Timmie on a clump
of moss and sat down on the flat rock.

Mandy loved rocks better than any other surface on earth.
Dirt was dirty and had bugs, sand got everywhere, grass had
to be cut and watered, but rocks took care of themselves.
The older they got, the more beautiful they were. These
were scraped into flat bits, slopes and ridges like oil paint

worked with a palette knife. The long wide slab of rock which ran from the front of their cottage two hundred feet down to the water was an abstract of an army, all shields and faces, lifted to the sun, in colours of pink and silver, black and grey.

Even more than their appearance, she loved how rocks felt. They were retentive; they held back the pace of the day. Now, they kept night in them and were cooler than the air. All day they'd store the sun, growing warmer until at five o'clock they bit the soles of her feet. Then at twilight when the air had cooled they'd be warm to touch, like fresh loaves of bread.

Quietly she told Timmie not to spill his juice; her voice blended with the bird chirp and low watery rustle. She had her coffee cup between her hands when she heard the raspy, piercing voice.

"My daddy says we used to use this dock."

A fish might just as well have risen up out of the water and addressed her. The hairs stood up on Mandy's neck. She turned around. An urchin with red hair stepped out of the trees.

"What's your name?"

"Thatcher."

"Thatcher Who?" It was not really a question. It was an expression of astonishment.

"Thatcher Barnstable Grange." He waited a minute and then plunged on. "My Daddy said this dock was for everyone, in the olden days."

The boy had pale blue eyes and freckles, and skim-milk skin. Mandy's heart was beating hard against her breast-bone. He had walked across the little wooden bridge, through the wild strawberry patch, and was within yards of their breakfast. "My daddy says there was a boathouse

down over there.'' He pointed across the rock to the side
dock, in the little inlet where Mandy went to read. ''We
used to tie up our boat there.''

''When was this?'' said Mandy.

Thatcher wasn't clear when, exactly.

''Well, Thatcher,'' she said. ''We're going to have our
breakfast now. Maybe we'll see you later on.'' She stared at
him intently until he backed up and clumped over the little
bridge.

''I think they want to use our dock,'' she said to Chip,
later.

''Do you blame them?'' The condition of the main house
dock was a standing joke. Nothing had been repaired for
years at Carscadden; the lower cottage was bad enough, and
it had the benefit of Chip's ''whittling and fixing,'' as he
called it. The first year he'd put a new swimming ladder on
the main dock. The next year he'd replaced the pilot light
under the propane refrigerator. Already this year the water
pump needed work.

''I don't blame them, I just — wonder what they're
like,'' said Mandy. All they'd seen of the adults so far was a
pale set of legs, crossed, on an aluminum folding chair
through a gap in the trees. They had not come down to the
water. There was no way to get down to the water, at their
end of the property; you had to either dive off a ledge or, farther down, manoeuvre along the rocky dock crib.

''We'll find out soon enough,'' said Chip.

Drinks were set for five o'clock.

Not that anyone ever looked at their watches, Chip added,
airily, standing barefoot on the edge of the rock calling over
the bridge to the heavyset, bearded man with deeply
shadowed eyes whom he had spied. You drank when the
combination of heat and sun passed pleasure and became
pain.

''Huh,'' said Donald Grange, in a declarative way.

"When you get thirsty, call it five," said Chip, becoming uncertain just what manner of man he was addressing, if he understood ordinary talk.

But they came, trooping Indian file along the path, first the husband, then the boy, then the pale, skinny dishwater-blond wife.

"Dora," she said; her voice was as thin as her neck. Her eyes were watery blue. Mandy found something painful about her and fixed her attention on Donald. His eyes were wide apart; he bore an unfortunate resemblance to Charles Manson. For some reason she was surprised when he said he was a roofer. Then she realized that she was meant to be surprised.

"Thatcher?" Mandy said. "You're a roofer and you named your son Thatcher?" Was she to take this for wit?

"In Ireland, they're revered. Like poets," said Donald, seriously.

"Absolutely," said Chip, rubbing his hands. "What about drinks?"

They settled in a semicircle facing the sun.

"It's *always* nice to come down to the Lower Cottage," Donald said from the wicker rocker. "Get some sun."

It was at its very best at this hour. Sun poured like blessings out of the western sky, over the surface of the lake, and bounced off the scraped rock face, directly to where they sat. Sunglasses did not dim it. They were haloed by it.

"Yes, you're a bit in the trees over there, aren't you?"

Donald paid no notice but took up his beer. "This was the honeymoon cottage," he said, "did you know?"

"You mean about the professors, and how they got it from the Crown?"

He smiled. "Professors! One of them was my dad."

"We thought maybe."

"No, I meant before them. About Carson and Scadding. Did you know about them?"

Thatcher had sat down with Timmie. He took one of his

trucks. "My Dad says there used to be a duck pond," he said. Timmie began to cry. Mandy raised her eyebrows at Jen. But instead of sorting out the toy problem, Jen got up, handed Timmie to Mandy, and walked off the porch into the wildflower meadow.

Donald leaned back on the wicker rocker and waved his hand around the Carscadden property, from McTair Rock up the narrow mouth of Fisherman's Bay, by the first point, to the calm inlet where (he said) the boathouse used to be. He included the grotto, the big dock, the long overgrown sandy beach which curved around and eventually ran down the other side of the lake to civilization. "All this was theirs," he said. "Can you believe it?"

"Who were they?"

"Carson was like all the guys who opened up Muskoka. A carpet-bagger. Except that he liked his privacy. He brought his family up here in the 1890s, when it was hours by boat from anything. The lake steamer used to tie up at the rocks here — see the metal pegs? — when it came up for day trips.

"You see, the house was never a cottage. It was a real house, with plaster walls and everything. The Carsons had servants, they had a duck pond. They had paths all over the three miles of shoreline — even up to McTair Rock — you know, where the Indians say two lovers jumped to their deaths? They kept the paths open; men walked them at the beginning of the season every year, slashing away the undergrowth."

"That's what we need," said Chip.

"How it came to be called Carscadden was, Carson's daughter married one of those rich Americans in the steel business who were up here. His name was Scadding. Car-Scadd-N was how it appeared on the early maps. This place was built for the newlyweds."

There was something dark about Grange. His words were

loving but there was a thick irony in his voice which made Mandy think there was something he hated, possibly his listeners. Dora fiddled with her fingertips. Mandy looked at her sideways. "Heard it before," said Dora apologetically.

"So it was happy times until the day Carson was down in Toronto, and his wife took ill," continued Donald doggedly. "She was alone with her entourage at Carscadden, see. The servants scrambled to get her down the path, into the boat, across the bay. But it took too long. And no road, no telephone, no doctor, no one within miles. Like now, only more so." He drained his beer with satisfaction.

"She died on the way down the lake. Carson never came back."

There was a silent moment, in which this was absorbed. Beads of sweat had broken out on Donald's forehead. "That sun's relentless," he said, and shifted his chair so he looked over toward the cliffs to the south. They waited for him to finish.

"I guess the daughter went to Pittsburgh or something, she never came back. It was left, abandoned, eventually let go for unpaid taxes. That's how come Tom Hulce and Dad were able to pick it up. For nothing, practically."

"How much?" said Chip.

"I mean like a few thousand." Donald looked him straight in the eyes.

"God," said Chip. "I can't even tell you what it'd be worth now."

"When they came into the house," said Grange, pulling his beard, "everything was as it had been when the servants rushed Mrs Carson down to the boat. Plates on the table. Even her pills and her medicine, scattered over the oilcloth." He smiled.

"Spooky," said Dora with a light thin laugh.

"It's always been spooky here," said Donald. "We liked it spooky."

Mandy shaded her eyes with her forearm. Jen was walking among the wildflowers in the little meadow beside the house, waving away the bees, picking the small daisies and blue stars. No one was allowed to pick the lilies. She fancied herself in a Swedish film perhaps. "That girl could let us down," Mandy said to herself.

They sat on, in the arms of the sun.

"Great story," said Chip.

"You do feel there's another side to this place. Other than this — bliss," said Mandy, her eyes closed. The others looked up at McTair Rock. There were trees on top of it, with contorted, eastward-leaning branches; the trunks bent acrobatically around the outcrops of rock. There were jagged rocks below. Even from here you could tell the force of the water, battering and sucking at them.

"Why did those Indian lovers leap?"

"Oh, you know. Why do they all?" said Donald.

There was a slight pause.

"You can never underestimate that water," said Chip, getting up.

Donald Grange took the second beer that Chip offered.

"Size," continued Chip. "Sheer size. How high is that cliff face, hundreds of feet? I don't know. All that bush. No one there." He was liking Donald Grange.

"I was the youngest of six," Donald said. "We came every summer. My father and Tom Hulce were psychologists. When I was about eighteen they had a falling out, over the double bind."

Everyone laughed, as if the tales about crazed disciples and weird psychodramas acted out at the house had never reached any of their ears.

He could have said it differently, thought Dora. He could have said his dad couldn't manage his share of the taxes, which was also true. How could he have, raising six of us, on a professor's salary? he could say, as if it were nobler to have lost than to have kept the place. But instead he held up his dad's failure to get a laugh. This Chip and Mandy must wonder about Donald. But then — she switched automatically to his defence — they didn't know what it was like for a kid, to tag along with these men and their followers up here. They even came in November, and slept on cots and held group-therapy sessions, screaming into the enormous implacable woods.

"We heard about Hulce," said Mandy. "Wasn't there something to do with his wife, too?"

"This place is hard on wives," said Dora. Donald smiled at her. Dora smiled back, startled, because he rarely acknowledged her in public.

"Weren't there stories about how she — didn't she go crazy or something?"

"That was my mother," said Donald.

And the sun kept on shining. At least over there, at the cottage. The house though was perpetually in shade. Dora made breakfast in a cold, dark kitchen. Only at noon did the first rays of sun filter into the screened porch. After a week, they were all still white, and half the time they were cold too. The must hadn't dried from the main rooms, and the mosquitoes were breeding only feet from the back door. Dora minded, especially when she looked across the rocks at the cottage and saw them turning golden, the hair of the baby now lighter than his skin.

She began to have Paul Bunyan fantasies. She wanted to take the boat over to the marina and rent a chain-saw and cut down a few thousand trees. She kept mentioning it to Donald.

"We never touched a tree, except for necessity. A fire," he said.

"Let's do it for a fire then," she said with uncharacteristic perseverance.

"We always have a bonfire at the end of the month. But

we use driftwood and dead branches. There's plenty of it.''

It was "we" and "always" and "never" as if Dora weren't a part of this but an observer, as if Donald were there on holiday with his past.

"It would be an improvement," she said.

Then he had another excuse.

"It's been sold. We can't touch anything. Whoever bought it from Hulce wanted it this way. They could pull out of the deal if anything, anything was changed.''

And nothing would be. Every day, as soon as the sun came over, Donald parked himself on the folding chair with a book. He wouldn't play with Thatcher on principle. "Think about me, the youngest of six," he said. "My brothers had forts everywhere. I would have given anything to have this place to myself.''

This was a bad morning. "What should I do, Mum?" Thatcher whined.

"How about making me a nature basket? We can do the names in French." She got him a basket and pointed him to the meadow. When he was at last on his way she wandered, uncertain what to do herself. She found the steep path down to what was known as the sandy beach. Most of the sand was under water, however; the undergrowth reached almost to the water's edge. If only we had a backhoe, she thought. But at least there was a stretch of a few hundred yards where she could walk. She paced to the end of it and found a log.

Sitting on her log, she looked slowly around the semicircle of rocks and shoreline. Beside a faded "No Trespassing" sign at the other side she saw movement on the rocks. It was Mandy. Dora stood up and began to wade in her direction. Without consulting Donald, she was going to invite the cottage people over for a drink.

In the immense, cheerless sunporch with its unpainted

gingerbread trim, the four adults sat with their beer. Thatcher was asleep inside. Timmie was asleep over in the cottage. Jen was probably reading with her torch-lamp in the room next to him. The loons had called their last half an hour before and had gone off to the back lake. Dora watched Mandy's generous lips form an expectant O as she raised her bottle. Dora was fascinated by Mandy. She acted as if she couldn't be hurt, couldn't be denied, as if she could get anything she wanted.

But rudely — Dora was sure it was rude — Mandy asked her what she did. Mandy wondered what exactly was this course she mentioned, and where was it offered? Dora was vague. Vague to the point of sounding like an idiot, she knew. Finally Donald answered.

"It's called the Forum."

"Oh."

Dora could tell that a forum in whatever didn't count, not with this kind of people. But Mandy wouldn't even leave it at that.

"The forum on what?"

It was late at night. The rocks to the left and right were blacker than the sky. The light was receding farther and farther down the tunnel the sun had made behind the trees across the lake. There were no lights anywhere.

"It used to be called EST," Donald said.

Mandy tried not to but she looked at Chip. And her lips twitched. She almost laughed.

Dora hated to tell people about her course. Everyone did something funny after they heard, either felt sorry for her or got hostile or acted like they expected her to preach to them. Some people in the Forum did that, but she would never. She wasn't even sure she believed in what the leaders said about empowering yourself, and being open to the possibilities. She didn't like the pep-rally atmosphere, and the way life was compared to a baseball game all the time. But it made her feel better to go to the meetings. She felt comfortable with the other people in her group because they were also a long way from self-actualizing. They were not better than she was. She spent too much time with people who were better than she was.

Dora tuned out of the conversation then and did what she wasn't supposed to do; she listened to the tapes in her head. It was all because of Donald, coming along like that and persuading her out of her natural milieu, dazzling her with his tales of the professors and five brothers and sisters and the poetry of a tight roof. Funny how when he came up to Carscadden he didn't care about the roof or the windows or the floors even; he didn't do a thing to them although they could use some work. Funny how he just sat there weltering in the house's slow decline.

It wasn't much of a place, after all. A bunch of scraggy trees and rocks was all. What it was, was a shrine. The memories of his childhood were there, resting, to be viewed by him, the last of the litter, in a kind of march past. And he, poor Donald, becoming important just by being the one on the spot, with his dad dead and who knew what his mother remembered and his brothers and sisters gone on to their careers as doctors and professors themselves, even the girls, terrifying as they were.

Dora hadn't thought she would ever see Carscadden. Donald hadn't been interested in coming; he'd been happy enough just to talk about it until he heard it was sold. Now it was more than a shrine, it was a shrine of a shrine. It too was marching past. And Donald was wasting his time hating Chip and Mandy, seeing them as some kind of inheritors when even she, dumb Dora, could see that they weren't part of it at all; they were just passing through.

Mandy had Chip laughing. It was pitch-dark, everywhere,

and they were in bed wrapped up together under the quilts on the porch.

"Did you believe that moment?" she said. "Did you believe it?" Tears seeped out of the corner of her eyes, she was laughing so hard, and ran down across her temples toward her ears.

"What moment?" he said, laughing already. He wanted to hear how she would describe it.

"I mean, there we are, the only two other human beings in how many square miles? Dozens, and it's dark out and the moon is just a thumb-print on the surface of the lake and it's going to be just us for the next three weeks and there's total silence, I'm about to take a sip of my beer and he says —"

She had to stop, she was laughing so hard.

"He says, 'It used to be called EST!' "

Chip put his head down between her breasts to smother his laughter.

"God! It's a *New Yorker* cartoon," she said.

They laughed until they couldn't laugh any more.

"Still," she said, "they're nice about it. I mean they don't seem like they're going to try to convert us."

Their laughter turned to nudging, and tickling, and then they made love. They were wakened by loud screeches and thumps from the kitchen. Flossie, conked out under the bed after accompanying Mandy on her long swim to McTair Rock and back, did not stir.

"What the hell kind of mouse is that?" Mandy whispered.

"A big one," said Chip. Knowing what shape the underneath of the cottage was in, he figured an animal must have got inside. If this were the city it would be a raccoon looking for garbage. But he wasn't sure if they had raccoons in the country any more. There used to be porcupines, he knew. Porcupines were attracted to new wood. Donald Grange told a story about how when they put up the two bunkies the porcupines had come out on the rock to eat the new wood. They'd had to take guns and shoot them, dozens of them, a slaughter, he'd said. But did they like old wood?

Lighting the candle in its holder, Chip got up and went to the kitchen. There in combined moonlight and candleglow he saw, swinging on the open door of the one mouseproof cupboard, a large red squirrel. It was utterly unapologetic, staring him down, shrieking.

"Shoo!" he said.

The squirrel laughed in his face.

"Get out of here!" He struck at it with a broom but only succeeded in causing it to move up the side of the cupboard. Then it popped into a hole in the ceiling. He went back to bed. With his newly adjusted eyes he could see Mandy sitting up, naked, shivering.

"A squirrel," he said. And then, "Brazen thing!"

"These animals are outrageous!" she said.

"We are in the woods."

"Did you get rid of it?"

"I think so."

They slept again.

"Thatcher hits," said Jen. She was washing a potato, which she was going to boil and mash for Timmie's dinner. She and Mandy were in the kitchen heating water. With a baby you need hot water all the time and neither of them had got used to the fact that they couldn't get it from the tap. Boiling the water did not need two people, however. The fact that they were both doing it demonstrated the problems developing between Jen and Mandy. Mandy wanted to do dinner herself, to give Jen a break, mostly because she felt like Jen was acting as if she needed a break, although Mandy couldn't see why she should be. Whereas Jen just wished Mandy and Chip would get in the boat and go away for a while and leave her with the kid. If she was going to be stranded up here in the bush with a baby, she'd rather be stranded without her boss watching her.

Mandy was holding Timmie, who was in a panic for his dinner. He had a cup in his hand and was banging it repeatedly against her face.

"Is that what happened?" said Mandy. She caught Timmie's hand. "Don't do that to Mummy."

"He just came up to him and slugged him in the side and took the truck," said Jen. "I didn't want to say."

"You can put that in now," said Mandy eyeing the potato, which was beginning to discolour, it had been waiting so long. "Is he around a lot?"

"I don't mind," said Jen. "As long as we're up at the cottage. But down by the water it makes me nervous. If he falls, I'd have to jump in and save him."

"But you can swim."

Actually Jen couldn't swim. She'd told Mandy she could swim, when she was being interviewed for the job. But it was a lie. How big a lie Jen was now beginning to realize. The water was deep off the rocks and it terrified her.

"Oh sure, I can swim. But if I went in after Thatcher I'd have to leave Timmie sitting on the rocks. Then he might crawl in himself."

"You're right," said Mandy. "I hadn't thought of that." Of course she couldn't rescue *two* drowning kids. She was amazed by her own thoughtlessness. "Thank you for pointing that out, Jen. I will talk to Dora and tell her to keep him at home." She felt sorry for Thatcher, but he was a whiny little thing. With all Donald's talk about learning to be self-sufficient up here, he didn't teach the boy anything. He seemed to be more interested in his own childhood than in his son's.

Chip and Mandy and Dora and Donald shared the good dock. Dora wore her old pale orange bathing suit with bones at the sides of the breasts. Mandy had taken off her bikini top and now threatened to remove the bottom.

"I remember when they put this dock up," Donald said. "They cut the trees from way back in the timber."

"These?" said Chip. The posts for the dock were three feet around. "How did they ever get them down here?"

"Down the logging road," said Donald.

"Logging road? Where's the logging road?" Chip did not tire of Donald's information. He appreciated what the other man had done for them, building a palatial summer estate of the mind at Carscadden. No one passed the strawberry patch any more without thinking of the duckpond. The wide porch of the house made sense now they knew how Mrs Carscadden paraded there with her parasol. How else would that decaying pile of wood become romantic, if they didn't know it used to be a double boathouse with a peaked roof? And they had the tennis court, the steamer dock, the wide walking paths. Chip appreciated imaginative ability in others.

"It goes back to the lake," said Donald. He wore a denim shirt over his bathing trunks and did not lie down.

"What lake?"

"There's a whole lake back there, that no one ever goes to."

Dora looked up as if he were giving something away.

"Hey!" said Chip. "Maybe there's fish in it. Let's take our rods and check it out."

"The mosquitoes will be wild back there, bigger than bees." But Donald got up and went to the house and came back with old mosquito helmets, green, with brown net veils which hung down around the face and neck.

"Why don't you take Thatcher too?" said Dora.

With the men gone the talk turned to children. "Are you going to have another?" said Mandy.

"Donald was so set Thatcher wouldn't go through what he did," said Dora.

"Oh yes?" Mandy was oiling her legs.

"You know, being bullied. No toys, no affection. That's what it's like when you have five."

"I guess."

Dora had the certain feeling that she was saying what she shouldn't. This kind of people didn't talk personally, or if they did it was to say something outrageous, scandalous even, like what Mandy said the other night: "Chip wishes I had big breasts because his mother does." She also had the feeling that she was boring Mandy. The latter feeling outweighed the earlier one and she plunged recklessly on.

"So he didn't want me to have any more children."

Mandy looked startled. "Oh, dear," she said.

"I don't mind, actually. Thatcher cried so much until he was one. We were living in a really small apartment then. One day a social worker came from Children's Aid. She poked all through the rooms and turned Thatcher upside down looking for bruises. Apparently a neighbour reported us for having a baby cry all the time."

"Good gracious," said Mandy. And got a look on her face like, what indignities these people have to go through, when they can't afford proper housing.

"I found it comforting, in an odd way," Dora added. "I mean you know, we weren't, um, hurting him, but just imagine if we were? Or if anybody else was. That they check up that way."

In a short time, Dora found the sun too much. She walked back along the beach, picked her way over the topless dock and began to climb the rocks. The trees were spindly with wispy needles like hair; they stroked her arms as she brushed past. She moved through a phalanx of straight trunks over ground that was dark although the sun was at its height, and found a few steps cut into the rocks. She took them, hoisted herself over a ledge and came into a circular clearing she'd never seen before. It was almost directly under the house, but it was not visible from above. There was a fire pit, and evidence of wide burning. The second growth was blueberry bushes. (Burns were best for blueberries, Donald had said.) Lodged against the cliff at the back was a small carved bench made out of a log. She sat.

The view down to the lake and water from here was new; it was neither the wide, conventional lake vista one got from the dock, nor the telescoped vista down two of the finger bays from the house porch. This was the mad view. From here Dora saw the dark islands with their two or three tortured trees, the narrow mouth of Mosquito Bay, and the front of McTair with its crop of trees shrieking off into the wind. Crazed, unrepentant, pitiless, frozen (despite the heat of a summer day), were the words that came to mind.

But perhaps she was not really seeing, only listening to her tapes, her opinions. Her Forum leader said that was wrong. But Dora thought perhaps the people she liked best listened to their opinions. Wasn't that what painters did?

Donald's mother used to paint. Dora had never met Donald's mother, but sometimes she missed her, missed her in the precise way you can only miss someone you love. They hadn't any place to call, to tell her, when they decided to get married. She didn't have a telephone. She didn't have a home to put a telephone in. She rode buses through the Southern States, that's what she did. It was — this was how Donald's father had described it — the symptom of her malaise. She travelled. Every now and then she turned up, usually late at night, and slept in the foyer of the family house in the city. Donald's father always left the outside door unlocked. The next day she'd go again.

There were some charcoal drawings by Donald's mother tacked on the pine boards of the cottage walls. Dora had learned about her from them. She chose constricted views, she looked at things that had no distance, went nowhere. There was one — "Woodpile, the House" — which was simply that, a clearing, a few stumps, a woodpile and an axe leaned against the one remaining tree. Dora had puzzled over it until she realized that it was the drawing of an artist who had been told she ought not to listen to her own opinions. Sitting here, looking at the mad view, she understood why a woman would listen to people telling her to ignore her ideas and concentrate on a pile of shavings. The reason was that she knew what was out here, and she had been scared.

At the end of the second week, Donald tried to teach Dora to drive the big boat which Hulce had let to Chip and Mandy but which was, he explained, for all of their use. She sat on the front seat, holding the steering wheel. He started it with the key and moved over. He sat watching her, his arms stretched out behind him along the top of the seat. She touched the throttle tentatively, pushing it slightly past neutral.

"All the way down, all the way," he said. She was afraid to push the throttle down.

"I don't like it when the front lifts off the water," she complained. "I don't see why you have to start that fast."

"Push it, Dora." The wind was coming in hard across the bay and the waves began to beat the boat back toward the crib. She twisted the wheel violently to the right; the boat swerved. She gasped and twisted the wheel back violently the other way. After a few seconds' delay, the boat swerved majestically to the left, then reeled back to the right. Now she was heading straight for the dock.

"Straighten it out! Push the throttle," he screamed, leaning over and doing it himself. They just missed the outside
corner of the rocky crib and sickled out into the bay.

"Now," he breathed, letting go of the till and dropping
back in his seat. "Take us over by the big dock."

But Dora was sitting with her face in her hands. "I can't,
Donald," she whimpered. "Don't make me."

Untouched, the throttle dawdled back toward neutral.
The boat was drifting backwards to shore now, idling into
the wide, shallow bay. This was the bay where, Donald said,
all the sand from Muskoka gathered. The water was less
than two feet deep. If she didn't do something soon the propeller would hit bottom.

"Do it, Dora," he said, remaining resolutely still, doing
nothing. "This is a perfect example of what we've talked
about. You have to be put on the line, you have to be forced
to account. You can no longer be protected, like a child.
Otherwise you'll never learn."

A wind which had not been there before licked the surface
of the water. It began to carry the boat more quickly back,
back to shore. Donald had his hand over the side, expecting
to touch bottom.

"Hit it, Dora!" Even in his fury he caught sight of Chip
standing on the big dock, scanning the bay, a bottle of sham-
poo in his hand. "God damn stupid broad!"

She hit it, hard, slamming the throttle fully down. They
heard a whine, high and desperate, and then a sudden clunk
as the engine cut out. The boat jerked once, and stood still.

"Oh, FUCK!" Donald jumped up and dodged between
the seats to the back of the boat. There was a great cloud of
sand in the water. The propeller was half buried. Dora looked
at him from her position in the driver's seat with something
resembling pride. He let his head drop between his shoulders
and shook it.

"Stupid cunt!" he said.

She didn't move. The boat, anchored in sand at the back end, had begun to turn in the wind, its nose circling inward toward the shore.

"I'm going to have to get into the water and lift the prop," he said. "You'd better pray it's not wrecked. Thatcher!"

The boy was standing on the rocky peninsula that was meant to be their dock, watching. You couldn't tell from the always cocked angle of his red head if he heard anything. "Got a job for you. Get the mask and the fins!"

Donald kept his head down, not looking at Dora. All he wanted to say was coiled, clotted in his throat. He was going to give up on her. He was going to shove her overboard in the middle of the lake. He looked at her thin, shivering figure, too small for the driver's seat.

"I hit it," she said.

"No, you didn't. You waited. You let it drift."

"I hit it," she repeated, in exactly the same stubborn, tremulous voice. "You didn't say anything about when."

"Dora, what am I going to do with you? You're just a goddamn helpless little loser, aren't you?" Revulsion filled him, and the desire to cry. He saw her pathetic shape. He saw himself, a child, an ignoramus, unteachable. He picked up a life-preserver and threw it at her.

She didn't move at first. Perhaps she didn't understand about getting stuck in the sand, how stupid it made them look. She was thrilled with herself because she'd had the nerve, finally, to push the throttle. It occurred to Donald that she was expecting praise. He couldn't believe it. He began to laugh. He turned his back on her, threw the rope overboard, and then jumped in after it.

"You're just never going to fit in," he said.

Dora flushed red. "Fit in with who?" she shouted, equally loud. "There's nobody here but us!"

Donald put his hand on the back of the boat and then slowly turned to look out at the lake.

All evening he tried to make up for his behaviour. He was even playing the guitar with Thatcher. His face hung low over the gleam of blond wood, a heavily fleshed face, its tenderness sunk in his beard.

"Just four chords, Thatch, C, D, G and A. '*If* I listened *long* enough to *you*, I'd find a *way* — ' "

But Dora sat resenting his thick figure, his low voice, as the light waned outside. He was like the trees hanging over her, blocking the light. He was not the wiser, older friend and lover who explained her problems to her. No, he *was* her problem. If she told Donald how she felt he would tell her it always happened at Carscadden. He would tell a story about some guest who got claustrophobic and ran out into the lake.

She watched how the mosquitoes batted against the outside of the screen, softly, soundlessly; weightless, hair-thin creatures but still a threat to life. If the screen went down her blood would be drained in minutes. The guitar stopped.

"Did I ever tell you about Reg Eckles?"

"Who was he? Another professor?"

"No. Reg Eckles was a patient. This was before my time, in the forties I guess. He had a thing for Hulce, used to come up early in spring and open the place up, cut wood for the stove, like a hired man really. He liked to row."

"No," she said shortly. "I think it's bedtime, Thatcher."

The boy looked from one parent to the other. He'd been crying before dinner. Donald had mocked him as he tried to walk into the water in mask and flippers to dig out the propeller, and tripped and fell. The boy couldn't understand his father shouting Backwards, Backwards!, didn't see that he meant to turn around and walk backwards in his flippers into the water. He wasn't crying now. He saw their expressions and went up the staircase.

"Well, Eckles used to row back and forth across from McTair Rock at night," said Donald, not missing a beat. "And one night he went out rowing late and nobody realized but he didn't come back. In the morning they found the rowboat floating up on the sandy beach but they never found him."

"Oh, Donald!"

"And at night sometimes after that you could hear the oars complaining in the oarlocks, you know? That wood on metal squawk. Dad used to talk about it."

"It could have been the wind in the trees or anything," said Dora. "It could have been a duck."

"That's not the point!" Donald's face was dark, darker than usual. It was almost as if he were pleading. "I'm telling you my dad SAID it was Reg Eckles. That's what he *said*."

Dora's face showed nothing.

"I'm telling you what it used to be like, for me." A kind of sob escaped him before he raised the guitar again. "Wretched woman!"

Dora lifted her book up to her nose. She would read tonight, even though in the light of the kerosene lamp it made her eyes ache. Donald said the darkness left you time to think. But she didn't want time to think. She particularly didn't want time to think of Reg Eckles, somewhere down there in the bottom of the lake. Down there with her grandfather's meerschaum pipe. She didn't want to think what Donald's sadistic old father had done to him.

A few moments passed.

"You have to learn," Donald said. "If you can't drive a boat how can I leave you here with Thatcher?"

"Why would you leave us here?"

He looked irritated.

"We could walk out the logging road."

He snorted. "You haven't seen the logging road. Anyways, what if he was hurt?"

"So don't leave us then. Why would you want to leave us here anyway?"

He reached for his finger picks. He wasn't very good, and he knew it, and Thatcher wasn't asleep yet, but he played anyway.

Mandy was reading in the sunporch. She knew exactly now at what point in the twilight the mosquitoes came out. A degree of twilight just past glow, and just inside an absorbent grey must descend. There was a hole in the screen somewhere, and a second after this crucial point they were dive-bombing her, circling her head, buzzing, and then stopping ominously, which meant they had landed somewhere. Then agh, the pinprick, the sting, her hand flying out almost of its own accord and slapping her own leg, or shoulder. The small warm squish of blood followed.

She moved inside to sit on the old reed sofa. The perfection of the place was failing. She strove for her usual contentment. Then the traps began to go, ruining her concentration. Every night Mandy loaded six mousetraps with brie and peanut butter. She began to listen for the small crack of the bar snapping. Sometimes after there was some squeaking. Once in a while you could hear the mouse dragging the trap around. It seemed like an hour, but maybe it was only ten minutes. Usually they stayed out of the kitchen until morning when the bodies were cold. But tonight she called Chip to reset them.

"There's too many," she said. "It's disgusting. This place gives me the creeps!" And she flopped into bed where she curled tense under the blankets, one human against a great wide world of vermin.

But the next day the lake was calm, an inkpot under the sun, and the peace was entire. As Mandy sat on the rocks she tried to reclaim the memory of the night before. The madness, viciousness of the place. She could not. Night and day could not be held in mind simultaneously; they did not meet. She could only think of her suntan, and what to have for dinner, and plan a long Scrabble game on the dock or a fort made of red and yellow Lego.

But instead they decided to ask Jen to stay with Timmie and took the boat out. A mile from shore they stopped the motor and drifted over by the diving rocks in Fisherman's Bay. Mandy had her bikini top off; they pullmanized the seats and pulled beer from the cooler. She spilt some on her nipples and Chip licked it off. He hadn't shaved for days and his stubble tickled her. He was trying to get the rest of her bikini off.

"Careful," she said. "Somebody will see."

"We're out in the middle of the lake!"

"But look."

Around the corner from the south came two long canoes, side by side. They were green, with high exaggerated curls at front and back. There were a dozen boys in each. The paddles hit the water all at once without making a splash.

"The war canoes!" said Chip, sitting up suddenly. "From Camp Wig-a-mog!"

Majestically, the canoes progressed, close to the rocky edge of the lake, following the curve of the bay. Now they could hear voices, a chant, rhythmic, matching the swing of the oars.

"Stroke, stroke, stroke!"

Mandy got up on her elbows. Chip was staring in utter fascination. He'd gone to camp himself. "Look at that! Great style! Good synchronization. Stroke, stroke!"

"Is that what they teach you at camp?" said Mandy, pulling at his bathing trunks.

They were so alone at Carscadden.

Before dinner, Jen was in the kitchen making Timmie's hot dog and scrambled eggs. Mandy was trying to get him to walk, but he kept falling on the uneven rocks in front of the cottage. Chip poked the coals under the lopsided grill that made their barbecue. A red boat turned the corner at the far side of the bay.

No boats ever came there. Sometimes one appeared, a white, aimed dart around the rocky corner to the west, its feathered white tail behind it. But inevitably it veered off into Fisherman's Bay, or toward McTair Rock, which was a favourite place for kids in their parents' speedboats. They climbed up on the rock, dived off and climbed up again, their cries faint and scattered across the water. Flossie barked if anything came too close; she even barked at the planes overhead and so far none of them had landed.

"Boat!" called Jen through the screen. "Coming here!"

"Sightseers," said Chip.

Mandy stood and looked over the water. It was geometry, from up here, like watching a pool ball on a table, or a tennis ball arcing over a court. You could extrapolate the line and know exactly where it would land.

"They're coming straight for the dock." She felt like hiding. It could only be bad news. A duty, a death. Something to end this.

In two minutes the boat pulled up at the big dock. Chip stood up and looked down the rocks.

"It's the kid who pumps gas for Roy. What's his name?"

Mandy didn't want to know his name. Together she and Chip strode down the rocks, barefoot, picking the best route without looking. Their walk was proprietary, their feet comfortable on the irregular sharpness and dips of rock. They were tribesmen meeting the first white man. The kid stood up at the wheel.

"Telephone message for you, Mr Hamilton," he called.

"Oh, no."

"Your secretary. Something about Crown Trust."

"Damn," said Chip under his breath.

"Wants you to call Mr Mayer at home. He'll be waiting." The kid was still calling out loud, although Chip and Mandy were now on the dock. He looked from one face to the other, checking their reaction. Neither of them spoke.

"Business won't leave you alone, eh?" he said, man-style, with a chuckle. Roy taught his employees to relish the fact that men like Chip worked themselves into early coronaries in order to earn enough money to come up here and spend a month living the kind of life the locals lived all year round.

"Yeah," said Chip. He had a narrow frown between his eyes.

"You want a ride back in?" The kid knew Chip had to use the payphone at the edge of the marina parking lot. The Hulce cottage was one of the last on the lake to have no phone.

"You might as well take the boat. You'll need it to get back," said Mandy quickly. She was holding Timmie on her hip. Conscious of defending her territory: wife, mother, keeper of home. He couldn't go, not now. But he meant to.

"Wait a sec, will you?" Chip said to the kid. He nodded affably and settled back behind the wheel. Chip took Mandy's elbow and guided her back up the rocks. Timmie was getting heavy. She stubbed her toe; pain shot up her shin.

"You know I thought that case might blow up while we were here."

"Mmmmm."

"I might as well just pack, and take the car keys, go straight to town, get it done."

She wasn't going to give up that easily. "Why don't you phone first? Maybe it's just something little."

But it wouldn't be something little. The harm was done, the trance broken. Chip might as well pack his bag and go.

He would be back, but he'd be different, he'd be on city speed. And after he came back — she counted ahead — there'd be less than a week left.

"Damn that marina phone," she said. "Why'd you give them the number? It was just asking them to call."

He pulled his sports bag out from under the bed.

"I might even be back tomorrow night," he said. "Listen, it's better than sitting here stewing about it."

She hadn't known he was stewing.

"Well, having it on my mind." He took her in his arms. "You know what I really want to do is lie down with you on the couch in the porch and watch the sun go down."

But the sun was going down and she was watching it all by herself, and it wasn't bad at all. Timmie was upstairs asleep and Jen was about to ascend with her flashlight and her P.D. James novel.

"You like it?" Mandy asked, gesturing at the book. It was the one about the adopted woman who tracks down her mother and finds out she's a convicted murderer. She liked the idea of Jen's reading good books. It was pleasant to think Jen wasn't exactly a babysitter, but a clever young woman who was just living with them before she went on to better things.

"Not really," said Jen.

"Do you like books by women?"

"If I wasn't stuck up here, I don't think I'd ever get through it."

Mandy retreated to the bath and luxury of that final light. "The hundred-thousand-dollar view," Chip called it. Chip was quantitative. He never knew he was cold until he found out the temperature, and changed Celsius into the old Fahrenheit, to boot. She wondered if he would know the view was beautiful if he didn't know what it was worth. It was good, for once, to bathe alone in this strange orange glow, be anointed with it.

She could hear Donald Grange's guitar from over the band of trees. If it weren't for the mosquitoes, she might have walked along the path, over the bouncing board, the little stream, and scratched on their screen. Even though he acted as if he owned the place and told long boring stories. She didn't mind the company of voices from an old tennis court and men leaning on their scythes at the bottom of the path. She took pleasure in knowing they had been there once, and that now they were gone. The bugs, the rock and the water had beaten them back, instead of the other way, which was what usually happened.

Gradually, as she lay there, the sun withdrew. Mandy took this personally; she felt deprived, abandoned. Chip had been gone four hours. Now that night was coming, she began to have faint recollections of the previous nights. She waited until the final tree-pricked curve of sun sank behind the opposite bank of the lake. As she stood up to go in she remembered that she'd forgotten to set the mousetraps. The kitchen would be dark and full of little creatures munching away. She'd have to forgo her cup of tea.

"Come on, Flossie," she said, standing. Her skin prickled from sunburn; she was charred on the outside but chilly within.

Penknife in hand, Donald was making sticks to roast marshmallows. They had a little fire, which kept the mosquitoes off; they had taken some dead branches off the nearest trees. The bigger ones they were keeping for the bonfire, at the end of the month. Dora watched his hands, dextrous with the knife.

"Mandy says she doesn't want Thatcher to play over on their rocks any more." She expected support for her slight offendedness. It was against the spirit of the camp about which, by extension, she had begun to feel proud. But Donald didn't seem to care.

"She says he might fall in and their nanny can't swim. She says their nanny lied to them about being able to swim." Thatcher was crouched behind their chairs running a firetruck over a track of moss.

"A kid drowned here once," said Donald.

Dora's heart began to pound with anger. Of course, she thought. A kid had to have drowned here; everything else had happened here. Every drama since the fall of man had been played out here on the rocks. And under the water? The pipe, the oarsman, now the child.

"You know what they do?" Donald said, looking up. "When they fall in?" He had a romantic look on his face. "They just disappear like stones. They're so surprised when they hit the water, they don't even scream."

"What was his name, Dad?" Thatcher was interested. There was no one to play with now, but once there had been. "Is he still down there?"

"Actually it was across the lake." Donald went back to squinting at his shaving. "I just remember my mum used to talk about it all the time."

Thatcher lost interest then and went back to his firetruck. Dora tried to still her anger by looking at Donald's hands. The knife glided slickly under the skin of the wet-green twig.

"Are they ready yet?"

"Yours is," he said to Thatcher.

The boy took the stick and examined the point. Dora saw with surprise that his blanched look was gone and his freckles integrated into a tan. He jumped up and danced a little, plunging the stick in the air. He was taller, too, his thin legs under the cut-off shorts longer. The holiday had been good, for him.

"Let's sleep on the porch," she said, suddenly to Donald. "Mosquitoes or no." Donald had wanted to all along but she had resisted. But now she'd become averse to sleeping in the bedroom. It was too old. In Rexdale you moved into a place just after the builder moved out. There were no overlaps, no stains, no trapped emotion. In this house there were pain and fear and ghosts. Not the ghosts Donald intended to frighten her with, not the likes of Reg Eckles. No, they were more familiar ghosts than that.

"Dad, do you think Grandma Grange will visit us here?"

Dora pushed herself off the webbing of the chair in a panic. She had no privacy. People read her mind. Last night she had lain awake in bed hearing the see-saw of the tall trees and imagined just that: that Grandma Grange showed up fresh from one of her bus trips through Tennessee.

She grabbed her son's arm. "Don't jab that stick around! You might hurt somebody!"

"She used to live here, didn't she?"

The dream had gone like this. Roy at the marina knew her, and put her in the boat with the kid who ran the gas pumps. It was a cooler night and mist came off the water in swirls. They pulled up at the bad dock. Grandma Grange sprang off the boat like a ballet dancer. She wore a hat with white netting, which draped over her face, and tightly laced boots, such as Mrs Carson must have had. She came along the bad dock, her face raised to the gable of the house, walking over the stones, not slipping, and the water didn't splash.

Donald looked at Dora who was standing ready to run. "I doubt it, son."

"Did Grandma Grange like it here?"

Dora swung herself up the rocks to the house. "Tea," she said, in explanation.

Donald was gentle, putting the marshmallow on the

spear. Its sticky white flesh parted over the pencil-sharp end he'd made. "Grandma Grange wasn't very happy a lot of the time," he said. "Elle était malade."

Thatcher put his marshmallow too close, and it burst into flame. He drew it out and blew on it. The flame popped out, immediately. What was left was an ashy, coal-coloured case with white glue oozing out. He put it in his mouth.

"Watch out! Hot!" said Donald.

The boy's eyes popped, he blew out his cheeks, made his mouth into a tight oval, leaving room for the hot molten thing to air. When Dora was there, Donald complained that the boy was coddled; he wanted to rough him up a little. But when she was gone, he became tender, like a mother. When Dora was gone.

Mandy woke to a scratching sound in the corner. She was in the upstairs bedroom; it was too cold to sleep on the porch without Chip. It was pitch-dark. A scratching and pattering of feet came from the other side of the hall. The red squirrel.

"Flossie!" she hissed. "Get it!"

The dog groaned. She'd been swimming that day again. In the old days Flossie went mad over little rodents; the slightest whiff set her into a frenzy of digging, leaping, pouncing. But she was out cold. Why did this squirrel not rouse her? Because it was not really there? thought Mandy, perversely, to frighten herself more. Because it was a ghost squirrel?

The scratching became chewing, and it echoed on the hollow board floor. The squirrel ate wood, just like a beaver. It had no trouble chewing out a hole the size of a tennis-ball in the pine floor and walls. Mandy had found one such hole by the closet door and blocked it with a piece of sailboat that had been standing in the corner. She propped the flat rudder in place with two large rocks.

The chewing culminated in a hollow bang: the rudder had fallen over. There were more patters. The squirrel was in her room, but she couldn't tell where.

"Agh! Get out!" she cried.

There was a thud on the bed. The sheet tightened over her chest. Her hands flew to her heart, which had stopped. The thing had landed on her. It sprang closer. She choked. Then it went off, the weight was gone. But where? Into Timmie's room? Would it bite him? Squirrels were just rats with fluffy tails.

Whimpering softly, Mandy reached to the side-table for the matches. Her hand brushed the package and it fell to the floor. She couldn't bear to reach her hand down under the bed. She waited one more minute for her eyes to adjust and then got up and opened the curtains to let in the moonlight. She went downstairs to sit; she couldn't sleep in here.

The next day, Mandy sat in the boat at the gas pumps. She had black circles under her eyes. Her head, covered with a kerchief, was at the level of Roy's knees. Her sun-glasses, pushed back, pointed to and reflected the clear blue sky in which one puffy white cloud sailed. Behind her, Jen held Timmie, who was trying to climb over the side of the boat. Roy laughed.

"Red squirrel?" His head went from side to side. "They're bad. You get one of them in your cottage, there's nothing you can do. Nothing."

"I was thinking of a trap," she said. "Like a mousetrap, only bigger. You wouldn't know where —"

"Rat trap? Won't do it."

"You can't catch them that way?"

Mandy had no intention of doing anything about the red squirrel. She wasn't entirely sure that the thing that jumped on her bed last night even *was* the red squirrel. Perhaps it was the ghost of Mrs Carson, who was said to be spry. Something was eating holes in the cottage, but then it wasn't her cottage. Basically she just wanted to sleep through the night. She thought talking about it might help.

"They fly," said Roy. "They're something. Bad, real bad." His eyes behind thick glasses were a murky brown, unblinking.

"So how do people get rid of them?"

The kid laughed. "Shoot 'em, mostly."

Mandy didn't like to say that she couldn't shoot. She was drawn, despite herself, to the notion of killing the thing. "I'm not sure a gun . . ." she said. "But if I got one good whack at it, I could kill it with, I don't know, a stick . . ." she said. She held the edge of the boat against the dock as Jen climbed out with Timmie in her arms. Then she reached back for the bags of laundry and lifted them out. Jen had brought her suitcase. She said it was full of dirty clothes. It was Friday, and they were going in to Parry Sound.

"Chip still in town?" Roy swung backward on skinny legs, down the dock. He'd had a good look down the neck of her T-shirt as she bent over.

"Mmmmm."

"Look in your toolshed," he said. "There's all kinds of stuff in there. Landing-net, who knows? Protect yourself," he said to Mandy. "If anything comes at you." It was a joke, of course. But it would have been funnier if Chip had been there.

In Parry Sound, after they'd done all the laundry and packed it into the pillowcases, Jen put her clothes into her suitcase, helped Mandy carry everything to the car, and then declined to get in.

"I'm going," she said.

"But Jen. You can't. How can you?" Mandy meant she had no car, no home other than their home. She also meant she couldn't leave her like this.

"I'll take a bus," said Jen. "I don't like it here. I don't like the cottage. I don't like the water, there's too much of it."

"That can't be the real reason," said Mandy, practically, thinking, I am dealing with an upset girl and I can get this situation resolved. "Is there something that you'd like to talk about?"

Jen stared at Timmie, who was clinging to his mother's knee.

"He'll be walking soon," she said, conversationally.

"We've got to talk this over."

"In my other job they didn't treat me so much like a nanny. I thought I'd be more like your friend."

Just like that, she headed to the highway. Mandy had never been so astonished in her life. And when she got back to the marina the kid gave her a message: Chip couldn't make it till Saturday morning. Was she wrong, or did he say it funny, with a leer? They knew she was alone out there with no phone, no road, nothing.

She only cried while driving the boat, so that Timmie wouldn't notice the tears; they ran off the side of her face with the wind. She felt very sorry for herself, alone on the rock with her child. She went out to the toolshed looking for weapons. She found a weathered, peeling set of croquet mallets and balls. There were no wickets. Who knows where they would have poked wickets in, with the ground so rocky. Perhaps the servants laid out a course with permanent wickets made out of tree boughs. She picked out a good mallet, two and a half feet high, with a solid head. The only other weapon she found was a badminton racket. Poncy professors! You could tell what sort of place this had been. She stood the two beside the door, in wait for the red squirrel.

Exhausted, she fell asleep on the porch with five old quilts on top of her to make up for Chip's warmth. She woke in the grey moonlight to see a frantic, fluttering shadow by the screen door. It was not the squirrel, it was something else.

It was a bat. There were bats under the eaves of the cottage, she'd seen them before. At least it was outside, she assured herself. She closed her eyes for a second and it flew over her head, creating a breeze. It was inside. Faintly mewling, it came to a stop on the wall behind her bed. That did it. She clasped the quilt around her breasts, leapt from the bed, ran into the main room, slammed the door behind herself, and with clenched teeth gave a low growl of revulsion.

What could she do? A mouse or the squirrel would run over her body if she lay down. The porch with the bat was out of the question for sitting. That very day she'd closed the gap in the screen that let in so many mosquitoes. Probably the bat had been sleeping inside and she'd closed him in as well. She had no idea how long it would be till morning. After Chip left she had realized that her watch was gone. It was probably somewhere in the bottom of her suitcase, and it was too dark now to find it.

She began to pace back and forth in the centre of the room.

Dora and Donald lay on their backs on the big dock, looking at the stars. They wore the mosquito helmets that Donald had fished out of the cupboard, and they were wrapped all down their bodies, like Romans, in netting. The bugs hadn't found them yet. They had smoked a little dope and drunk part of a bottle of wine. The stars were all over the sky, scattered thick and thin, in waves, lines and clusters.

"I'm tired," said Dora.

"I hear something," said Donald. "It sounds like crying."

"Tired," Dora repeated, more loudly. "Of your awful stories about dead people at this place." Donald said nothing; he was lost in contemplation. "Tired of the way you try to scare me."

"I can see the Big Dipper," he said.

"Anyone can see the Big Dipper."

"I can see Reg Eckles," he said.

"I'm also tired," she said, sitting up, "of the way you don't listen to me!"

Donald turned his head slowly. He looked like someone she had never met, under that pith helmet thing, with the draping over his face. He looked like a very sinister person. "This is good, Dora," he said. "You're learning."

"You only want me to learn," she said, "so you can have more fun trying to keep me down."

She lay down again, and fell into the waltz of the blue-black depths up there, all that great black privacy beyond.

"Look," said Donald loudly "A light!"

An enormous indignation filled Dora. He was not going to do this to her any more, with his scare stories, his drowned acolytes, his dead matriarch. He was not going to get away with it.

"Don't disturb me!" she said. He was sitting up looking at the cottage. She noticed that he was wearing his Walkman. She had no idea what tape he was playing. That was funny. It was what her leader said at the Forum. "The tapes you play" in your head are what keep you from being equal to the risk of life, keep you from committing. But she did know what tapes he was playing. They were the tapes of poor Donald, the last of the litter, with the mean father. It surprised her to think this about Donald, to be on top of him this way. Perhaps she was self-actualizing.

Donald took off his earphones. "There's a light moving around in the cottage," he said. "Chip didn't get back, did he?"

Dora was enjoying the black and whiteness of the sky. Nothing indefinite about it. Nothing pink or red or yellow, in between, weak. It was going to be her new vision.

"She's probably just up with the baby," she said, without

wanting to. She didn't want to talk to Donald ever again. She didn't want to let him know what she knew: she had a sudden great selfishness about it. She didn't want to mix it up with his vision, to tangle the two of them together in a dialogue, because hers always got broken up, distorted, thrown aside.

"No," he said. "It's going from side to side, all over the place, fast."

"Then she's doing her Jane Fonda by flashlight." Dora laughed heartily. It felt good to scorn Mandy's Barbie-doll shape.

Donald lay down again. "I have the feeling something is wrong," he said. But he put on his earphones again.

Mandy turned off the flashlight. She took the badminton racquet in her hand and stood beside the doorway into the screened porch. The sky was clear and the stars brilliant; moonshadows of trees danced down the rock. There were two long things on the dock which she took to be towels left from swimming.

She could hear the faint, persistent munching of mice. Also she could hear the squirrel journeying between the floorboards. The place was infested. "None of these things will hurt you," Chip had said. "They're just animals. They're more afraid than you are." She doubted that was possible. Their hearts were small. If they were this afraid, they'd be dead.

She knew the bat was in the screened porch. She knew it would fly out again, she only had to wait.

The bugs had found Donald and Dora. There weren't many places in the net shroud where they could get in, except around the ankles, but they ruined the peace with their high-pitched faltering whine, their alighting and taking off and alighting again, trying for a crack in the net-armour.

Donald decided to light the fire. He began to run back up the rockface to the cottage to get the barbecue lighting fluid from Chip and Mandy.

"They won't mind," he said.

"They'll mind if you use up the driftwood." All four of them had collected it, and dragged dead branches into a pile. The pile had been carefully placed, a little back from the water but not close to the trees.

"Thatcher gathered half of it," said Donald. "You'll see how the smoke keeps the bugs away."

"It's too windy," she said, but he didn't turn back.

She lay there alone, and became aware of the long curve of their solitude encircling her: to the left, across, behind, to the right — no one. The night opened to her. The trees became a ragged back curtain, the water an exotic floor, with a sheen, like the Persian rug she'd once seen in Donald's father's house. The ghosts came out of the water, the dead man floated on his back halfway out in the bay, phosphorescent. The meerschaum pipe hung hugely over his head; the drowned toddler walked on the rocks beside her. And she saw the other ghosts too, the sick old lady carried by servants down to the waiting mahogany boat; the mad mother-in-law at her introverted easel.

She didn't mind, didn't mind at all.

"Domain," she said, out loud. It was a word out of some childhood story. A beautiful word for something large and lost; once granted by divine right. Carscadden was her domain now, she loved it, loved it the right way, she alone. She could imagine the rest of them gone and it belonging to her.

Donald came scrambling back down the rock with the lighter fluid.

"What about the camp tradition? Don't we do that the last night?" she said.

"I could give a fuck about the camp tradition," he said. He seemed in such a hurry tonight. He began to pour the lighter fluid on the pile of driftwood.

"What about Thatcher? I don't think you should do this," she said. For three weeks he'd told the boy about the bonfires they used to have at the end of the season, the way the flames sprang up higher than the trees and everyone had to jump back and the roaring, the shouting over the roars, how a party started when the flame died down.

He did not answer.

"If you're going to light it," she said, "I should get Thatcher. Don't you want Thatcher to see it?"

Still he didn't answer.

"This is very selfish," she said. "Should I get him up?" And then more to stop him than anything else, "All right, don't move until I get back."

She walked up the bald face of the rock, on Chip and Mandy's path, because it was easier, and jogged through the strawberry patch and over the board bridge. She saw no light in the cottage. But although this was crazy — it must have been by then the very depth of night, maybe two o'clock — she thought she saw movement. At Thatcher's bedside she whispered, gentle.

"Thatcher, dear, it's the middle of the night. Daddy's going to light the bonfire. Do you want to come down with me and watch?"

The boy jerked straight up, a marionette. His eyes popped open, then shut again. Dora put her arms around him. "I could carry you."

"Mmmmm," he said.

"Do you want to see the bonfire?"

"Mmmmmyes," he said, burying his head in her shoulder.

She began the more difficult walk down to the water.

"What about Mandy?" she said to Donald.

"What about her?" He was standing in front of the wood-pile, with his match, ready. The gas tin was behind him on the rock. It was no use. When he decided to do something, you couldn't talk to him, couldn't turn him around.

"She's banging around in the screen porch up there," said Dora. "I thought I heard her when I went by."

Donald lit the match and threw it in. There was an enormous clap and the flame burst like a sail in the full wind, fifteen, twenty feet high, orange, white, stretched, banging. He jumped back. Now he began to shout over the din.

"That was it, you see. You never stood as far back as you should. You always thought you were far enough back but you never were."

Everything was orange, the details gone, just masses of tree and rock and yes, their own shadows. A man twelve feet high leaning over them. That shorter one with the bump in front, Dora and Thatcher. They couldn't hear what he was saying. He backed around to see Thatcher's reaction.

The boy was crying "Mummy, Mummy," and hiding his face. "I don't like it. I want to go home."

Donald's face was livid in the flame light. His clothing seemed to be swelling and shrinking; he looked like a wraith, a genie out of a bottle. He turned back to his fire. He only wanted one thing, to see it go up. Dora was saying something about Mandy, then she turned, and, carrying Thatcher, half crawled away from him up the rock.

"She'll be down now," Donald shouted, "she can't miss this."

The fire had already consumed half its bed of dry wood and was getting no smaller.

It went right by Mandy's nose, a fluttering thing, like a handkerchief in a stiff breeze. It came and went. Mandy squinted at it. She looked outside into the pewter moonlight. The bat was darker than the sky. Easy to see. She took aim with her badminton racket. Chip always said she had good hand-eye-ball co-ordination.

It was flying from one end of the porch to the door, hitting the screen, and then flying off at a ninety-degree angle down the other side of the porch. She waited. It had to come back.

It came around the corner a foot from her head. She swung the racket and screamed at the same instant. She caught it, on the sweet spot too. Thwack! It fell to the floor, squeaking. Not dead.

She peered into the darkness under the Scrabble table. There it was. She was prepared for this. She had a broom and a Loblaws bag. Holding it open with her finger, she swept the quivering thing into the plastic bag. She got the croquet mallet and began to pound it, pounding it until she knew it was dead.

Even as she was looking down at the floor she saw the light change. She thought at first it was dawn, but the night hadn't been long enough. She looked up then and saw the huge orange light down by the water.

From her vantage point Dora could see the flames at the top begin to curl over toward the tall trees with the many dead branches that clung to the cliff face in front of the house. She could see exactly how it was going to travel, from those tree-tops to the house, and then across the bridge behind her to the cottage. No further, because of the bog and the lake behind. A contained conflagration, geographically contained, as if Donald, safe on the water side of the fire, had designed it with a map. All of this came to her mind in a clear vision and she knew she was safe where she sat, and Thatcher too. The fire was a magnificent thing and would harm nothing innocent, only that stretch of old and tangled timber that stood between the two of them.

She would quit the Forum, which had not helped her step

up to the home plate of life at all; it had kept her in the dugout. She would go back and finish high school. If she did something for herself she might at least become immune to Donald even if she could not like him.

Mandy stepped up beside her on the rock. She was carrying Timmie in a basket. Dora was not angry with Mandy now. She didn't have to be, because she was not angry at Donald, and she was not angry at Donald because she was over Donald. She was glad to see Mandy. Mandy alone here with her child, without Chip. And Dora with Thatcher. They were the ones who managed, after all, weren't they? It was just the two of them, had been, all the time.

"The bonfire," said Mandy.

"I'm afraid it's out of control."

Mandy seemed to understand at once. She was calm.

"I wonder, should we run around saving things?"

"It hardly seems worth it, just for a few summer clothes and some old dishes."

"Chip would worry about the pine furniture."

Dora laughed.

"There are those mice in the traps. To be killed twice," said Mandy, grimacing. She didn't mention the bat.

"That's not fair," said Dora.

A curious slowness had invaded their limbs, a luxurious feeling of fate. "I believe there's a volunteer fire brigade somewhere on the lake," said Mandy.

"They'll see the flames right away."

The fire grew. Timmie slept in his basket. Thatcher slept, or hid, on Dora's thin shoulder. The women began to edge their way down the rocks to the left of the fire. They'd have to wait on the dock. Chip would arrive in the morning.

"I'm not really worried about anything," said Dora. She smiled at Mandy. "Are you?"

Where Are You Calling From?

Where Are You Calling From?

"I have joined the lower classes," wept Althea.

She was lying across the purple bedspread in their apartment in married-student housing. It was morning. The room was grey like a lit television screen; a weak winter sun barely penetrated institutional curtains of blue jute. Althea was in despair. Last night, Michael vomited outside the door of the Masters' Dining Room during a graduate seminar on the plays of Yeats. And already today a threatening man from a credit agency had telephoned.

"The working classes," Michael corrected, his eyes closed.

"Working" didn't sound right to her; she and Michael did nothing that seemed like work. They only read and went to class and talked and drank wine. As a lawyer, her father worked much harder. But Michael laughed at her when she said "lower" class. The term was archaic, like many of her notions. Thank goodness she was only twenty-two; there was still time to straighten her out.

Michael got up and made his way to the bathroom.

Around the seminar table they had been debating the

romantic image with the aid of several bottles of wine provided by a thirsty professor. Without warning Michael burst
into a song of his own composition. He sang a number of
verses, with refrain, and then stopped abruptly, turned
white, and excused himself. When Althea went after him she
identified a body curled around the banister at the bottom of
the staircase. His dashiki and ill-fitting jeans, his Kodiak
boots with the laces tied around his ankles gave him away. A
nun was stroking his head. Nuns were always turning up
around Michael. This one had cleared up the mess already.
Only the smell remained.

The sound of Michael retching again came from the
bathroom.

Althea sobbed some more, thinking of the looks that must
have gone around the table when they didn't come back.
They walked home across the field. In the middle of this
Toronto winter there had been a thaw, rain and a freeze.
The tall grass was coated with ice and clattered around their
waists. They took the elevator to their eighth-floor one-
bedroom. On the way up Michael dissected the other
students whose papers had been under discussion. "Karen's
so earnest. Did you see how her perfect little pink buffed
fingernail moved along under each line? Like a kindergarten
teacher!" Edward with his typed-out pages of critics'
remarks came in for similar scorn. "I've got more art in my
little toe than he'll ever understand," said Michael.

Althea enjoyed the walk. The mockery unleashed by in-
ebriation was the only part of Michael's drinking that she
did enjoy; when he was sober, her husband was kind and
humble to a fault. But as soon as they got home he dropped
heavily in the middle of the bed and fell asleep, stinking and
snoring. She lay beside him and worried about her life until
she fell asleep too. This morning the telephone call from the
credit agency woke them.

Althea heard the dizzy rush of the shower. It was time to

get up. She went to the bathroom herself, stood in front of the sink and looked in the mirror. But Michael's shower had steamed it over: her face was obscured, blistered like some Byzantine madonna's. As she reached out with a handcloth to wipe the glass, the noise of the shower stopped.

Michael stepped out. He wasn't meeting her eyes yet. She examined him objectively. He looked young for his age. His collar bone was thin, his arms and legs long, his trunk like a lozenge, without a waist. "This is my husband," thought Althea. "This is what I have married." She felt sick.

People always said Michael looked like Jesus Christ. Perhaps he tried. He had been an altar boy, he even spent a year in the seminary training for the priesthood. In 1965 there was a shortage of young men with vocations; as inducement, the priests allowed the seminary boys to go down to the main campus for classes. The freshettes found Michael's sapphire eyes and mournful Renaissance face irresistible, and soon he gave up the Church.

Althea met Michael in drama class. Later he came to play accompaniment for the drama-school production of Samuel Beckett's *Play*. Althea had one of the two female roles, specifically, W1. She was to sit the entire production enclosed to her neck in an urn on a dark stage. A garbage can had been all they could find for the purpose: she was wedged in it halfway down, her back against the back, her knees smashed into the front. When the light came on her face she said:

"I can do nothing for anybody any more, thank God. So it must be something I have to say. How the mind works still!"

Althea had a forceful voice, she spoke with utter conviction. Olive-skinned, with masses of coarse dark hair and a long face, she had the face that her decade, the sixties, had declared beautiful. Everyone in her class was sure she was going to be famous.

Althea loved the play. She thought Beckett was the best

writer in the English language. It was Beckett's logic, or rather his fatalism that sounded like logic, his illogic with the rhythm of syllogisms, that was best about Beckett, she explained. Michael agreed. He thought Althea extraordinary. She was a temperamental woman from a sophisticated family, a double major in drama and philosophy. She had a boyfriend in New York, who was going to be a businessman, but she didn't want to marry him. Althea saw through things like that. She saw through everyone, understood everyone, and consequently was often disturbed and unhappy.

Michael admired Althea's strange woeful look. He found as they spoke that he was able to say to her what he had always known, which was that he too was exceptional, sensitive and talented. He confided to her that he was going to make a record; he was in negotiations now with a company. He dreamed of conversing on a friendly basis with Bob Dylan. Althea could see all this coming true. She applied her imagination to his condition; from her position of superior worldly knowledge she made his hoped-for future seem real. In exchange she asked him to take her troubles seriously. There was a professor who tried to seduce her and then gave her a low grade, an awful man. They made a tacit pact. In exchange for her faith, Michael would listen to Althea even when it meant taking a certain amount of abuse himself.

Michael was used to taking abuse. He was the oldest son in a family of five children. Early on his mother put Michael in charge of seeing that father didn't drink up the grocery money. Before he was a man Michael had rolled down the back stairs in a pugilist's embrace with his father. He protected the younger children and his mother. Althea found all this vastly appealing. His eyes contained a kind of benediction. He had such talent, and his family had never even been able to afford to give him music lessons.

Michael took Althea to the pizza cellar where he sang. She sat in her expensive sweater and smiled at the table; his voice entered her. In spring they skipped classes and took a bottle of wine to the park. Sitting at a picnic table under the black wet leafless trees enclosed by the steady drip of melting snow, dazzled by the glitter of standing ice, they fell in love. A more or less chemical exchange, a purification took place there in the cold melting April afternoon.

They were equals, they thought, equally scarred and equally starred for brilliant futures. If Michael conversed with Bob Dylan in his dreams, then Althea met Sarah Bernhardt in hers. They imagined that together they would make a fantastic child, a child who would combine their separate powers; they owed the world this child. When the sun dropped behind the hill they walked up the path to Althea's house.

It was a big house, overlooking the park. It was warm and dry; there was a fire crackling in the grate, and sherry in a decanter. Michael, who had already taken more than half the wine, had several sherries. Dinner was a formal affair with roast beef on a blue and white china platter and scalloped potatoes. Althea's parents liked Michael. He wasn't what they had in mind, was all. He came from an unstable background. Also, his clothes were cheap and didn't hang properly; he was not presentable. Althea knew what they were thinking, but she also knew how deliberately Michael chose that old cardigan from the pile shared by his brothers because he liked the look it gave him. Passing his coffee across the linen tablecloth Althea's mother asked him why he didn't give up smoking. It was the only one of his vices open to comment.

"I'm making a study of weakness," said Michael, smiling slowly under his moustache, and taking a deep drag on his cigarette.

"Well, why don't you make a study of strength?"
retorted Althea's mother.

All of this would have been fine, if only they hadn't married.
Everyone was against it, and it seemed inevitable. The
priests were upset because Althea wasn't a Catholic. Indeed
she was a nothing; she hadn't even been baptized. Father
Upshall threatened to throw water over her head right there
in his office, but she ducked. They had it in the church
without a mass. Came the wedding day he was wavering
around at the top of the aisle as Althea, propelled by her
father, made her way up between the rows of church pews.
Her friends were sightseeing, and his were grieving.

But Michael's face was creased with tenderness; he folded
her hand against his heart. Althea felt the cold on her back
when her father stepped away but Michael supported her.
Together they faced the priest. But the ceremony did not go
ahead. Father Upshall did not start. Instead he gave a very
corny grin.

"Well, Mikey, what do we do now?" he said.

Michael, former altar boy, pointed out the passage where
the ceremony should begin. Father Upshall peered out at the
assembled people, opened his mouth and closed it. He was
drunk.

Poor Michael, thought Althea. No one ever looked after
him. Even at his own wedding he has to take charge. Right
then and there Althea vowed to look after him always. At the
reception Althea's mother was heard to say, "I give it four
years." Nevertheless, they gave them money to go to
England for a honeymoon.

There, among other monuments, the newlyweds visited
Althea's grandparents. "I don't understand why she didn't
want china," said the grandmother deafly. "She wouldn't
take silver either." On the wide lawn stretching out to the

moors the old woman asked Michael how he kept his feet clean in the sandals.

"I wash them," said Michael.

The grandfather laughed and laughed. Althea hugged the old man when they said goodbye; he was old and he was the first one of either family who felt like a friend. The fact that everyone regarded her marriage as a mistake made Althea very busy defending it. She could not let on her own resentment of the expectations of married life. She was horrified by china, silver, vegetable choppers and woollen blankets alike, which were presented as if they and they alone would serve her future. She stopped reading Joyce and took up *The Golden Notebook.* Since her marriage the lives of women had begun to obsess her, and depress her. At this point in time a serious student did not betray interest in women's writing. A serious student was above issues of gender. Before she was married, Althea had thought that this was as it should be, but now she had doubts. She was a woman. She was affected by being a woman. She could not escape the condition or the consequence.

For instance, they came to this university because Michael had a scholarship. He would carry on with university until his music made him famous. The same record contract was pending. There was no theatre school, so Althea was taking a couple of drama courses. People kept getting her name wrong. An absent-minded doctor had told her to use foam and forgot to mention the condom. As it happened she only used the foam sometimes. It was hard because they made love all over the place, on the rug or in the van, as if to prove they were carried away.

And now, of course, Althea was pregnant. Food disgusted her. Yesterday morning even the steam from the teapot caused her stomach to turn. She had lost fifteen pounds in

the last six weeks. She looked at Michael standing naked on
the bathroom mat, his penis dropping like a worm over his
balls, and she lost faith. Lost faith in the perfect child they
might have, lost faith in his goodness, lost faith in the
idea of completion that this marriage had represented.
There was nothing special about any of this: it was the most
ordinary, most terrifying dilemma. Michael was a nice guy
but he was going to be an alcoholic. He was always going to
be in debt. She had lost her family, lost her footing. She was
sliding down, down the ladder. Feeling faint, she reached
out to grasp the edge of the sink. She would save herself.

"I'm not going to have it," she said.

Michael didn't argue. He was in no shape to argue. He
cried instead. He had all those brothers and sisters; he was
used to babies around. But he understood, Michael always
understood. Althea had no brothers and sisters but her
whole life to worry about. She wanted to act, to be useful, to
do things.

They both went back to bed and cried. They loved each
other so much. They could have had an amazing baby, a
baby that could save the world. But perhaps it would have
been too perfect, for it was not to be.

After the abortion, giddy with relief, Althea worked up a
résumé. She went downtown and had a photograph taken.
In this photograph she looked hectic, thinner; she looked as
if she had a secret. She had cut herself from Michael's messy
future but she had not told him yet. Just having this secret
made her stronger. But when spring came, and the little pale
buds began to fatten on the bone-white branches, her mood
went black. They had stupid fights about who did the cooking; she refused to clean the bathroom. She lay on the sofa
eating Jello. Everyone was applying for grants for next year.

"I cannot imagine what I'm going to do next year," Althea fretted. "I cannot even imagine next week."

"You're beautiful, why don't you just be content with that?" Michael said.

"I am not beautiful and anyway if I was it's not a thing to do," she said. She thought it was their one-bedroom apartment in grad. res. that depressed her, so they gave notice and moved to two high-ceilinged rooms with stained velvet drapes, in Chinatown.

There was neon and noise down in the city. Across Spadina, Meat and Potatoes was open till four in the morning. Althea and Michael went every night. Sometimes Michael sang a set or two. They met Max and Aida who drank and smoked up every night and slept all day. Aida wore old satin dresses with lace at the hem, and a velvet cloak. Michael admired her style. They talked about going to Europe, the four of them, living in Italy. They drank and smoked some more. Sometime during that spring and summer, Althea's fevered photograph got her an agent. Max and Aida giggled hysterically when she said she had to go home to bed because she had to be at an audition early in the morning.

Then Michael's scholarship ran out, hastened by their having to keep up with Max and Aida who had a mysterious supply of cash. With a feeling of the injustice of it, Michael started reading the ads in the newspaper. One day he found a job at a junior college in North Bay. They had one hundred and thirty-three dollars left. When the offer came it said be there in a week, and we'll pay you nine thousand.

In five days he was gone. Plucked from her side, that's how it felt. Althea reeled in the space all around her. Voices came through the walls of the boarding-house. Her parents got on the telephone and told her she should follow him, set up a drama group at a local library. She knew she was meant for better things. That very day her agent phoned; she'd got a place in an acting company funded by a local initiatives grant. The company went around to schools proselytizing against the use of drugs. It was an ironic disguise for a miracle, she told Michael on the telephone (he called collect from the coffee house near the campus). They laughed and laughed. She couldn't wait to get to Meat and Potatoes, and tell Max and Aida.

But it wasn't so funny in winter, when the acting job ended and there weren't any more. After Christmas Michael wrote a complicated letter about his fuel expenses and the second-hand car he'd bought. There were too many details for Althea to absorb; in her embarrassment she only skimmed the paragraphs. But she understood that he did not want to support her; he did not feel he had to.

She was too proud to ask her parents; they thought that if she was going to be on her own she should pay her way. Besides, helping her now would be interfering with her marriage (they would think) and that was something they wouldn't do, particularly since they'd never approved of it in the first place. The other aspiring actors she met worked as waiters and sometimes shoplifted but she couldn't. Just in the nick of time her grandfather in England died and left Althea some money. It wasn't much, just a few thousand dollars a year, but in those days you could live on it. Michael didn't ask Althea to come up; they agreed it was better for her career to be in the city. But the rents were too expensive; she found an old farmhouse for rent not far north of the city.

Max and Aida went to Europe. Althea wrote to Michael; all kinds of people like her were living around Stouffville; the country was very social. She bought a second-hand truck to get down to the city for auditions but she didn't go there much. She put a lot of miles on the truck.

While she drove she remembered Michael. There was one night in a café in the Townships, where he sang two sets in exchange for two hot dinners. He leaned over the mike, brows puckered up high in the middle like three-cornered hats. "If I listened long enough to you, I'd find a way to believe that it's all true."

Althea wondered which of her decisions had been the wrong one, to come east, to want to act, to marry? She decided none of them were wrong. She believed in Michael, and their marriage. There had been that moment of panic, when she had to cut loose from him, get rid of the baby. But that had passed. She was sorry she ever doubted Michael. It was summer when he showed up in her driveway by surprise, and went to work installing a good cassette system in her truck. He'd bought her the new Bonnie Rait album. They sat in the truck and listened.

There was no scrawny boy in him any more. His skin was opaque; a layer of fat over his cheekbones changed the shape of his face. His voice was rough. (He thought it was an improvement.) When he talked about his songs a note of bitterness was discernible, even to Althea. He said that although the guys in the music business had long hair they might as well have little briefcases and business suits. They were awfully organized. Being organized was not cool. "Organized" meant keeping an appointment book, shining your shoes, shaving every morning, *trying too hard.* The organized ones had not seen the light, and justly became the butt of those like themselves who had sloppy clothes and forgot to pay their bills but were rightful artists. But look what was happening in the world: those who were organized were getting ahead.

They moved into her bed under the farmhouse gable, in the one room that was warmed by the chimney. After they made love Michael told Althea about a very special student in his class. She was called Laura. Apparently she was sweet and undemanding, not at all like Althea. Laura was that much younger (she was eighteen; Althea twenty-six), said Michael, almost a different generation, really. She had no problems about her role as a woman. By that he meant they had no fights about money or cooking or her job. Althea said she was happy for him. Then they sighed and hugged and kissed and Michael got in his car and drove away.

Thanksgiving weekend Althea drove up to visit Michael and discovered that he and Laura were living together. Althea was touched by the way Michael tried to stop Laura from revealing the turkey defrosting in the kitchen sink. It was just like him to know that signs of their domestic ritual would be painful to her! Michael was so kind. But just after Christmas, the sheriff turned up at Althea's door to serve her with divorce papers.

"There I was in my bathrobe," she said, "and I saw this cop tramping up the driveway." Breathless, she had telephoned Michael at the college. "I thought it must be for my parking tickets." Althea was notorious for staying too long at meters in town. They had a good laugh, and then Althea started to gulp and cry. "It's just that I wasn't expecting it."

"I didn't want to bring up the subject at Thanksgiving because I didn't want to hurt your feelings," said Michael. He explained that it was Laura who wanted the situation cleared up.

"But doesn't she understand about us?"

Apparently not. Although Laura was free of the conflicts that had plagued Althea, she had problems of her own. She was insecure and felt threatened by Althea, said Michael.

Standing there in her cold bare feet by the wall telephone in the kitchen, looking out the window to where her truck tilted on its frozen muddy ruts, Althea realized that she did not want to hear this. She did not want to hear about Laura's problems. Althea had a lover, another actor named

Nick, even less in demand than herself. That night, as they played Scrabble at her kitchen table, he accused Althea of drinking too much. She said he had never understood her, not like Michael. Nick walked away out into the starbright country night, but there was no place open, so he had to come back.

When the divorce went through Althea's family blamed her, having decided at last that Michael might make something of himself. With Laura, he had bought a book and record store in North Bay; they were impressed by this. Althea still wore her hair long and untidy; but her stock of beautiful sweaters had run out. She wore men's shirts or sweatshirts. She lived on her inheritance and hardly ever worked. In the old truck she drove east and west and south, staying with friends, stopping at bars. Althea would have a few drinks and find a man and put her head on his lap and say that she needed to be loved.

"Don't you think I'm a textbook case?" she would say, when she was drunk. "Don't you think it's interesting, the way I've gone down?" People worried about Althea and were glad when she left.

She visited Max and Aida in their expensive apartment over a store in Yorkville. They both wore evening dress and looked as if they never went outside. "Althea!" they said, with genuine disapproval. "You were supposed to be in movies by now!" Althea didn't care, she didn't figure a couple of drug dealers had the right to judge her. Perhaps they even asked Michael to do something about her, because he called and called and finally got her at the farm and said he was coming down for a weekend. Althea didn't know, but it was the week after his marriage to Laura.

Michael kept saying how much he loved being in Althea's farmhouse. The kitchen was bright with bulbs forcing their way through earth in clay pots. The other rooms had a feeling of enchantment, deep in dust and cobwebs, the windows greyed over, tattered throws spread over the indentations on the sofa where she habitually threw herself down. Now he liked it that she refused to do housework.

They played Cat Stevens and John Prine. Michael quizzed her about her life. Althea confessed that her agent didn't send her on many auditions any more; they wanted a new face, cool, hard-edged.

"I'm out of date," said Althea. "It has all passed me by."

"You are not. Never think that."

But he suggested that she consider teaching. They lay side by side on the sprung sofa in the parlour and sunlight made the dirty windows look like marble.

"I love you very much, Althea," said Michael. "But I'm glad I'm with Laura and you're with Nick."

"Why?" said Althea.

"You make me nervous. I feel like when I'm around you I'm going to drink too much, or end up in debt."

"Silly," said Althea.

"But now I'm not worried about myself. I'm fine."

Michael went home and told people that Althea was fine, too.

And then, despite his best intentions, Michael did not see Althea for a long time. It was nearly a year later when he got the letter, covered all over with red and blue stickers and marked Special Delivery. It contained very little news but reeked of private knowledge of him; it was hung together with unavoidable memories. "That day in the park," Althea wrote, "when we discovered we were the same people inside. . . . We weren't wrong. Remember the baby we still owe to the world."

Michael hid the letter and said to himself that he would write back. However, six months went by and then another letter came the same way, pasted all over with stickers indicating urgency. And inside, their continuing intimacy was assumed. He read the letter twice. Once he fell into the spell of their earlier love, thought of her lying on the old sofa crocheted to the wall with spider webs. The second time he stood apart, thinking that Althea was a stranger and the letter was mildly pornographic.

Then the telephone calls began. She never made them from home. She was always on the road. She would call from a highway coffee shop most often. Once it was eleven o'clock at night. He was in his study, marking papers.

"This reminds me of that Joan Baez song on Diamonds and Rust," he said, sternly. "You know, where she says, 'Where are you calling from?' and he answers 'A booth in the midwest'?"

"Only in the song it was Baez who stayed home and Dylan who kept going from place to place."

"So what have we done, traded lives?" said Michael, looking out the door of his study to the round white clock with black hands that hung in the kitchen. In two minutes Laura would call out that he should come to bed. He had the idea that Althea knew this, and was trying to get him in trouble.

"Who was that on the telephone?" said Laura later.

He told her.

"It's a shame about her," she said. "I mean how she's gone down."

Michael said she was likely to settle down soon. It was hard to get over thinking Althea was the one who knew what she wanted and he was the reprobate. "I don't know what happened to her," he said, finally.

"It was probably all that money."

"It wasn't really very much money," he said.

"You always stick up for her."

"Three thousand a year," he protested.

"Enough to ruin her life," said Laura.

Michael defended Althea. But Laura got more angry.

"You pretend to be so good to her but all the time you're putting her down. That's why she calls here! You haven't let her go. Why don't you just be mean to each other like all other divorced couples, and get it over with?"

Michael began to realize that there were no women who didn't have problems being women. There were only stages of life. He'd met Laura at an uncomplicated stage. Now she was complicated.

"Maybe Althea was just someone who couldn't cope," he said, desperately selling off his first love to stop Laura from proceeding in the dangerous direction her reason was taking her. Then he was ashamed of what he said about her. After the dishes were put away he went out to the bar. The pain seemed too great to drink away but he did. There was silence from Althea for more than a year. Then Michael, in a spasm of missing her, wrote her a letter and covered it with stamps and stickers and sent it Special Delivery. He enclosed a picture of Laura and the baby, only eight months old and you couldn't tell but she was pregnant with another.

When the telephone rang he was upstairs in his study. Althea said she was on the road from Cobourg to Toronto. She had just pulled over at the Voyageur for coffee.

"You'd think you didn't have a home," he said.

"I just felt like talking." She'd got the photograph. She went on to tell him how proud she was of him, that he had done well, that he was all set up in life now.

Her voice stirred the pit of his stomach in the old way but it ruffled him, it made him angry, it was an intrusion. But he didn't tell her, instead he talked about Darin, who was already cruising around the furniture, and told her about the other one coming and how Laura was tired. Althea was in no rush to get off the telephone. Michael had the sense — he'd had this sense ever since they first separated, but so far she had never proven him right — he had the *sense* she was going to ask him for something.

"What ever happened to Nick?" he said.

"Oh, that's over," said Althea lightly. And she began to tell a story about how she'd been in hospital for troubles he understood to be related to her menstrual cycle. The long and short of it was that she couldn't have children. And Nick had wanted them, so he left. Michael had the impression Althea did not blame Nick for this.

"I'm sorry," said Michael.

Then for some reason he could not fathom she began to talk about the abortion she'd had way back in the first year of their marriage. They said that her cervix had not closed properly and that when she got pregnant again she would miscarry. There was an operation you could do with a string to tie it up like a little purse, but there was no guarantee.

"I'll never have children now," said Althea.

"Never's a long time."

She continued as if he had not spoken. It was gynaecological talk. Michael heard a lot of it from Laura and he had learned to tune it out. From Althea it was almost as boring but not quite, because there was a tantalizing threat of violence underneath.

"So that's why I was so interested to see your baby," she went on. Her voice was soft and frightening.

But now it was almost midnight. Michael was tired. He thought for the first time in many years of the peace and silence of the seminary the year he had lived there among men. The bells that marked the hours, the low murmur of voices in empty halls, books on the pillow at night. He imagined Laura feeling tired too, standing there in the telephone booth on Highway 401 and then getting back into the truck and maybe falling asleep at the wheel and the truck careering over the rail into the stream of cars going the other way. But it was not Laura on the phone. It was Althea.

Finally he cut her off, saying he had to go to bed. Darin got up at six. When he said goodbye he knew she wasn't finished; there was a patient, languid sound in her voice.

Hours later he thought what it was Althea wanted.

She wanted to blame him for destroying their perfect child. It was his fault, but he had a baby now. Therefore he owed her something. He was in debt to her, the damaged and denied woman. That was the reason for her casual voice, her ease in demanding.

Michael had loved Althea. He had tried to be kind to her. Perhaps Laura was right, perhaps unkindness had been needed. But it was too late now. He had a feeling that time after time the telephone would ring and it would be Althea and he would not know where she was calling from.

Big Game

Big Game

Tomi ran her fingers through her straight short hair, still damp from her swim in the sergeant's apartment pool. "If I were a girl that's how I'd wear my hair," he had said to her years ago when they saw one of these no-nonsense boyish cuts on a woman in a line-up outside a movie theatre. Only tonight did it strike her what a strange remark that was, considering the kind of woman he favoured.

"Where are you off to tonight?" said the sergeant.

"Judy's."

They had had this agreement from the start, that when they spent time together her social life would continue. She had gone back and forth between his city and her mother's so often that she had matching sets of friends, one in each place.

"What will you do for dinner?" she said.

He winked, meaning he would be naughty and have a Lean Cuisine in front of the TV. The sergeant had a perfect slow wink and a head of ruffled brown hair at sixty, with only a few strands of grey at his temples. His eyebrows were

black, white and red. People asked him if he was Welsh,
they were Welsh eyebrows apparently, horned. They were
part of his allure, along with the height, the firmness of his
movements, his small even teeth and the deliberate outmoded
courtesies. After the divorce he wasn't so much Dad any
more. Sergeant was only his nickname; he was military only
in style. He worked as a civil servant in the Department of
Education.

"And after I eat I'll go out to the liquor store and then
maybe do a bit of work at the office."

"The office." The sergeant did not change, he even used
the same excuses. Tomi didn't expect him to be alone here
all the time, the way her mother was at home, except for that
crazy United Church minister who visited. But she had expected him to give up his excuses. It turned out though that
his excuses had nothing to do with the marriage that used to
be, or with her mother, or with Tomi herself even. They had
to do with him, the sergeant.

Ten years ago he emptied his tie rack of the long striped
silks and removed the many dark suits which hung like a
stopped parade behind the sprung doors on his side of the
master bedroom. He took a promotion to the provincial
government and moved to Edmonton. Her mother gave up
the night school he'd insisted she wanted and got someone to
look after the garden, and in some ways it was better. Then
too it was not long until the other husbands began to die,
leaving Tomi's mother a good supply of widows to shop and
even travel with.

The sergeant, however, was less dead every year. Tomi
never met any of his women now. They were evident only in
the sweet-smelling hairspray and sponge powder puffs she
found in the bottom drawer of his bathroom cabinet. She'd
seen more of them when he was still at home. Then it had
been Rita accidentally met up with in a downtown bar at

lunch time or even, daringly, Sharon, encountered the day he'd taken Tomi to the High River Stampede. "Look," he'd said, pointing across the fairgrounds, "there's Sharon from the office. Shall we ask her to join us?"

Oh, he had played a dangerous game and although not wanting to be caught, exactly, had wanted her to know, Tomi thought, eyeing his long fingers with the blunt white nails on his glass. And the nature of his game was to be above suspicion. Such a correct man, so exacting, so moral. If he brought some beehived tart to Tomi's graduation ceremony, shortly before the divorce, surely there could be nothing in it. She must be a family friend. But Tomi knew. She knew without knowing she knew. After the dance she borrowed his car to drive up to Banff with her girlfriends. Some boys were expecting them. That time the sergeant said to her dryly, coiling up the backyard hose in the neat way he always did, like a sailor, for what he must have known was the last time,

"You really think you're putting one over on your old dad, don't you?"

And she thought she might cry but she didn't. She was sorry to betray their understanding but he had done it first.

"If it weren't for Judy," said the sergeant, "I'd have taken you out to dinner and a movie."

She stood examining his face while he finished his drink. His profile was as beautiful as ever, the light downturning line at the end of his lip the only indication he wasn't getting what he wanted. His head was poised, looking across the carpet like a bust, a work of art; for the first time she imagined the bleakness of that bust presiding alone in his apartment.

The apartment was spare and rigorously ordered, the pens by the paper, the hat and gloves solitary on the shelf. A pair of binoculars that used to stand on the bookshelves at home now lay on a glass table by the balcony door. A ship's barometer from some early job; a lacquered flying fish. At home these had been flotsam, heavy in the weave of her mother's ivy, the flowered tablecloths ("treatments" the decorator called them) and French watercolours. Now they stood out, unfamiliar in relief.

These objects belonged together, on their own. They looked masculine, purposeful, part of a story — binoculars, pot, clock, barometer. A story about adventure, discovery, measurement. Their new coherence showed up the gap that had always existed at home. The separate levels, separate depths of his life and her mother's. Two species with habitats which did not meet, without sacrifice of one or the other. Her net, his fish. Her sewing together, his standing apart. Her being, his doing. His going.

It was time for Tomi to go. She tidied her things from the bathroom and stowed her kit to the side of the pull-out couch where she slept. She tied up the laces of her fur-lined boots and put her shoes in a bag. Winter had come to stay. It was fifteen days before Christmas and the snow was falling thickly. She rummaged in her purse for her keys.

"Taking your car?" said the sergeant, now hovering in the hallway awaiting her departure instead of watching the news on television as he always did, as he was supposed to do.

She nodded.

"There's going to be a blizzard," he said. "Why don't you take mine?"

His was heavier and safer, he meant. The sergeant was not in favour of small cars, he said he'd never drive one, not as long as the other drivers were in large machines. It was asking to get the worst of any accidental meeting. He reached to the place on top of the shelf where he kept his keys and handed them to her. How thoughtful he was.

"Forty-five," he said. It was the number of his parking space in the underground garage. She left.

Long, and the colour of a peeled almond, the car fishtailed on powdery wet pavement as Tomi turned into Judy's street. She needed yards and yards of space in which to park, and had to go halfway down the block to find it. Running back into the wind, she could barely pick out the covered front porch of Judy's little brown-shingled house. The snow was turning mean, stinging as it struck her face.

She stepped into the living room. It was all red and black cushions, embroidered rugs with little mirrors in them, hand-woven hangings. Judy and Reid kissed her; their faces burning and dry. At first she didn't see the man sitting in the corner chair. His face was pale and his hair thinning, mouse brown, his thin legs were crossed at the knee. Judy said he was Luke from England, teaching at the university on exchange. Tomi took a glass of white wine and quizzed him distractedly.

"Have they found you a good place to live?" (No. It's in a tower block and the only good thing is that the owner left a great record collection.)

"How are you liking Edmonton?" (The river valley is great for walking. Enigmatic smile.)

"Are you going back home for Christmas?" (No. We rented our house.)

We, she heard, and pressed herself to her feet. She went to the kitchen to visit Judy, who was making Hungarian dumplings in boiling water. The kitchen was tropical; the windows were steamed over and all the plants on the sill were plump, not scraggly, like Tomi's in her apartment in Calgary. Judy kept things alive. She built a web of living things around her, she connected people to people. But then Judy didn't travel; she had time to cook, to get supplies in. Judy didn't have a business. And Judy had Reid.

"Wife didn't like Edmonton?" said Tomi, reaching for a raw carrot.

"She left a month ago. I gather they'd been about to separate in the first place," she said.

Tomi examined Judy's profile. She had a flat forehead, a deep scoop between her eyes, a turned-up nose with a slight bulb at the end, and a beautiful, strong, forward-reaching chin, a chin to envy. It was difficult to tell what Judy did on purpose and what she did by accident.

"I hope the snow stops. I have to drive back to Calgary tomorrow," said Tomi, draining her glass of red wine.

"When did you get here?"

"Yesterday."

"Oh, Tomi," said Judy, and Tomi turned away from the criticism.

They had shared this meal before. It was hearty and full of colour, pure Judy. Cherry soup and then a deep brown stew with the little yellow dumplings, and purple-cabbage salad. Judy's beautiful tawny neck as she leaned over the table setting down a heavy tray. Reid filling up the glasses with more burgundy wine. The rolled-pancake dessert with its white lace of powdered sugar. Everything served in silver, something that reflected.

For tea in glass mugs with brandy, they all moved from the table to floor cushions in front of the gas fire. The firelight made the mirrored rug, the shiny pillows, the pewter goblets move and shimmer and wink. The wind burst black against the windowpane and then withdrew, returning all in white. When they looked out they could see that the snowflakes had become smaller, tighter together, more desperate; the temperature was dropping. Neither guest spoke of going home.

Tomi was quiet, leaning back on her elbows next to Luke. Luke had expanded, pillows under his back, his goblet balanced on his breastbone. Like a lot of Englishmen he wasn't nearly as wimpy as he'd first appeared. In fact he was full-blooded and outdoorsy, with a deep rolling laugh. He was telling the story of how he met an Indian in a hotel beer parlour and went to his house on the reserve where he learned to play the fiddle.

"I told my students next day," he said. "I could see they were deeply shocked. One doesn't go drinking with Indians, does one?"

Nobody said anything.

Luke laughed again.

"But it's why I came here. To hunt bear and moose. There's not many places in the world you can. Except Africa, and Africa's no good now. This Indian's my pal. We go to the country bars and amuse ourselves stealing the tall hats from Hutterites. They're shamed, you see, if they show their heads."

He roared again, and looked at Tomi. She smiled dubiously. "We always give them back, you!" He gave her a soft punch in the shoulder. Men often punched Tomi's shoulder. "She's too serious, this girl. It's a dangerous thing." He reached out and pinched her leg above the knee.

Tomi was certain now that Judy intended to set them up. And she could see it wasn't entirely insane. He did have a certain animal magnetism. But she could not imagine this intellectual big-game hunter would be interested in her. She lacked the necessary feminine charms, she was too small, not substantial enough. It was what always went through her head when she met a man.

Where her hand lay on the carpet she felt his shoulder approach. It moved in her direction on its own by subtle half inches. How did he do it without changing his position on the floor? Finally the top of his arm touched her fingers.

In the familiar living-room the strange man's warmth turned the tips of her fingers into glowing coals. Tomi wondered what Judy thought. She hoped Luke wouldn't move any closer. She couldn't pull her hand away without attracting attention. Finally Luke spoke.

"Look, Judy's yawning. It's after 1:30. We've got to be going." He said this as if they'd come together, erred together in sitting in their comfortable spots too long. And Judy's face showed only its bright affability.

Luke donned an enormous army-surplus parka with a fur trimmed hood. "You can't imagine how glad I am to see this purchase justified," he said. They hesitated a moment in face of the violence at the door. "Look at your weather! It's wonderful, it's truly magnificent."

And then they were off the porch and into it. Luke said he would drive ahead of Tomi and watch out for her in his rear view mirror. Two, three inches of snow had fallen. The sergeant's car was rounded by a thick layer. It had ceased to be a vehicle that moved along the surface and had become an outgrowth of the street. Tomi dug out the door handle and slid into the hollow centre, and Luke shut the door behind her.

The street light above made her car pale blue inside, like a snow cave. Now the red wine hit Tomi. She could easily go to sleep sitting there in the driver's seat, with the cold glow lending a final perfection to the evening.

The cave broke open as Luke's rough ski glove wiped the snow off the windshield in great black sweeps. He was revealed in her mirror; a man's shape without a man's detail, dark in the white whirl. He waved, took a few steps, and disappeared toward his jeep. She turned on the ignition and started the car.

He honked when he got going, and when the tail lights of his jeep passed her, she pulled out. It was very late, and she'd drunk a huge amount of wine and brandy but she knew the encounter wasn't over yet. She would like to ask Luke in for a nightcap. But of course there was the sergeant.

Luke's jeep pulled over in front of the sergeant's building at the edge of the river valley. Tomi didn't stop before she descended the ramp to park. The overhead fluorescent tubes shocked her eyes. Gone. No more Luke. But she stopped the elevator on the first floor by the front entrance. He was standing there, hunched in the tumult.

"Why don't you come over and see my place?" he said. "Have a ride in the jeep."

"I don't see how. I'm staying with my dad, I told you. With the snow and all, he'd worry."

"Oh come on now," he said. "I can't persuade you?"

She could just see the outline of his face within the fur trimmed hood. She didn't want to see him get in that jeep and disappear.

"All right, you come up for a drink. But we'll have to be quiet."

It was 2:05 by the clock on the stove in her father's galley kitchen as she poured some of his brandy into a snifter. She took water for herself. They turned on no lights. The outdoor whiteness was visible through the windows at the end of the living-room, a ghostly display of turbulence across the great black open sky sparked with lights on the other side of the river.

"That's me over there," Luke whispered, pointing across the river valley. His shirt had come loose from his belt.

Tomi giggled. It was really too funny to have smuggled this bush hunter into the sergeant's perfect box. Her father

slept not easily or soundly. She and Luke sat side by side and
talked in whispers. He asked about the handmade paper she
produced. She asked about his wife.

"She's a dangerous woman," said Luke.

He asked her why she didn't have a boyfriend.

"I move around too much."

"And that's not all."

"No, that's not all."

It was easy to be frank. They talked till they were almost
asleep.

"Come to my place."

"How can I?"

"Why ever not? He knows I'm here," said Luke. There
had been no movement from the sergeant's room.

"Because if I say I'll go it's like saying I'll go to bed with
you . . ."

"Aha!" said Luke, his gusty voice getting almost to normal volume. "Methinks she doth assume too much. It's only
so we can talk without you thinking of your dad. You
mustn't assume we'd make love, if it frightens you. And
anyway," he said, "I might not be able to."

I might not be able to. Tomi let her head fall back on the edge
of the couch. It was the strangest come-on she'd ever heard,
and the only one she could respond to. She took their glasses
out to the kitchen. The clock said 3:45. She picked up the
pad of yellow paper with the adhesive strip and wrote a note.

"Dad. Gone to Luke's. Back later."

She stuck it on the refrigerator. It hung there, so civil, so
adult. So bald a cover-up. Gone to Luke's. Hah! The note
was a parody of her domestic relations with her father. She
beckoned Luke. They replaced their overcoats and went out
the door. She was aware of a certain gravity in her
movements, aware of the moment being charged, freighted
with more than the cold and the heaviness of their clothing.

She paused at the sidewalk.

"Come in the jeep."

"No." She wanted to be able to get back any time she wished, not to have to depend on him to drive her. She looked down the street. By now her own car was nothing but a suggestion of a hood under a drift.

"I'll have to take the sergeant's."

She drove up the ramp from the underground parking-lot and saw the jeep's lights boring into the white haze of snow. She pulled out onto the street. It was like manoeuvers. She and Luke were enclosed with the artillery of their past, they moved in these heavy closed tanks. This was how approaches were made, by those past youth.

Slowly the two cars like a cortège followed a route along the river-valley drive up to the High Level Bridge and onto it. They were not alone in the wild early morning. Other motorists were out in the operatic scene, moving between blank flats of snow and wind.

One thing she was grateful for, thought Tomi. Edmontonians knew how to drive in blizzards. It was a skill one acquired. The skill was to travel over a surface that was totally treacherous, never knowing whether there was a grip underneath or not. It was like a slow-motion dance, you made no sudden stops, no quick turns. You did not step on the gas to accelerate. Momentum was your only power. Braking was worse than useless. You got the car in motion and used its slide forward as well as sideways, turning the wheel slowly on a turn and after the fact. You gave in to the road and let it drive you.

At the foot of Luke's tower on the south side of the river they parked and locked their cars. The building was dark and silent. The elevator stood with the door open. Luke's apartment was as awful as he had said. But he put on one of the wonderful records — Elizabeth Schwarzkopf, singing lieder. He offered tea. Tomi watched him move in the kitchen, efficient, practised, as if he had always been alone. But Judy said his wife had just left him. Perhaps like her mother and the sergeant they lived on different planes in the same house.

She set her teacup down on the floor. When he came to sit beside her she hit it with her elbow. The clear liquid spilled all over the floor.

"I'll wipe it up."

"Oh, screw it," said Luke, wrapping an arm over her shoulder.

He had no children.

"It just didn't happen," he said.

"You played around."

"It was part of the agreement."

"I wouldn't know about agreements," said Tomi. She leaned against his chest, under the weight of one big arm. "Tell me how you hunt a moose," she said. It gave her something to listen to. Over the hour the threat of sex had gone. He had been disarmed, he was just comfortable. Listening to him she imagined the apartment across the river, the sergeant getting up and pulling on his silk jersey kimono, going out into the living-room to see if he'd heard correctly. He was going into the kitchen and seeing the note. "Gone to Luke's." He had never heard the name before, and she had used it with an assumption of familiarity. "Well, who the hell is Luke?" the sergeant was saying to himself.

He was asleep, his head propped half on the wall, half on her shoulder. There was the ragged line of his bearded chin, a sharp Adam's apple. Luke — it was a soothing, biblical name. But the sergeant would not be impressed. He was unkempt, a man who drank with Indians, who shot animals in the wilds. She too slept a little.

At five o'clock she woke because it was quieter. The wind had lessened its assault on the sealed windows. Tomi stood and found her purse. As she was putting on her boots he appeared in front of her. Luke: a muscular man with a pot belly and pants which hung low, a beard, a bald forehead. Goodbye.

Again the driving was like coasting and this time she was alone on the High Level Bridge, its black girders flashing rapidly slash slash slash across the giant white empty view of the river valley. As she turned the last corner onto the sergeant's street she miscalculated and the car fish-tailed. She pumped the brakes, she was hardly moving, but she couldn't stop. The back end of the Oldsmobile swung into a parked car. There was a thorough, prolonged crunch.

As Tomi put her foot on the ground to survey the damage she realized that she was very tired, even light-headed. Her tail had swung into the rubber bumper of the parked car. It was a jacked-up car, probably belonging to a teenager. It was not damaged. But the sergeant's back fin was seriously dented. He hated a dented car, even a scratched car. He wouldn't be seen driving it.

Now the rhythm started. She got back behind the wheel and drove the rest of the way to the parking garage. At first she didn't know what the words were that went along with this three-legged rhythm — duh de duh, duh de duh. Matthew Mark Luke and John, she found herself saying, Bless this bed that I lie on. If I die before — what was it? Something about my soul to keep. She let herself into the apartment with the sergeant's own quick, silent moves. His door was closed. That meant he had been up, had seen the note, and did not want to know if and when she came in. She pulled out her bed, lay down, and fell instantly asleep.

The kitchen clock said eleven. There were his juice glass and his egg plate, the remnants of the yolk gone hard. Tomi's mouth was dry, her eyes full of sleep. It was late, it was far too late to be in bed. She had to get back to Calgary. What was the reason? She had to think a minute. That was it. The owner of the gallery in Kensington was having a reception. There would be people there who might want to carry her paper.

She and the sergeant had talked of having lunch, but now she had no time. She called him at the office.

"Morning, Dad."

"Good morning, Tomi." His voice was correct as always, but he sounded tired.

"I don't think I've got time for lunch. I have to get back for this thing tonight."

"I doubt the highway's open." He became stern, fatherly. It was his first error in tone. "They may well have closed the highway with all this."

"The wind is down from overnight."

"It was down but it's getting up again. You might think of taking the train."

"But I need my car."

"Call the motor association," he said. "You'd be foolish to set out in that little car if —"

"Dad," she said. "I had an accident with yours last night. I caught a bumper."

The silence was too long. He was angry, in his contained sergeant way. "I really am sorry. Didn't you notice this morning?"

"It was all over snow," he said, somewhat pathetically.

His second error. You had to notice everything as a matter of self-defence. If you noticed everything, then nobody could put things over on you, you were never unpleasantly surprised. She had learned this from him. Now she would have to teach him all over again.

"Let me know what it costs and I'll pay it. I really want to."

"You didn't have any sleep," he charged. This was the third and absolutely the worst error, showing that he cared. You never let yourself be hurt, you made sure none of it mattered. You noticed, you knew all, but you did not allow it to matter.

Tomi was looking out the window. The blizzard was not less, he was absolutely right, it was still going strong. She was rather looking forward to getting out on the highway.

The highway to Calgary is closed, said the radio announcer. Do not drive on Highway One to Calgary. "I hear you but you ain't talking to me," Tomi sang back to him, warming up the Honda after she'd dug off its great hood of snow. "You talk a bad story, don't you, don't you always."

She had a little trouble getting out of the side road but the main streets had been cleared by snow-ploughs. She stopped at a gas station and got herself a large black coffee to go. She bit off two little squares out of the rim of the plastic cover, one for drinking from, the other for letting the air in. She opened the glove compartment and set the cup in the circle on the tray.

And she drove south.

"I know this road like the back of my hand," she said to herself, "better than that." The Edmonton-Calgary highway was the straightest road in the world. One hundred and eighty-six miles without so much as a curve. "Since university I've driven it how many, probably two hundred times?"

The fact that there were almost no other cars made it safer. Her high beams diffused into the snow swirls about fifty feet in front of the car. She leaned over the steering-wheel and peered into the dizzy whiteness. She couldn't see the white line. Of course she couldn't; it was snowing. Why didn't they make highway lines orange or green, like tennis balls, so they'd be easier to spot?

She couldn't see the shoulders either. Now and then there was the dark block of a building or a sign, giving her to know that was the edge of the highway. You just pointed the wheel straight ahead and drove. The road wasn't slippery, that was a good thing. Her tires clung to it, gripped it as they spun. She finished the coffee. The radio went on with its blizzard warnings, record snowfall, high winds.

"Blah blah," said Tomi. "Thanks but no thanks." She snapped it off.

She passed, or thought she passed, the windbreak just north of Red Deer. She planned to stop at the Juniper Inn, but then she wasn't sure if she had passed it; she couldn't tell how far she'd gone. The landmarks had all been wiped out.

The rhythms started again, this time in the wipers. Duh de duh, duh de duh. Matthew Mark Luke and John, Bless this bed that I lie on. If I should die before the dawn — what was it? 'Magnificent weather,' he had said, 'this is what I came for.' 'You're crazy to drive back. In that little car?' 'When did you get here, yesterday? Oh, Tomi.' Why was she so keen to get back? It wasn't as though there was anybody there she wanted to see. She had never known anyone named Luke before. It was a reassuring name. Not an English name. Perhaps he had only been pretending to be English. He was probably German, listening to lieder.

White is the worst colour to look at. It makes people anxious, like a page to be filled, like a stretched sheet. Her eyes were aching. She couldn't pull over, couldn't stop, or read the distance signs because she was afraid to take her eyes off the road. If she stopped looking at it for one minute it would be gone. It would disappear into the general whiteness of air and field, her car wheels would take off, the jolts would be felt through the floor, and then a fire in the snow.

It was nearly three o'clock. She'd been on the road two hours and hadn't had any food that day, and not much sleep the night before. The light began to go. The storm became thicker and greyer and settled around her. She thought she saw the Juniper Inn. By now she had to be half-way. Once she was half-way she knew she would make it. After all she'd had her accident already, with her father's car. The law of averages meant she wouldn't have another one.

Matthew Mark Luke and John. It seemed important to remember the words of the prayer. Not that she ever prayed, not that she ever had prayed. But the music of it, the rocking rhythm was nice. And repeating his name. Something about waking and sleeping. About God keeping. Matthew Mark Luke and John, Bless this bed that I lie on. If I should die before I sleep, I pray the Lord my soul to keep.

Perhaps she was crying. She was certainly travelling blind, meeting screen after screen of snow and the wipers going by blackly clap clap clap on the built-up ridge of snow on the windshield. With the child's rhyme she remembered being a child. How large the task was, too large, and she was too small. Like this road, too long, too straight. This going back and forth was too hard, it was too far. The winds were too strong. This country was like a board marked out in squares and straight lines, and she was thrusting herself from here to there, from there to here, playing it, trying to fill it up. But it was too great. If I should die before I wake, I pray the Lord my soul to take.

At six o'clock the snow stopped. The dark was firm and

solid. The lights of downtown drew dipsy doodles through the sky as Tomi's head wove back and forth. She had just been holding the wheel, she might have been unconscious, but once she turned off the highway she had to think where to turn. Here right, and right again, and over this ridge and down past the gas station. She made it into her driveway. Her bladder and her hands screamed from holding. But she had made it. The other place was away behind her.

Monte Carlo Night

Monte Carlo Night

Ken was standing at the door of her narrow house, his hand on the latch, his cheeks blown full of air. She had her palms against the far wall, her fingers spread out.

"But I don't want to spend Christmas with your family! I don't even know them."

"If you don't come," he said, turning the old brass knob until it clicked, "you'll never see me again!"

Ken was younger than Althea. On their first date she ordered a cheese soufflé, and in the long wait before it came he found out everything he needed to know. She was thirty-three, fully recovered from an early marriage and a slow divorce, independent, happy in her work. Even though she was in business she took time off for holidays. Children were not out of the question. He gave her a wide, moustached smile; his eyes rose and fell appreciatively from her breasts to her eyes and back again. He took her arm on the street, at the door he kissed her lightly on the lips. At once she felt the comfort of him, his solidness, his cautious searching. When he called again she thought, why not? All the men in theatre were gay. How often was she going to meet a single straight man without the complications of an ex-wife, or children?

Althea was, of all things, a casting agent. She was tall and dark with shorn black hair, a long face mournful in repose but more often, these days, wide open with laughter. She had three pianos in that eleven-foot, two-storey row house. She and Ken were introduced by mutual friends. "He'll play those pianos," they said. At first she thought him a Mummy's boy, with his courtly manners and his narrow lapelled suit, his tie for the sake of it. But his mother was dead. He dropped out of business school, travelled in Europe, and came back to become a television reporter. It caused a rift with his father, as it was intended to do.

Old man Blossom wasn't so old, old was only what Ken called him. He was a discount retailer with a permanent tan, an athletic stance, and beautiful clothes, his own label. Althea would have used him in a period film perhaps, as a religious patriarch whose followers had strayed. Moses in *The Ten Commandments,* coming down with his tablets of stone. He'd like that, probably. The sister, Barbara Blossom, had blond curls and a faintly shattered air. Althea would have cast her as some kind of victim, a prostitute perhaps or a faded child star. Casting them was the way she entertained herself, meeting his family. There seemed no other way to understand them.

Now here was Ken, enraged. "Make up your mind," he said. "Do I stay or go?"

Althea clenched her fists and pressed them into her eye sockets. Christmas! It was out of the question. She hadn't even spent Christmas with her own family in years. She lifted the heels of her hands from her eyes. She was not going to cry; she would make a joke of it.

"I can think of a lot of things I'd rather do," she said. "Like have a nervous breakdown and spend the week in hospital."

The door opened. There was Ken's back, angling out. She couldn't take the chance.

"Oh Ken," she said. "If you absolutely insist."

Christmas was always the same for the Blossoms. They spent it at an old stone lodge on a lake near Mont Sainte-Anne, where they had apparently passed many happy times before Mother died. The lodge was picturesque. Antique sleighs draped with ropes of pine waited for the children to ride. In the giant log hall the Christmas tree reached the roof. The family always took a separate cottage, a little way up the mountainside buried in snow. The log walls were a foot thick, and whitewashed in the chinks. There were windows looking down the ski slopes, and a little alpine balcony in front, with chairs.

There was an awkward moment when the bellcap dropped the bags beside his hairy mukluks, and waited for instructions.

"Who's sleeping where?"

"There's not enough rooms for all of us," said the old man. "I booked a single for Althea in the lodge."

Althea turned sharply to look out at the snow as the others carried their suitcases into the bedroom. "Do I come knocking at the door in the morning for breakfast?" she hissed to Ken. "Does he think I'm the merry widow?"

Ken went back to his father and said he would go and share the single with Althea in the lodge. The old man thought about that for a minute. "We'll keep her here," he said. "But she'll have your room. You'll have to take the couch."

The family called Ken by his full name, Kenneth. Then there was little Sarah and her mother Barbara, who wore matching pants and sweatshirts in turquoise and pink, with flat pumps; they wore fun furs and had barrettes in their hair. Barbara's husband stood on the sidelines making random sour observations; he was a political science professor.

Ken, or Kenneth, was different, Althea noticed. He was not
warmly enough dressed for the snow, in his trench coat. His
narrow wrists stuck out above his sleeves and his long fingers
wove absently when not holding something.

Althea and Ken went down to the lodge, to the whirlpool.
Hand in hand they stepped in. The heat was searing, the
water hissed and bubbled, the jets were a persistent thrum at
the base of Althea's spine. Ken said he loved her. We're
together, forget about them, he said. Althea looked up and
there was Barbara, out of breath, sliding into the hot bath.
She had run to catch up. "I got Berto to stay with Sarah,"
she said.

At dinner, the old man's silence dominated the table. He
seemed to be eating in his sleep.

"You're a matchmaker, you introduce people, is that it?"
said Barbara to Althea.

Althea laughed. "No, no, I do casting for commercials,
films, the theatre."

"Oh, that's different, I suppose," said Barbara dubiously.
"I really have nothing to do with that world."

"Tell them how you got started," said Ken.

"I was an actress." Her hands flew up; all the humourless
eyes went to them; it was as if she had let a bat out of her
skirt. She noted they were going to be a tough audience, and
carried on. "But not a very good one. When I auditioned for
a part I could always think of someone who'd be better for it
than me." She laughed in a self-deprecatory way. Then she
wondered why she had to.

"Did you see 'The Fast Lane'? On CBC?" said Ken to
his father. "Where the kids are out driving their uncle's car
and then hit an old woman at a crosswalk?"

The old man's head went slowly from one side to the
other. He hadn't seen it.

"Well, Althea cast that."

The old man looked down at his plate. So did Barbara. And Althea thought how an actor, no matter how skilled, how right for the part, can be frozen out of a scene. If the other actors don't like him. They won't include his gestures; their eyes and his don't connect. Of course it ruins the production. Nobody wins. But they'll do it anyway.

Ken subsided. Berto smirked. The women had to carry the conversation. Althea began to talk about how styles in faces changed.

"For years, I've represented Maureen Fay. Did you see her, in 'Top Girls'?" Of course not. They hadn't seen anything. What did they watch? It was like talking to people from outer space. Althea soldiered on. "She never made it as an ingénue, her features were too strong, she was too intelligent. But now that Barbie-doll look is out. Maureen's thirty-five and her career is just taking off; everyone wants one of these savvy, forceful career women as romantic lead."

Althea blushed as she realized what she'd said. But Barbara hadn't taken offence. Her mind had caught earlier in the conversation. Her curiosity was roused.

"Do you make much money?"

"Barbara!" snapped the old man. He was eating his lettuce with his eyes closed. Althea was not clear what the old man was objecting to, Barbara's asking questions out of turn, or the mention of money. She hadn't minded, herself; she was glad to talk about it. She was so proud of the living she made. She had invented her business, and herself. It was what rescued her from being crazy, before.

"Enough," said Althea. She trusted Barbara for a moment. She expanded on her theory of money. She made enough to buy herself a fur coat after a big job, enough to stretch over the inevitable slow months. Enough to cover lunch one day with a poor actor at the Zero café, the next with a producer at the Courtyard. Enough to buy her Lurex jackets and jeans, and the occasional dark fitted suits, for her Barbara Stanwyck moods. She was pleased with her living. She was not stuck anywhere, planted. She had what she needed, and freedom besides.

"No but — " persisted Barbara. Her weary young face took on a stubborn cast. There was something here she really wanted to find out. "Do you make enough, for instance, to go to a dentist?"

The old man retired early and so did Sarah the brat, so nicknamed privately by Althea. Perhaps she did not want children after all. In short order the rest disappeared. Althea went to her room. She looked at her teeth to see if anything was wrong with them. Nothing was. She smiled broadly at herself in the mirror. The sadness of the rich, she thought. Their power is to carry their world with them, to control the outside of things. To cause others to live in this world they define. But oh, how they hate it.

Ken came in. He slept with her until he woke with a jolt at five to move with the bedspread onto the sofa. For the old man, he said, half asleep as he stumbled out the door.

A low cloud got stuck on the mountain peak and snow came down so thickly all Christmas Day they didn't try to ski. They had no tree, they didn't need one, trees carrying armloads of snow marched by the windows row on row, disappearing upward. The family gave each other items which the recipients had ordered, exactly, by size and colour. Sarah got a bowling set which she played in the middle of the room. When she was finished with that, she jumped on Ken's lap and began pulling his moustache.

Barbara let on that she'd signed Althea and Ken up for the Boxing Day ski relay.

"But I've only been on skis once before!" said Althea.

"Not to worry," said Barbara, disappearing out the door. Her voice returned faintly. "It's just a social thing. We enter every year. And you need a team of four."

"What about Berto?"

Berto had a bad leg.

In the bar later that night, they were alone. Althea fretted. Ken played the piano, Gershwin. He hummed along.

"I can't possibly," she said.

He stopped humming. "Just ski the best you can."

"It won't be good enough. Why is she doing this to me?" Althea said.

"Who knows? She feels neglected? She's afraid of losing me?"

"Then you go in the race with them. Why should I have to go too?"

His fingers wavered above the keys, wanting to go back down again, to get this over with. His face had that blown-up look, it was a mass of little knots and hidden muscles. "Are you going to let them win? Don't you want to fight back?"

At two o'clock the teams collected on the south-facing slope, where there was still sun. All four members of the Blossom team were given green armbands. They would pass a red polka-dot bandanna instead of a baton. Barbara skied first, then the old man. Althea was third. She stood at the edge of the easiest part of the hill and looked over her shoulder to see him coming. He skidded up beside her and nearly knocked her over. She regained her balance as he attached the bandanna to her armband. The old man was laughing. She had never heard him laugh before.

She snowploughed off downhill, looking down at the moguls that cropped up in front of her. She fell. She got up slowly and wiped the snow off her back. In all the whiteness, she forgot it was a race. Self-preservation seemed to be the thing. Ken had tried to teach her a stem turn in the morning, but she forgot all about it. By the time she got to Ken he was the only remaining fourth skier standing in place.

"I guess we lost some time," she said, as he untied the bandanna. He just laughed and dug his poles deep into the snow. He shot forward straight downhill, to cross the finish line second to the last.

Afterward the contestants came together over mulled wine in the bar. The recreation director gave a speech before the prizes.

"Oh, the mighty have fallen!" he said. "Six years in a row the Blossoms have taken first prize!" Ken seemed inordinately pleased about it all, squeezing Althea around her shoulders, smiling. Althea began to feel that she was something he was doing to his family.

Certainly they weren't in a party mood, and the old man and Barbara soon stood at the door to leave. Another man came up and clapped the old man on the shoulder. "Didn't know you were up this year," he said. "I want you all over for cocktails. How about tomorrow?"

"I'm not sure," said the old man, waving in Althea's direction. "It's a situation . . ."

The next day after skiing, Althea retired to her bedroom and draped one arm over her eyes. The old man had explained to her that only the family was invited. She was curious, in a perverse sort of way, as to whether the family included Berto. But he dodged the question by offering to stay home and babysit.

She thought about how, being in their place, she became their creature. Whatever they thought she was. A little-known fact, she thought, was that she had a family too. She came from some place, she had work and friends. But she was stripped of that now. She was without context.

"That world," Barbara had said. They didn't know any-thing about people like her. Perhaps they thought she was a call-girl, Sally Bowles with her black garters. Or a 1950s career woman, Eve Arden with her black-rimmed glasses saying "all men are brutes"? Marlene Dietrich as Lola-Lola, in *The Blue Angel*? Gorgeous, disdainful, incapable of remorse? Out to ruin the burgher's son who was infatuated with her white thighs. What was that song? "Falling in love again, never wanted to, what am I to do?"

Althea heard padding feet, and a light tap on her door.

"Are you all right?"

It was Berto speaking, Berto with his bad leg, his detached sardonic voice. Berto staying home to babysit.

"Come in," she said, and didn't move.

He opened the door partway and leaned in. He saw her watery eyes, the raised arm protecting her face.

"Can I do anything for you?"

They looked at each other. Information passed. Berto understood. He too was a situation. How did he stand it? Althea despised him for putting up with it.

"It's OK," she said. "I just have a headache."

He lingered in the doorway. What did he have to say? Words of sympathy? Some apology for the family? She would not let him say it. He closed the door and went away.

The old man invited Althea to Monte Carlo night. Blackjack dealers had set up downstairs at the lodge. Barbara had taken over Ken. They strolled arm in arm ahead.

"Here," said the old man, taking out a small roll of bills. "I'll stake you. Play it. See if you end up ahead." He smiled. His smiles to her were muscle reflexes, like the smiles of a monkey.

"That's OK," she said lightly. "I have money."

"No, no. This is my treat."

She watched the roulette table. She counted the money.

He'd given her twenty-four dollars. She stopped in front of the wheel and put a dollar on the black eight. She lost it. She put another on the same place and lost it again. She thought after four more tries that she shouldn't move. She had an investment in that black eight; the more times she lost on it, the greater her chances would be of winning with it the next time. It had to come in sooner or later. (This is how it works, she realized. The gambler commits herself to a folly so specific that abandoning means even greater risks.) Finally after twelve losses, she put two fives on the black eight, and it came in.

Now she began to put her money all over the wheel. She made back all that she had lost, and was even again. She looked at the clock. Only half an hour had passed. Ken was with Barbara. She guessed her date for the evening was the old man's money. But this twenty-four dollars was not much fun. Perhaps she could liven it up. Get up a little act with it. Friends and admirers in Althea's head cheered her on.

She was on stage with the money in her hand. She rubbed it and stared at it, goggle-eyed. She stroked it, held it up to her cheek.

A space was clearing around her in the casino.

She squeezed the money, flattened it out again. But she couldn't get a feel for it, work out a relationship to it. It just lay there in her hand, like lettuce. She put it between her teeth, and bit down, but it didn't taste good.

Ken was still at the bar. He didn't notice. She put it on the floor behind her, as if it were a dog. She walked a few steps forward.

"Go home, money," she said. "You don't belong to me!"

The money did not move. She tried to reason with it.

"Look, you and I, we've got nothing going. You were just handed over to keep me busy."

The money just lay there on the floor. People were staring at her, laughing. But they were laughing with her, not at her.

She had an idea. It was foreign money! That was the problem. She and it didn't speak the same language!

"Français?" she said to the money. "Español?"

Nothing. She shrugged. The audience laughed. There were enough people around her now so she couldn't see Ken even if he turned around.

"It's Italian," someone said.

Oh, Italian. She smiled helplessly. She could not speak Italian. She went and picked it up.

"My date," she said, to the man who'd spoken. "A blind date." She held it up in the palm of her hand. She didn't know how to behave with it, what to ask it. She couldn't get through to it. "This whole thing is very embarrassing," she said. The people moved away.

She took it to the gambling table. She'd have to play to lose it, every penny. But as she played she thought perhaps she could turn it into a fortune, and then throw it back where it came from, to prove that she was clever.

Ken was still at the bar with Barbara. She moved from roulette to a horse race. This money just wouldn't play. She couldn't win with the money, and couldn't lose; no matter what she did, she ended up with the same twenty-four dollars. When the old man said he was going back to the cabin, she handed it over.

"I only came out even."

"You keep it." He gave her a long smile this time.

"Come on," she said. "It was your money."

He just shook his head and walked away.

Finally it was New Year's Eve.

The curtains were open to the night sky. The dark was

clear and thousands of stars fell across the open sky between the softened grey peaks. A sickle moon hung over the mountain, directly above the oval platter that lay on the cream lace tablecloth and carried a perfect crown roast of lamb. Barbara had brought it up in a freezer bag and spent the whole day cooking it.

They all drew up their chairs to the loaded table. Hoping to achieve an effect of gaiety, Ken and Althea had gone to a convenience store and had bought party hats and crackers. Althea snapped her cracker with Berto. A small plastic whistle and a rolled fortune fell out.

"Play your cards close to your chest. If you do, your best efforts will be rewarded."

Berto's said, "Beware a stranger bearing gifts. He does not have your best interests at heart."

Ken got the giggles. His laugh went high and out of control, he leaned weakly to the side, tears running down his cheeks. The stiffer the faces around him, the more he laughed. He held the toy that came out of his cracker, a miniature top. He wore a small, frilled cone hat.

"Have you read your fortune?" said Althea, offering him a hand across the table.

"I don't want to read my fortune," he said. He put the thin paper in the candle, where it flared for a few seconds. His family watched this. They seemed to be getting a message. "What's yours, Dad?"

The old man looked at his narrow piece of paper as if it were a stale-dated bus transfer, and threw it down.

"Hhhhmph," said the old man.

"He doesn't read them. He writes them," said Althea, beginning to giggle with Ken. Together they went on and on, in high shaking giggles. That was it, thought Althea. Fortunes, not movies, were the old man's scenarios. They were simple, lethal, truthless. "You will meet a dark stranger." People differed only in degree of usefulness or potential to disrupt.

"You were talking business," said Barbara to her father.

The table was plunged into sobriety.

"I'm not getting any younger," said the old man. "I've been patient, Kenneth. We've got to get someone in there."

"Get Barbara," said Ken.

Barbara blushed and looked at her plate. She had made a beautiful dinner. She was dressed in her pink sweater with pearls sewn on it.

"Barbara!" scoffed the old man.

She burst into tears and ran from the table.

Althea drank a lot of champagne. They walked over to the lodge; against the snow it looked like a children's pop-up illustration. Everything was reduced, faraway and old. Althea was reduced too, to a minor, in custody of the old man. How could Ken stand it? Maybe he didn't know any better. Althea used to be ashamed of the mess she'd been when she left home, and got divorced, but now she was proud. She was nobody's daughter, she was just herself. How they envied her!

When the Blossom party arrived in the dining-room a form of dancing was under way. Elderly couples, touching hands, paraded the dance floor up one side and down the other. The walls were mint green with white plastic ribbons draped over the windows. A band of prematurely aged men in dinner jackets played soft, unidentifiable songs.

The old man had been drinking all through the meal; his eyes hung lower than ever. In the others a grim silence had set in. Sarah had been promised a dance, but as a result of the late hour had begun to misbehave, and was being threatened with bed. Barbara had wiped away her tears, and was holding hands with her father.

They took a table by the dance floor. The old man thrust his chin toward Ken.

"So, Kenneth, how's Penny?"

The table fell silent. Ken flushed.

"I said, 'How's Penny?' "

Ken gave a yelping laugh. "Don't listen to him," he said, under his breath, to Althea. The old man watched Althea's face and laughed.

Althea turned her head away, and watched the dancers. "Who's Penny?" But she knew, of course. Penny was a daughter of the families who holidayed here. Penny had been at the cocktail party to which Althea had not been invited. The little white lights in their wall sconces swam. Ken took her hand under the table.

"Don't listen, he's drunk."

The old man ordered another drink. He turned his attention to Barbara, whose face was glowing.

"I'm not listening," said Althea clearly, looking over Ken's shoulder.

"She put the money on the floor and talked to it," said the old man. His low cracking voice carrying across the table. "And she's been married before."

Barbara murmured, earnestly, up to something. The old man waved her words away and went on.

"He's infatuated. He's not himself."

"Who are they talking about?" said Althea to Ken, knowing.

"Us."

"That's what I thought."

The old man's voice had grown louder. "It won't last. It'll be over in a year. She's all wrong for him."

Everyone was listening. The old man was speaking. Barbara nodded and nodded.

Althea sat very still, waiting for the impact to make its

way to her feelings, the way she might have looked at a long gash in her skin, seen the blood spurt out, and waited, seconds, even, before feeling the pain. It wasn't so much what he said. It was that he did say it, aloud, in front of her. He probably didn't even think he was being rude, she was not real to him. They were in two different movies, and it wasn't blood, it was ketchup.

"What should we do?" said Ken, softly, in her ear.

Althea's legs and arms felt warm, ready to flex, to run and leap. Her chest filled with air. There was so much of it, and it felt so good. She had her own power. The power to name. The power of not needing.

"What shall we do?" whispered Ken again.

His father was pushing Ken into her arms. She didn't even know if she wanted him yet. But she knew she could have him. She had earned him, through all this. She could tell Ken to walk out on the old man. She could make sure he married her, soon. And the old man would be furious, he'd be stuck with this madwoman for a daughter-in-law.

Or she could walk out, now, go to the front desk, ask the bellcap to get her a cab, pronto. Crack a few jokes. Breathe some nice fresh air out the open window of the cab. "It's over," she'd tell Ken, "You're a nice guy but your family is impossible." And down the mountain she'd go in the dark night in her dancing dress and no coat, right to the airport. Free.

"Let's get a cab to the airport," said Ken. "I'm walking out."

And Althea thought, there he goes again. The hand on the doorknob. Threatening them like he threatened me.

"If you didn't walk out years ago, you're not going to do it now."

She looked at Ken. She saw the stubborn jaw, the long fingers on the piano keys, felt the questioning kiss. She saw the cab in the darkness dashing down the mountainside without her.

"Let's dance," she said.

The band was playing "Tiny Bubbles." Ken and Althea joined the dainty couples. His hand was large and firm, it covered the whole of her back, from one side to the other. Occasionally, when he turned her at an angle, she could see through the pillars to the family table. There was some kind of skirmish going on. In a few minutes Barbara took the old man away. When the song was over they sat down at an empty table.

Back in the cabin Ken, Althea, Barbara and Berto sat around the fire. Sarah and the old man were in bed. Midnight had come and gone without merriment. It was the next year already, and Ken's long body swung around the cabin like a lariat. Passing the wall, he slammed the fat logs with his fist.

"This place is built like a jail!"

Barbara's eyes were bright, her colour high. "I think you're overreacting."

He turned on her, his rage looking for somewhere to go. "You egged him on!"

Barbara's eyes grew wide. She included Althea in her gaze. "I thought it was better if he talked it through. Rather than just buried it."

"What are you, his therapist?"

"I understand him." The more ragged Ken became, the calmer Barbara grew.

"You meddle, that's what you do."

Barbara widened her eyes. "I just wanted to help."

Ken swept around to the window and stood, one hand on each side of the frame, pressing them apart with all his strength. Nothing even creaked.

"Tomorrow," he said. "I'm really going to give it to him tomorrow. I'm going to tell him he can't get away with it this time."

Berto yawned. He was going to bed. "I hope you don't mind," he said, on the way out, to Althea. "You'll see, in the long run, there'll be room, for you."

When Althea woke up in the morning she found Ken in the kitchen frying eggs and bacon.

"I gave it to him," he said. "Boy, did he get it from me!"

The sun was brilliant on the snow. Ken and Althea took their coffee out to the balcony. There was going to be a thaw: the sun, reflecting off the snow, was warm enough for tanning. Sarah brought her bowling balls. They were all there, faces raised to the sun, when the old man slid the glass door open.

He was pale. The lines in his face all pointed downwards. He was smoking a cigar. Its foul odour disturbed Althea's nostrils as he sat down beside her. He drained his cup and placed it on the wooden railing. It was a plain, ordinary day. All the movies were over and no one had much to say.

"The best snow will be this morning. After lunch it'll turn to corn." Ken said to his father.

Althea stood up to go in and get more coffee. She was about to offer him some but when she looked she saw the old man had flicked his cigar ash in his cup. He lifted it to his lips. The cup was full of ashes. As she opened the door she looked back at them over her shoulder. They were after all just ordinary people, just an ordinary family.

The Bomb Scare

The Bomb Scare

It was two o'clock in the morning. Ted lay between ironed sheets in an ample, soft bed, the green and yellow flowers of the wallpaper leering slightly out at him in the darkness. The motorcycles that passed like marauding insects under Ted's window all night had finally stopped. She had left his room an hour before.

The alarm sounded. It went on and on, like the horn in a car when a body falls against it. Thumps came up the hall, voices rose and in a moment, a knock. A matronly voice, frightened, sounded through the door.

"Excuse me, sir, it's a bomb scare. We'll have to ask you to please vacate your room, if you please."

Ted, being awake, was wrapped in his trench coat and at the door in a second. He had already picked up his wallet from the bedside table. He opened the door, and then darted back to the desk for his notebook. He knew that tomorrow would come, even if at that moment, for a variety of reasons, he felt that it wouldn't. And tomorrow he would need those notes.

At the door again, he put his feet into his new pale-yellow topsiders, a bad purchase and an uncharacteristic one; they would get dirty and soon begin to slip off his narrow feet. But when he saw them in the store window he had thought them beautiful objects. He reminded himself that, unlike before, he could afford them. He didn't want anything else from the room.

In the hall Ted's breath was short. It was not that he thought there really was a bomb, it was something else. He was going to see her again. Hand on the banister, he swung around the circular stairs to the lobby. He crossed the polished local flagstone, pushed open the heavy door for two grey-haired women in nightdresses, and stepped out into the deep, cool night. Ahead was the mill-pond. Around its rim the yellow post lights were magnified in the mist to look like a row of small moons. The sluice ran alongside, dropping lower between rock walls as it passed the mill itself.

Most of the guests were out already, well back from the building, hunched in sweaters and shivering. How obedient they were. They could be summoned from their beds to meet their makers, you could tell them anything, they would not complain. There was no sense of urgency. In a leisurely way he walked away from the front door and joined the growing assembly. He remembered the evacuation of Mississauga, five hundred thousand people in hours without a hitch. Evacuate: you might say it was what Canadians did best.

He was almost happy, in the outdoors at that hour, as the cool mist laid its pearls on him. He had an idea why people enjoyed these dramas. Moments of crisis forcing everyone out of doors provided unexpected benefits for the voyeur. For instance, he saw women in curlers; he hadn't known they still wore them. And it came to him that those two old ladies who laughed so much were lesbians; he'd never have guessed it if he hadn't seen them in their matching nightgowns, holding each other's arms. The blind girl came out the front door as neatly dressed as always; long ago she had learned not to panic in darkness.

Slowly, she walked thirty feet in front of the building and like the rest turned to face it. There were perhaps forty people now, staring at the austere outline of the stone mill against the fuzzy charcoal sky. Were they waiting, as Ted was, for it to light up, for the sudden yellow line to run behind the edge of the roof, along the timbers at the door, a laser breaking it out from its background, for the orange flower to burst inside the foot-deep window sills, and the great grey slabs of stone to fly through the air like empty boxes?

Visualizing it, Ted stepped back, and at once there was Marian, looking angry, even angrier than when she had left his room, and somewhat wild with her hair all undone and her smudged makeup turned to violet bruises under her eyes. She stood alone, her arms around her ribs, her hands tucked under her opposite arms.

"I was sound asleep," she said crossly, not looking at him.

The innkeeper, a large woman with smooth black hair normally in a bun, now in a loose pony-tail, was fully dressed. She spoke into a megaphone. Mrs Stoddart; he'd come to know her slightly since he'd begun to take his sanity week in the country twice a year. Darlene didn't mind his going. Darlene was good about things like that.

"No danger," Mrs Stoddart bellowed into her megaphone, "no danger at all. Just a nuisance call, we're sure. But you understand when there are guests in the place, we can't take chances. Especially with the international situation."

"Exactly," said one flannelette lesbian to the other. "Why do you think we didn't go to Europe this summer? This place is supposed to be *safe.*"

Ted moved closer to Mrs Stoddart. "Are you that sure there's no bomb?"

"The call came from inside the inn complex," she said, quietly.

Together they looked out at the assembled guests. A still, quiet lot, they were, their faces puffed with sleep, and hair dishevelled. The mist seemed to thicken by the minute. Ted felt clammy. Perhaps he was, after all, suffering shock. The years ran on in their slow, pleasingly empty way, and then in one night overturned; before he knew it he was standing on the pavement at two-thirty in the morning only five feet from Marian. The careful scaffolding of his life, its rewards and refuges, suddenly felt like cardboard and matchsticks, as if he could fall through and it could come down all around him.

Ted Bezny had met Marian Frost thirteen years before when she was a student in painting at the Ontario College of Art and he a poor ("impoverished," he called himself) young painter. They had fallen wildly, morosely, for Ted, in love. By a series of improbabilities and miracles — that was what Ted had considered each stage of the relationship to be — this falling in love stretched over three years and became a serious affair, well-nigh a marriage. It ended with Marian pressing to have children and Ted, panic-stricken, dropping into bed with a Hungarian waitress from the Tarogato who wore white lace-up ankle boots.

It devastated Marian, and, coincidentally, finished her for the art world. She was a student of great promise, but naïve. Although he praised her work, he had not expected her to paint, not really. In fact he had expected her to do just what she had done — retreat to the arms of a man with money and security so that she could raise her children to be just as advantaged and sweet-natured as herself.

One of the women in curlers was in front of him, asking something.

". . . they should do something *for* us? Don't you think?" she said. "If we're going to be kept standing out here? Some tea at least?"

He looked dubiously at Mrs Stoddart.

"Perhaps the cook doesn't want to get blown up."

The woman, who had long red hair and square brown glasses, turned her gaze back to the still-standing mill as if to make it answer for this situation, and said nothing. Years ago no one approached him in public asking for help. It came with age and success, he supposed, although one felt just as useless inside. Marian's presence was reminding Ted of how he used to be. He could see himself in filthy jeans, brow screwed down in a terrible frown. He would have been in a temper because he'd been interrupted, even if he had, in some way, asked for the interruption himself.

Out of the dim driveway loomed two yellow fog lights: the police. Doors slammed, and in the darkness two German shepherds materialized, straining on their short leashes.

"Imagine them even having such dogs, way out here," he said, loud enough for Marian to hear should she choose to.

"The peaceful countryside isn't that peaceful," said Marian.

The blind girl stood with the lesbians, nodding and nodding. People talked to her endlessly. It was something to do with being blind. They thought she needed the constant commentary.

"If I were blind I'd want silence," continued Ted over the garrulous woman's head to Marian. "Noises in the dark are always more irritating than noises you can see."

But Marian wasn't saying anything else. And Ted could not turn and look at her. It had startled him so when, going into the patio for lunch, he saw the back he knew, and

recognized it as Marian's. At his inn. Confused, he lurked
in the doorway until she and the two women she was with
were seated. Then he made sure he got a table on the other
side. They were used to him here, a man alone. In fact he
didn't doubt he was one of the attractive features of the inn.
"*Artists* come here in spring and fall, for the quiet, for the
walks," Mrs Stoddart probably told prospective guests.

To see Marian, at his retreat, what a coincidence! He'd
only laid eyes on her twice in the last ten years. When she
first met Angelo he followed her onto the train to Hamilton,
and rode all the way down with her, trying to convince her to
get off. A year after her marriage he took her for a drive in
his truck along the Escarpment where, without premedita-
tion, he accused her of ruining his life. Then he met Darlene
and got married himself. He drank his tomato juice and
decided she must have known he was here.

He watched until she got up to leave, and followed her.
He cornered her outside the front door while her lady friends
were investigating the General Store. She had on one of
those wide-brimmed floppy straw hats women wear in summer; she had never liked the sun on her face.

"Marian."

"Hello, Ted, how are you?" Her voice was milky, her
face smooth, it was impossible to gauge her surprise.

"Let's walk," he said immediately. It was taking a lot for
granted. But suddenly there was a tremendous amount to be
had, where there had been nothing an hour before. And he
had always talked better walking.

"Your hair is longer."

"I grew it so I could wear it up."

He laughed. Her hair was down. It was typical. There
was something childish about Marian, backwards and non-
sensical, more so about the way she tried to make everything
she did seem logical. Or maybe it was just that he was older
than she was.

Even after all this time, there were things to tell. He had sold the farm. Darlene hadn't liked it. This was his compensation, a week out of the city twice a year. They walked along for a while, over the cobblestones, until one of her sandals twisted under her foot. He caught her elbow.

"It's so strange to see you here," he said.

"It doesn't feel that strange to me." She looked at him simply, her head a little cocked, the grey of her eyes untroubled. Then, "Although Angelo might find it a little odd."

"Darlene's terrified of you," he said.

"Of me? Why on earth should she be?"

"She'd never believe we met by accident."

Already it was a conspiracy. Marian stared impassively at his face.

"I keep wondering how it would be to be in a room with you, alone," he said. He said this instead of asking. Asking would lay himself open for a refusal.

"We could try it," she said. The hat was laying tiny crisscrosses of shadow on her cheeks. "I'm staying over."

He ate dinner alone, a long meal, chewing slowly and squarely. He liked to eat alone; this had bothered Marian; she thought there was something uncivilized about it. The whole time he was careful not to smile at her, not to show what he felt, which was that they should be sitting down together. Could she be divorcing Angelo? Could it be some kind of trap, perhaps (fantastically) laid by Darlene?

Then he went to his room. He always got the same room, here, in the top of the old part of the mill, rather than the new annex. He stayed in a lot of hotels, and knew how hard it was to find a quiet place with a desk. This one was old oak with deep gouges in it. He sat and opened his notebook.

Marian had agreed easily, too easily. Perhaps she had said she would come just to get rid of him. Perhaps her coming here was a total fluke. Perhaps he meant nothing to her.

At eleven o'clock she knocked on the door. He returned to his notebook on his desk. He had pretended to work too when they lived together on Spadina. He pretended to be working when he was really fighting back the fear. Each time he made a mark on the canvas cancelling her needs, what she did to him. She made him raw, new in a way that was painful, and (he considered then) bad for his art. He had not managed to fight off her influence. He could go through his work from then and count all the little M's, and find all her colours, the thick rusty black of her hair and the pallor of her skin.

She stepped into his room quickly, as if someone were behind her. He shut the door. They faced each other without speaking. A motorcycle wound off around the base of the mill. She was not wearing her hat. She lifted her strong chin, the white angles of her cheeks to his face.

"Nice quiet place you got here." A motorcycle went by.

"I picked the wrong weekend. There's some convention of motorcycles at Wasaga Beach." It *was* something different, to be in a room with her, just them between four walls. It was like experiencing a change in the force of gravity. His arms felt light at his sides.

They moved to the windows. The curtains were open. They looked down on the millpond. A man was on the path, looking up. They both stepped back, instantly, apart. Once they had been anonymous and unimportant with nothing but time and no one cared what they did. Now they were illicit. But self-consciously so, as if it might be a pose, as if they were the same untroubled pair and their lives now fabrications.

Ted was aware of his hands, large and empty beside his thighs. He wanted to circle her with his arms but not to touch her yet. She moved away, and began to pace out the edges of the room. He stood still and rotated, looking at her full hips, her large, long legs. This tension was always the beginning with them.

"What are you doing here?"

"Why did you ask me up?"

He had never been able to intimidate her, though he had tried. He knew the answer but didn't say.

"How is Darlene?" she said, turning to look straight at him.

"Pregnant," he said.

She stopped. With a soft hand she touched her hair at the side of her face, and wet her lips. She smiled, and drew a circle with one hand. Onward, said the hand gesture. You have permission. Although they both knew he'd sworn he would never be a father.

"She gets what she wants, doesn't she?"

He ignored that. "Your kids are OK?"

"Fantastic," she said, and now he got the full glorious smile. He was fiercely jealous for about three seconds. Then he thought, a woman like her, she probably loves them more than she loves her husband.

"What are you doing here?" he said again, and this time she laughed, and shook the hair off her shoulders.

"I do interior design. Those women are looking for antiques."

Marian looked at the electric kettle, the teapot, the little saucer of packets, tea, coffee, sugar, whitener.

"Why don't you make me some tea?" The first evening they met at the late studio class and went with a group for beer at El Mocambo. Snow was falling, big fruity half-melted flakes, and his truck skidded on the slushy wide street as they passed through the neon cloisters of Chinatown and arrived at his studio. He was like something left over from the sixties with his earthen pots around. He made tea and it sat on the floor untouched.

"Oh, Marian," he said now, and reached for her.

Marian arched out of the range of his arm. He had left her for that waitress.

Marian was protected, as a child. Her parents sent her to a special school which fostered creativity. She was allowed to spend weeks making a tree-house or a castle, then to do all her lessons inside it. Her affair with Ted had been one of those tree-houses, and they both lived in it. Then he came along and smashed this perfect creation over which he had no rights. She sat in the ruins and cried until Angelo came along. Angelo who was honourable and could be trusted and had beautiful skin like butter. Then Ted wanted her back. Saying no to Ted had been easy.

He held out his hand, as you would to an unfamiliar dog.

"I had forgotten what your hands were like." What she didn't say was how different his hand was from Angelo's; how different it was from what it had been, because now it could only exist by comparison with Angelo's. Angelo who at first counted the times they made love, counted months and years until he was sure he had been with her more than Ted had. Angelo who had finally been convinced that Ted was no danger.

Ted's hand was small and fine, with papery lines in it. She picked it up and turned it over in her palm, as if it were a cookie or a coin. All those years ago, this hand had been everywhere on her, in her. It showed no sign of it. It was just a hand. A youngish hand, still colourless.

He put it up on her face, his palm over her nose, his fingers splayed over her eyes, reaching through her hair to her scalp. She pressed her face against his hand. Her eyes were forced to close.

"So this is what it's like in a room alone with me," she said. "Are you satisfied?"

"Of course not." His fingers stretched over her head as if it were a basketball. She knew he just wanted to make love and then he would be afraid or satisfied or both and he wouldn't talk any more.

"I don't do that sort of thing," Marian said. "I didn't when I was with you and I don't now that I'm with Angelo."

"Women are such dumb loyal creatures. Like dogs," he said. "But you're happy."

"I am," she said. "It's right for me."

"That's what I thought," he said. "You have the children."

"And even a little career," she said, mockingly.

"Not painting?" he said, smiling steadily.

"No, Ted."

"You still could, I guess. You were awfully good."

She laughed a little unkindly and said nothing. Then, "You're making money now," she said. "I saw the prices at your show."

"When they sell."

"But they do. Now."

"Yes," he said. "Hard to believe, isn't it?" Now he had his other hand behind her head and was pushing it back and forth between his palms. Some people holding a basketball never hold it still. She kept talking.

"I told you it would work out. You just had to get through that time. You see I was right, wasn't I?"

"It was a bad time for me."

She nodded.

"You don't know how much I've thought about that," he said, carefully. "If things could have been different."

"That things would have been different if things had been different?" she mocked.

"No one means as much to me as you do."

His hands dropped from her face. Marian was not surprised at what he said. She thought of her children, how beautiful they were, and fragrant and always growing, like plants, and full of colour, not neon.

"But you're all right," Ted said.

" 'Course I'm all right." Although people sometimes asked her. There was Angelo and the house and her office telephone with its bright recorded message. "Marian is not available at the moment but she would like to receive your call." She always sounded stilted on that machine; she had never got the hang of it. She made an effort to confess.

"Sometimes I feel as if it's all a job, you know, the house, all the arrangements. As if I've gone into business with someone."

Ted nodded. "It's the same with us. An institution."

"It has to be, I guess."

"We were ridiculous." By now they were feet apart across the room. "We couldn't even decide where to live. There was no way."

They lived in the studio for a while but that hadn't worked. They'd rented a house, a compromise she didn't like and neither did he. Then they moved to his farm. Those were the times when people lived at farms. At the farm the days had no departments. Ted and Marian ate and made love and bothered each other when they tried to work, and put thousands of miles on the truck driving to the city. But the nights in the country had been starry and absolutely still.

"All the *time* we had."

He shook his head.

"Sometimes I think about it," she said, carefully, "how much we slept out there."

Their sleep was rich, long, nourishing, a variety of sleep unknown since. They woke up from it making love, without knowing they'd begun. He'd been an insomniac before.

"True sleep. I taught you that."

"You did." It had all been true with them. There was

nothing hidden. In his notebook he drew a diagram of the parts of her she couldn't see. (He still had it, somewhere.)

"I taught you a few things too."

Marian smiled.

Ted turned out the light, and stepped over to the window again. The moon was up. There was a mist over the grounds; the day had been hot, but the night was cool.

"We talked about everything, too," he said. "I hardly have time now."

"It's like it's gone out of style. It's like people don't do it any more. Everything has to be forward-moving, for a reason."

"I feel old," said Ted.

"You always did." There was a silence.

"Speaking of which," said Marian, shifting her feet. They had been talking long enough. "What are we doing here?"

He smiled. "Maybe testing."

"What's to test?" she said. It sounded flip. What she meant was that there was so *much* to test, her children, his wife, his coming baby, her husband.

He stepped toward her. "All these accoutrements we've got. To comfort us for the loss. One can't help but want to know. Do they work? Do they blot the other out?" A motor-cycle went by. He turned his head slightly. "I was terrible to you."

He seemed to need to say this, for once and for all. "It scared me how bad I was to you. We had it, didn't we?"

She nodded. "We had something."

"We had it and we blew it," he said.

She nodded; the bottom of her eye filled with a tear. They had it, and they blew it.

Marian sat on the bed. She felt the air in front of her face.

She could feel her ring on her finger, her hair on her neck, her blouse over her breasts. Ted wanted to make love. He wanted her to do the thing that he had done with the waitress who had served them their goulash soup all those times. He wanted her to make Angelo into herself. It was not the kind of thing she did. She had not done it to Ted, after all, who had probably deserved it. Why should she do it to Angelo, who did not deserve it?

Marian and Angelo had a traditional marriage; he was Italian. She wore a white veil from a spray on top of her head. It fell thickly to her feet, studded with handmade roses. Despite what had gone before she was still only twenty-six.

She felt something now, against her face. A cobweb. It was her present life. She brushed it away, and leaned forward, into before. She looked into Ted's eyes: narrow, with an impression of depth. Brown with black around the edges.

And then they were making love. Without obvious consent, or decision, just as there never had been. All the necessary intermediate actions like unbuttoning happened in a way that made it seem that clothes had no substance. They were making love without haste, or memory, or shyness, and then there was no time or place to any part of them. It was as it had been then and as it should always be and as it must be.

The moonlight lay thrown across the bed. First was the sweat, and heat. Then Ted becoming Ted again, a man with texture, weight, odour. Marian began to think about betrayal. Perhaps he never betrayed her. Perhaps he just misbehaved. Perhaps the real betrayal had been hers, in refusing to take him back, in growing accustomed to living without the something this was. Whether love or another quantity, less refined.

She stretched out her body; it felt new. They slept. They made love again, and this time it was conscious, exacted pleasure. She cried out his name. He cried out hers. After, she felt herself going down into sleep, the old kind of sleep.

"Marian," he said. "Marian." He dislodged his arm from under her breast. "Marian, wake up."

She opened her eyes unwillingly. What was he saying? She had been swimming, or drowning, in this thing that she had lost, and reclaimed, and now was clinging to. He leaned over her.

"I've got to do some work tonight."

"You're kidding," she said, and closed her eyes again.

"I can't let you sleep here, Marian. I have to work."

Her heart began to pump, as if she had just come up a steep hill, pursued by something ugly.

"I want to stay," she said.

He was sitting up now. He was nervous. "I can't, Marian. I — Darlene might come up."

Marian did not understand, at first. She got up on her elbows, covering herself. "You want me to go?"

He looked at his lap. "They know me here."

He was talking in a rush.

"I can't start again. It nearly ruined me. I just couldn't function, when we were together."

Marian began to cry. He had been expecting it. He put his hand on her face. "What's wrong?" That old tender concern, after he had hurt her.

"I'm sorry," she began to say, "I'm so mixed up, I'm not used to — I'll be all right." But her heart was still pumping, she was angry. She was blinding angry. She jumped out from under the sheet, stood before him in all her streaming nakedness, her streaming hair.

"I made you everything you are! Those paintings you

did, they were the best ever. Since then it's been shit! You never gave me credit for anything. You took everything you could get from me and went off and painted and never gave me a thing.''

''You were too —''

''You sent me back — to where I belonged. That's what it was all about, wasn't it?''

''— vulnerable. I couldn't afford to have anyone dependent on me,'' he said. ''Not then.''

''You couldn't afford to have me painting. That's what you couldn't afford.'' She jerked her blouse off the bed, and put it on. The underwear was on the floor.

''Marian!'' he said, bending to pick it up. ''Be quiet! People would see you go out in the morning.'' He handed it to her.

''And now you're afraid of Darlene,'' she said, running down. ''You're ridiculous.'' She had her slacks on now. She stuffed the underwear in her bag.

''Don't you see, Marian?'' he pleaded at the door. ''I can't. It would send a bomb right through my life.''

The blind girl tapped her cane on the stones. The police dogs were being dragged down the road to the waiting van.

''They didn't find anything, did they?'' she said.

''Terribly sorry, terribly,'' Mrs Stoddart said. She was just talking now, without the megaphone.

''I didn't figure they would,'' said Ted.

Moving back toward the still intact inn, its lines etched more permanently than ever against the sky and the fields, the group had become convivial. Mrs Stoddart mentioned opening the bar, giving everyone a free drink before they went back to bed.

''It would have been a shame to see it go, apart from any

inconvenience,'' said one of the old women. ''Such a solid old place.''

''Yes, and the food's good.''

Marian was close to the door, ready to go in the moment she was allowed. Her look at Ted was masked. He was filled with remorse. He could not catch her eye again. His feet were sticking in the topsiders, there was sweat all over his body; he was a man who got away with it when he never wanted to.

''Now I can go back to bed.'' She spoke not to him, but in his hearing, looking straight ahead. She had understood the message. She spoke her answer, a new language they'd learned (how much they'd learned in one short evening, a whole new way of being), this public way of showing private knowledge, private failure. ''I was sound asleep.''

''Will you go back to sleep?''

''Absolutely,'' she said.

The Open Door

The Open Door

The evening had been romantic. The hotel was on top of a hill, in the ruins of a star-shaped castle. The turquoise sea rose and fell in sighs around a red-rocked shore. They dined on lobster and champagne in a firelit cellar, surrounded by ruddy sailors in guernsey sweaters. They walked embracing on a foggy path to their cottage on the castle grounds.

But there, without a word, he clicked on the overhead light and pulled out his papers. He sat with one leg crossed over the other at a small table, erasing careful pencil marks and writing in new ones. It was a computer print-out he worked on, the results of some poll. He cast a shadow over his page, squirmed to avoid himself.

She dropped her cardigan over the armchair and then dropped herself on her back the same way, across the end of the bed. She picked up the guidebooks to amuse herself. The sights and conveniences were alphabetically listed — Bicycle hire, Bronze Age village. After that she picked up the novel she'd brought. Someone was murdering cripples according to the spelling conventions of ancient Sanskrit. It was hard slogging, but she pushed herself through to the end. Then she stood up, undressed, and got into bed. His light glared at her.

Noisily she flipped from her right side to her left. The room was big, as these rooms go. It was called a housekeeping suite; one end was a kitchen, with toy-size stove and fridge, and ruffled curtains. Just whom was it meant to please? It presumed to be the set for a game of house, surely exactly what the married wished to escape. And to the unmarried, like them, it was a kind of satire, what they were not and would never be.

The room was big but not big enough for her to forget him reading, and blowing ("whew! whew!") the little flecks of exhausted eraser off his pages, and then scratching in more numbers with his high-tech automatic pencil.

"When are you going to turn out the light?"

"Is it bothering you?" So polite he was, and continental. Forgetting she was not a fixture or a wife.

What was he trying to prove? He had never said he was going to work tonight. They held hands across the devastated little lobster rib-cages. They nuzzled down the path in the fog. But he had turned from her the second they entered the room. She snorted.

Making no attempt to interpret this snort, he continued quietly folding the papers. He put his little stapler, his eraser, his high-tech pencil back into the little case called a travelling office. As he closed it the zipper snarled like a pocket-sized dog.

"Working at night is a form of passive hostility," she said.

"I'm coming to bed right now. It's after eleven." Carefully, precisely, he placed his papers and his kit in the centre of the table. "I always intended to finish at eleven."

He was coming to bed, but not because of her. He was

coming because it was the time he set himself. Bed was on his schedule. He went to bed to meet his expectations, not hers. She flipped from her left side to her right, like a fish on a dock.

"Drive me crazy," she said. "See if I care."

He popped his contact lenses onto the tissue where he put them at night. He didn't use one of those screw-top cases with the two basins for storage. Why did he not bring a place to put his eyes, as he called them? Would a case have been too easy? Too premeditated? If he used a case would he not be able to convince himself he was the travelling professional who had accidentally tripped off his itinerary? He would not be able, either, to go blank with rage when she tossed out the tissue and the lenses dropped invisible as teardrops onto the carpet.

He went to the bathroom and came out naked, raised the sheets on his side of the bed and got in. The mattress sank. She retreated up the incline, closer to her edge. Then fell the stiff silence of the untired.

The trouble with him was he would go right off to sleep. Even if he wasn't sleepy. Even if he was angry. He was so relaxed he could go to sleep on a mountain top, on a camel back. Even if he had a problem. *Especially* if he had a problem. She couldn't stand the idea of his going off to sleep without hearing about it first.

"Turn the light back on!" she said.

"I thought we were going to sleep!"

He rolled over and the mattress on its sleazy springs tilted up, then down. It made her seasick. As well, his shoulders dug a great hole in the surface of the bed, causing her to be off balance. She had to cling to her side of the bed, or roll up against him.

"You wanted to work, so why don't you work? You didn't want to come to bed."

He wasn't good at her reverse way of speaking, her pig Latin, as it were. But now he understood.

"Everything can't stop just because we're together," he said. "I still have —"

"Don't," she said. It seemed to her she hardly ever saw him, and that everything should stop.

He turned to her with courtesy. He put out his hand to find her in the dark. It was just a tiny island, with a few hundred people on it. The night beyond the uncurtained windows was deep and went on for miles and miles.

"OK," he said. "OK. Let's." His hand lit on her breast. It was a large hand, and gave a generous squeeze.

"Are you kidding?" Her voice got louder as he came closer. "Turn on the light!" She saw herself in the hour during which she'd waited, slung across the end of the bed looking ridiculous. She was not going to make love with him in this most perfect darkness. Not now that she'd had to wait for it so long. Not now that he'd implied that she had been asking.

He put his face up to her ear. Kiss, kiss.

She raised her hand and pretended to erase his eyes. "Whew! Whew!" she said, and then brushed the imaginary little bits off his cheeks.

He didn't know what she was doing.

"Turn on the light!" she sang.

When he didn't she jumped out of bed and touched the switch for the overhead. It made a small click like the sound of a trigger and suddenly the room was *there*. The room, with the bed, the little table, the ugly open curtains, the half-open door to the bathroom, the sink, the miniature refrigerator. His clothes, her clothes, the suitcases. The night had become a flat piece of black where the window used to be.

He squeezed his eyes shut. He hunched his shoulders under the sheet. The black stripe across the royal blue coverlet cancelled the centre of his body.

"It's on," she said. His eyes were shut. Perhaps he couldn't tell. He coiled up on an elbow then, squinting.

"What the hell are you doing?"

She climbed back into bed.

"The light's on. You can work. Don't come to bed."

He lay back and let out a great whack of breath. Now he had a sense of what was to come. "I hope you're happy about it."

"You're the one who wanted it on."

"No I didn't, you did."

"Just pretend it's not eleven yet. You can go on working," she said with satisfaction. She lay on her back, looking up. The light drove painfully into her eyes. But at least she knew he wasn't sleeping.

"Will-you-turn-that-thing *off*!" he said with perfect, even inflection.

"No!"

He rotated, the other shoulder going down, his back rising up to face her. She could feel his tension as he tried to burrow into sleep. He put the pillow over his head and pinned it on either side of his ears with his arms, like someone with his head in stocks. She laughed.

"How do you like it?" she said.

He said nothing.

She nudged him.

He didn't move.

"How do you like it?"

No answer.

She took the question herself. "I like it, it's good. Moreover, it's *us*. Contemporary, but with a kind of fifties shape. The age-old convention, of course, but in a new context . . ."

He said nothing.

"It may have been done before, but it *feels* new," she said. She was not getting a laugh. His breathing began to draw out, his body to sink more heavily into the bed.

"All right. You can turn it off, if you want," she said, indulgently. "Just get up and turn it off." She didn't care about the light, she decided. It would be enough to have him obey her.

He began to snore. A corner of desolation exposed itself to her, a page about to be lifted. She pressed it back.

"Maybe if you ask me *very* nicely to turn it off, I will," she said. She was not going to let the evening go. They had so few, they had so little time. Life and its obligations encroached everywhere but here, on the island. And now regret for the unfinished, the wasted evening spread through her. Making love — sex — was only one of the pleasures they had lost. There was the old garden with the crumbling statues they hadn't even looked at. A moonlight ramble down the coastal walk, too.

"Darling?" she said.

The pillow bulged over his head, tied down at the sides by his long arms.

Yes, a moonlight ramble was the thing. She could go alone. With any luck she'd meet one of the armed guards for the royal hideaway out on the point.

She swung her legs out of the bed, took two steps and turned off the light. The room disappeared; the night retrieved its depth. Then she took another two steps and opened the door.

Theirs was one of a row of little cottages that faced a swimming-pool. Swimming was not permitted after eleven o'clock, said the sign. But the underwater lights were still on. Shining from holes in the pool sides, they turned the water into a great square diamond. Beyond its tempting dazzle the old stone wall with its dark archway cornered the abandoned garden. Over all hung an enormous, pale, pocked moon.

She swayed in the doorway. Her white nightgown was luminous.

Now he sat up, pulling the pillow off his head.

"Oh, God," he said. It crossed his mind that she would run out, show herself, dance, or drown.

She hovered on the doorsill, teasing. She imagined his fear, that she would run out into the dark. She wished to, but she was afraid. Just looking was enough. She drank up the velvet of the air and the upside-down sky-blue shimmer of the pool and the gamut of darker blues that ran into black between. She felt the breeze through her nightgown. She smiled. Then, without closing the door, she walked slowly back to bed.

Holding his pillow bunched at one end, like a club, he stared at her with fury and incomprehension. She lay on her back looking up. She was bright, electric, she would deliver a shock if touched. Oh, she was happy. She loved everything about this moment. She was awake, freed. And he was hooked. He wasn't going to drift off now. The open door changed everything.

The room was large, and included the pool, the dark presence of the wall, the gardens. The open door made an avenue to the cosmetic glamour of the water, the pebbles of light that led along the path to the castle. It let in the odour of rich loamy blackness, unknown plants on the moor. It let in, from farther yet, the sea, an invisible rummaging over stones.

She turned her head to the side and looked out the door. A faint glow indicated light coming from under the door of the nearest cottage. Supposing the door of that cottage were to open too? What might they find? A matching pair, mirror, twins to themselves? How marvellous that would be, what a relief, what a comfort! It was so difficult to be two, in a room, like this, cut off, not part of the world. She wanted to tell him she understood.

"What in Christ's name are you doing? Shut the bloody door!" He was leaning over her, staring.

"I like it."

"Bitch! Shut it!"

With an effort, she brought her eyes back to him. He was big, sitting like a rock in the semi-darkness.

"No. It's nice. Listen."

But he would not be able to hear. A stranger, she thought, might walk down the path and stand looking down into the water. If the stranger turned his back on the pool he would see the open door, walk toward it, peer inside. There she would be, floating above the sheet, her white nightie gleaming like scales. As he drew back she would be sucked out feet first, in the vacuum his withdrawal created, her nightie flying over her head.

She sighed. How happy she was to have lit on this novel solution to the problem! She breathed in and out slowly. Her hair spread behind her on the pillow. She loved the open door. She rested.

But he had become very lively. He was thumping the bed beside her head. "Shut the door!"

"The door?" she said, as if she had forgotten it. "The door is marvellous. It's perfect." She put her hand on the side of his face. She forgot about computer print-outs and gum erasers. "Don't you see?"

His hands were clenched somewhere in front of her throat. Perhaps one day he would throttle her. "Are you going to shut it, you fucking little bitch?" he said.

Very well. She didn't need him. She could enjoy it herself. "Poor you," she said gently.

He rolled away from her, swearing some more. She heard him regulating his breath, sensed him trying to relax his shoulders.

"Just go to sleep," she said.

"Not with the door open!"

"Why not?"

He merely groaned.

She was lying easily now, awash in the scent of heather and gorse, the breeze with its chill from out at sea.

"I love the door open," she said, more to herself than to him. "As a matter of fact, I regret the walls. Wouldn't it be nice just to be on our beds, in the open air? part of the night, part of the world? Doesn't it excite you?" she whispered.

"Don't you touch me! Bitch!"

She patted him with sorrow and turned away. He wanted the door shut but he was damned if he was giving in to her. She understood that well. She was only sorry.

He yanked the sheet and drove his big shoulder down into the mattress, turning himself again away from her. Whatever the open door was to her it was the opposite to him. A challenge. A threat. It exposed the privacy of his lair, made his hackles rise. He might have to get up, drive off animals. Oh, that was ridiculous, but still. It was an affront.

Dreaming of dark figures on the moor, she drifted. She floated several inches above the bed. At some point he got up, went quietly around the foot of the bed, and shut the door. The room was pitch-black now. He tripped on her purse, and his arm brushed her.

She woke. She caught his arm, felt for his face, touched his cheek. He found her mouth and pressed his lips down on it.

"You're awake."

"Madwoman," he said, finding the hair at her temple.

They were so good together. Their bodies were ready and fit in an instant. It was the grand diversion and admitted no other.

After, it was as if birds had gone off in a great flutter of wings, leaving this stillness. Where else can you get this, and when, she thought. What we have to go through to get to it.

"Diversion of angels," she said.

"What's that?"

"A dance. I only know the beginning," she whispered, "I never saw the end of it."

The Good Samaritan

The Good Samaritan

Ace placed his Russian fur hat and gloves on the shelf and
bent to remove his snowboots. He stored a pair of leather
slip-ons in the cupboard despite the fact that he didn't live
here any more, hadn't since we were married. I hung up my
coat myself, listening to the stillness. It was always still in
this house.

In the big room beyond us was a tableau: Miss Amy
standing in the centre of the living-room with a glass in her
hand; Block and Brault occupying stuffed leather chairs in
the opposite corner. The walls were burdened with landscape oils; overhead the beams of the cathedral ceiling
crossed and crossed and crossed.

We walked into the room. No one said hello.

"What's up?" said Ace.

"I'm getting a job," said his mother.

Now Block yanked his leg down, and thrust himself to his
feet. Behind his dad's back, Brault rubbed his nose. Then he
twisted his heel and took a slug of his drink. Miss Amy too
lifted her glass to her lips and smiled. Suddenly a drama was

aimed at us, as if we had made it begin, as if they had been waiting, in their places, for our entry. I had the disconcerting realization I had never been given my part.

"What kind of job do you think she's fit for?" Block demanded. He set his glass on the coffee-table, and took two steps to the open fireplace. He seized a poker and began to jab the logs, which were crackling away nicely with the aid of natural gas. "She's never had one."

"That's why I *want* one."

Miss Amy had been beautiful once and still retained the air. She was very thin, her costume of fawn silk jersey wispy around her calves. Her cheeks were mottled red and white, her hair colourless from a lifetime of peroxide and carelessly propped over the bald spot at the back of her head.

"I'll tell you what, let's get you a full-length mink," said Block into the fire.

I advanced to the edge of the rug; my stocking-clad toes were attacked by purple and green oriental daggers.

"I don't need another fur coat. I need a job." Amy whined, but there was her archness too, the exaggerated hand curls with the cigarette, the lowered jaw, lowered eyelids. She was either making a joke of it, or anticipating that they would.

Block's long arms swung sideways from his perfectly pressed flannel pants in a gesture of helplessness. "I ask you," he began, and then sighed and replaced the poker. "Boys . . ."

The boys said nothing.

"Your mother's a bright woman," said Block, "but she has this tendency to go off half-cocked." As if that finished it, he drained his drink and set off for the far end of the room.

"You haven't even asked what my job is!" cried Miss Amy. Her voice chasing him, he strode on to the far windows and looked over the backyard. It was lit by spotlights, pure white, the snow unspoiled. There weren't even any of the small three-toed bird tracks that sometimes ran across it like faint embroidery. The suet must be gone from the feeder.

We used to play pie out there, run around in a huge circle, then mark it out in pieces, and have a game of tag up and down the slice marks. I met my husband when we were both seven; we were as if betrothed all through school, which makes us some kind of rarity now, like the great whooping cranes. What it didn't do was make me part of the family, despite the fact that I'd been around so long. They started out treating me like some sort of foster-child, there temporarily — kindly, to be sure, but with condescension, no doubt expecting that Ace would go on to some more glamorous creature. By the time we were married it was too late for me to become a full member of the family, and I knew enough about them to be glad.

Block took a walnut from the silver basket on the bookshelf, put it between the jaws of a tool that resembled an instrument of torture, and squeezed. Bits of shell spattered on the rug.

"Well, what's this job?"

"I'm going to be a Good Samaritan," said Amy, smiling.

Block tossed the nut in his mouth. He jiggled the ice in his drink and kept looking out the window.

"Much money in that?"

Everyone laughed.

It was destined to become what was known in the family as a moment. A moment was retained when the hours around it, the days and months, receded. A moment was a snapshot, a view out the window of a train. Or perhaps not a train, since that implies motion. A moment stopped time, it was still, as if the curtain was raised at the high point of a drama on stage, held a few seconds and then dropped. That was all you got.

Why the Cummingses had moments when other families had more extended periods of reference was unclear to me. Perhaps what went on between the members was too awful to contemplate in larger units. Or perhaps the Cummingses were no more awful than most families and simply had a flair for the dramatic. Moments were expressive of complex and tangled emotions; they put what was unsayable into acceptable form, and they took on height and resonance as time went by. Moments tended to become funnier as they were reduced and simplified by frequent reference, but they were not, essentially, humorous. They had a note of tragedy, more of the Marx brothers than the Three Stooges. And they always seemed to have Amy at their centre.

The moment that came back as I stood looking over my father-in-law's shoulder into the snowy garden was the one in which Miss Amy crashed the CR group. My women's-liberation cell, as Ace liked to call it. At that time, which was before we were married, the cell met in the Cummingses' rumpus room. One night as we sat around in our black sweatshirts and our crumpled Indian cotton ankle-length skirts, our Roots shoes with negative heels, sharing thoughts on how best to link up with our oppressed sisters in Latin America who had only a few pesos a day to feed their eight children, Miss Amy walked in.

She was an apparition, lurid in some rainbow-hued, rhinestone-trimmed diaphanous négligé brought back for her by Block from a business trip. Her hair was dry and full of electricity and she had been drinking. "Look no farther," she said, "I am the wretched of the world."

"Come again?" said someone.

Amy wavered on the last stair of the conversation pit.

"What's that poem, Sukey? 'Look on your works, ye mighty, and despair'? I've done everything a woman is supposed to do and now I'm old and I have nothing to call my own but the clothes on my back. I'm what happens to women."

Of course it was ridiculous: her husband was a millionaire. The women of the CR group told Amy she was lucky, that if the good things of life hadn't brought her fulfilment surely it was her own fault. It got a bit nasty — someone even accused her of trying to cadge sympathy from the deserving, if I recall. I tried to help make a case for corporate wives — Look at Ducks Triblanc, I said, and Mimi O'Brien, one had a breakdown and the other got dumped by her husband and then she got cancer and had to go to the Mayo Clinic all alone. But the others didn't know Ducks or Mimi.

Miss Amy had another drink and was carted off to bed. Now the story of how Miss Amy crashed the CR session was wont to cause Brault and Block and Ace, and even Amy — heck, even me — to go red in the face and laugh until it was either stop or die. Like all our laughter it verged on tears. In the laughter was recognition we could not otherwise give. We had become accustomed to reading our lives this way.

Block stared ferociously at the unspoiled snow. I was not really surprised by Amy's announcement. After the CR session moment, I had expected some follow-up, even if it took this many years to come. In the silence Amy began to talk about how Ducks had started a service for drivers whose cars were impounded by police or caught in snow, or having mechanical difficulty. The service was to be called Jericho Road.

'It's the name of the road where the citizen was attacked by thieves," she explained proudly.

"Spare me," said Block.

"I think it's very clever. There's always something wrong with a car. And what with the weather, and the traffic, and the construction, and the police, well, people need help —"

I walked to the brass tea-trolley, which was laden with crystal bottles, each wearing a brass name-tag on a chain. My feet scuffed on the carpet, and I got an electric shock as I touched the trolley. I carried my Scotch back to my position at the entrance to the room. It seemed very warm in there. I stepped over to turn down the gas jet that animated the burning logs. The dark beyond the glaze of the picture window was like that of outer space, pricked out with lights at distant points but all-encompassing. My in-laws' house was beyond the farthest-flung outskirts of Calgary, on a hill, turned west in full contemplation of the mountains. All encroachment over the years had come from behind where it did not disturb the view.

"I don't know what Ralph is thinking, letting this sort of thing go on," Block was saying. Ralph was Ducks's husband and one of Block's poker pals. "And what the hell could you do for this outfit? You can't even *drive* worth a bean." He ran his fingers backward through his hair.

Amy said she'd answer the telephone and take down the membership number and the car licence and then put a call in to the police on that special line, reading the number from a card right on her desk. She said all this as if she had been carefully rehearsed in her duties and had all but taken them up. It caused Block, finally, to turn on his bandy legs from the window and growl.

"I hope you aren't presenting me with a *fait accompli.*"

I think it is fair to say that Block Cummings was a man who never met with a *fait accompli.* His air of authority was such that his approval was sought far and wide before matters were set in motion. Total strangers had been known to stop him and ask for his opinion of their planned route through town. When he backed into a car in their cul-de-sac the other driver, a woman, jumped out of her car and begged his pardon for being there in the first place. Certainly we knew enough to ask him things first, or never tell him at all.

"I start next week."

Amy held the floor for another minute and then tiptoed — an odd habit she had, as if a baby were sleeping on the sofa in the room — to the trolley to put down her glass. "I'll go and see about dinner."

I caught up with her in the kitchen just as she was about to lift a pot of boiling water off the stove. Her wrists, ribboned with purple from her last operation, were not strong enough to support it. The handle twisted and the noodles plopped out into the sink after the cooking water, where they began to make their way toward the drain. I stuck a fork in the tangle just as it oozed down the garburator. Shaking, Miss Amy found the tongs and began to pitch the noodles out of the sink into a bowl where, cooling instantly, they began to congeal.

"Don't you think he ought to be glad to have me earning money?" she hissed.

But Block's voice cut between us from the doorway. "You couldn't earn your way out of a paper bag!"

Block was a sentimental man; he liked to be fed by the women in his life. When we sat down to eat, the Stroganoff had simmered dry; the meat was like shredded cardboard; the noodles had joined into a giant gluey wig. Miss Amy dished out frozen peas, smiling grimly, with her look of having retreated to an inner debate. Food was always the vehicle for her revenge.

I saw in my father-in-law's face the hungry boy of sixty years ago.

"What happened to the meat?" said Block pathetically. He had been a poor boy and married a spoiled girl. He'd made his children rich too: now he was all alone with his memories of not having enough dinner. If I ever had sympathy for him it was when he looked at his plate that way.

"With a career woman in the house you've got to make allowances," she snapped.

By spring Miss Amy was working four hours a day, five days a week as a receptionist at Jericho Road. She had a desk and two telephones and pads of paper and pens of her own. She joked and let out her smoky cocktail-party laugh and flirted in her southern way on the telephone to stranded motorists. She sent out the limo stocked with drink and set the forces in motion to get the impounded cars out of hock. Ducks hired a young man called Hamish Brew to do the books. Hamish Brew kept odd hours and was nervous but Amy paid him no attention. It was said people called up just to have a giggle with Miss Amy.

Now we had intimations of change from the Cummingses' house. Brault reported that his mother had begun to pop out of bed at seven every morning. Block had always done this, but over the years Amy slept later and later, so that he was used to having breakfast alone and letting himself out without seeing her. Now she competed for the shower and the bathroom mirror; she hummed over her coffee and wanted a section of the paper. She was particularly cheerful on days of minus-thirty-degree temperatures or icy road conditions because she knew business would be brisk.

Her two dozen négligés drooping in the closet, she went in for Lurex sweaters and tight studded jeans. She had a salary now, money of her own. It was only two hundred and twenty-five dollars a week but she made it seem like a fortune: she bought champagne and potted plants and sent telegrams. When Block wanted a good dinner she had it catered.

Not long after her career had begun, we were up for dinner. Even the conversation was different. Before, it was Block who introduced topics at meals; he had done this for so long he regarded it as his right. Where he had been for lunch and who he met, from which city they came. The remainder of Block's conversation was really a set of instructions, a list of things to be done. With no instructions to give and no accomplishments to report Amy had been reduced to saying yes and no and not much else. Such information as she had to offer — the cleaning lady's problems with her delinquent son, for instance — met with his scorn.

"That's enough about that," he would say.

How many times had I listened to this, for how many years? The wonder of it was that Amy had never subsided, she had never given up. She still had her weapons, and we had all felt them. Another sort of woman might have cheerfully accepted a subservient role, at least where he could see, and invented a life out of his sight. But not Amy. She brooded and scowled and drank. She was a woman who just could not believe she wasn't going to get her due.

Now all was altered. Amy was full of news that the practical man could not fail to regard as valuable. Fourteenth Street would be closed for two weeks beginning Monday. The traffic jam at Tenth this afternoon was caused by a truck jack-knifing on the Trans-Canada. Judge Rawlins had his car towed from the front of the Courthouse where he habitually drew up in a No Parking zone, and you ought to have heard his language, she said, as she zipped a frozen lasagna out of the oven and onto the table.

"I beg your pardon," said Block. "I don't think you ought to talk about what you don't know."

"Oh, I know," said Amy gaily.

His frown blackened. Block professed belief in, and especially liked his wife to profess belief in, the correct and upright behaviour of all highly placed individuals, including himself. You could see he disapproved of Amy's having independent sources of information as much or more than he disapproved of her having an independent source of money.

"You wait till spring," he said. "Then your business will drop off."

"Oh, no, it won't," she said. "In spring they start road repair and there'll be rear-enders galore."

"I'm not sure I like this new language you've picked up either, young lady!"

Ace and I guffawed but Block saw nothing funny.

Sometimes Amy had lunch with the young fellows who ran the tow trucks or the secretaries and office-boys from the law firm on the next floor. Word got back to Ace that his mother was a kidder and a great old gal. Block too must have heard about what a character his wife was. Perhaps it suggested something insufficient in his appreciation of Amy. It exposed her in a way he didn't appreciate, heck, as he said to Ace in the locker-room after a golf game, it exposed *him* in a way he didn't like.

The next time we saw them was Father's Day, and I knew something was up. Block was cooking the steaks himself. Amy was sitting crosswise in a lawn chair, dangling her feet and talking about how some people pulled off the road and called a limo and some drinks, inviting her out to join them for a party.

"I'm not even sure this is legal," he complained, "I won't have my wife involved in fraud."

"Oh honey, it's not fraud," said Amy. "It's just fun."

But there was something wrong with Jericho Road and Block with his nose for these things got wind of it. Not long after, Amy telephoned to say two policemen had been in looking at Hamish Brew's books. Wasn't that a bit odd? she said, her voice quavering. I agreed that it was odd and put down the telephone with dread. When you suspected the worst of Block you were normally right.

The very next week the office was raided and Hamish Brew taken away in handcuffs. It appeared that Mr Brew had been using the American Express card numbers of the members to put through false claims. It made for a quick end to Miss Amy's job as a Good Samaritan.

"I still can't figure out how Block got onto that one," Amy grumbled to me. In no time she went back to sleeping till noon and lost the ten pounds she'd gained over business lunches. She began to drink again in the evening and to leave the dinner table in the middle of conversations to which she made no contribution. Block seemed neither pleased nor concerned, and before too long all that was left of it was her "working girl" bank account, which she referred to as if it were a precious heirloom from a past life.

Then came the day when Block said, "Remember when Miss Amy announced that she was getting a job?" We couldn't help ourselves, we started to chuckle, then to rock and shake, letting out nervous little blasts of laughter. Eventually we all just let it out, we roared. Miss Amy herself laughed so hard she peed her pants. When the laughter stopped I took in a shaky long breath. It was obvious now that moments were not independent events, each to itself. They were like bubbles coming up from under water, a series, proof of a chemical exchange under the bottom which had to lead to something.

Once a month the boys consented to be the opposite pair to their parents at bridge. I never played; I couldn't get onto the bidding. I brought a book and sat nearby on the couch.

It happened to be August, hot, dry; Ace and I had brought over take-out Chinese. The card table was set up under the swag lamp where the breeze came from the balcony. Block was shuffling the cards when Miss Amy stepped up to the table and spread her papers in front of her.

"Move that letter, Amy," Block said, without looking at it. His hands sowed the cards in four piles, steadily, flick, flick, flick, flick. I looked at the paper. It was deckle-edged ivory vellum with black lettering on it, very pretty. Amy had put on fresh lipstick. She stretched up her long neck and drew in her chin.

"It's for you," she said. "Something I should have given you long ago."

"What is it, dear?" Block signalled us to begin and picked up his cards, drew them to his chest, and pushed them out again so he could see them over his bifocals: expertly, between his thumb and fourth finger, he spread them to an even fan.

"A bill," said Amy.

"A bill?" That caught his attention.

You've got to know these people don't talk about bills over the bridge table. They don't talk about bills, because Block doesn't like to. Bills are Amy's job. She pays them out of the household allowance. If she runs out of money she goes to him for more. He had made this procedure difficult for her when he was younger; he had practised strict economies through her agency and made her fear to ask even for an extra fifty. Now he had too much money and wanted her to spend more, but the old habit of defensiveness over anything approaching extravagance held on.

"Is it legit?" he said.

"Oh, yes."

"Then you pay it."

Amy smiled. She always smiled when she was about to say
something unpleasant.

"I can't," she said. "Only you can. It's a bill for my services." And she stretched her hand across the table to give
him the sheet of paper.

Brault slunk down in his chair and Ace craned his neck to
read over his dad's shoulder; I leaned nearer, sensing a moment in the making. Block began to read aloud.

In Settlement of Account
between
Mr Block Cummings

and

Ms Amy Ashley Cummings

"*Ms?*" said Block.

Brault spurted laughter and then began to scratch his ear
rapidly in the silence.

For Services Rendered
April 15, 1945, to June 30, 1985

"First time she's remembered our anniversary," said
Block, lifting the top sheet. He always bought flowers.

Forty years is 14,600 days, plus 7 (leap years), totalling
14,607 days at a rate of pay averaged to $60 per day —

"That's a very reasonable daily charge, I'm told," said
Miss Amy with satisfaction. "I could have asked for much
more."

To an amount of $876,000.00

The amount was underlined twice.

The paper began to rattle. Block's hand was shaking. I hadn't noticed before that he shook.

"Is this some kind of joke?"

Amy, slender and curved, cast her eyes modestly to the table, as if she had produced something magnificent and were refusing the glory.

"No joke, no, of course it's not a joke," she said.

At this point Brault scrambled to his feet, causing the bridge table to wobble and the ice to knock the sides of the glasses. "Oh, *Mo* — ther," he said, in that pesky childish twang, "Mo — *ther.*"

"Didn't really feel like bridge tonight," said Ace, the tradition for comedy in the face of family trouble getting the better of him. I headed for the drinks trolley for a refill, and found Amy there ahead of me. She poured herself a glass of brandy. Block steadied himself with one hand on the table, and looked over at her.

"Just out of interest and not because I take this thing seriously for one minute, how did you arrive at your rate?"

Brault's normal look of watchful malice blossomed red as he was struck with an idea. "Dad! Dad! Listen, I've *heard* about this sort of thing," he said. "She didn't even think it up. She got it out of a book somewhere. I *took* this, in Sociology 443."

"Brault, shut up," I said.

"No, really, Dad, women trying to get paid for house-work and stuff —"

"Look at the inside sheet," said Miss Amy.

We all crowded around. Block lifted the page. On the left side of the page was a list of functions. In the centre was a column with the hourly wage put down, and on the far right an estimation of the number of hours over the years Amy was taken up with this function. I thought it rather neatly done. But the functions, as far as I could see them, were not the expected — cook, nursemaid, cleaner. Come to think of it they'd had women in to do those jobs. Amy's had been more skilled work — Household Management ($20 an hour); Loan agent (a percentage charged back thirty years); Ego-Stroking ($9 an hour); Dining with Fools (a bargain at $5 an hour). There were others even less delicate. I stepped back, out of respect for my father-in-law's feelings.

"I don't see how you got down to a mere $60 a day," Block murmured.

"It's not serious, Dad, I think she's making a point," said Ace.

Miss Amy ignored him. "I've been very, very easy on you. I asked for top rates for last year only. And I basically gave him the first decade free, because I knew he had no money then."

Block threw the paper on the table. "It had better be a joke."

"It's not a joke."

It was true, Amy appeared to be utterly serious.

Block was riled now.

"What do you want, Amy?" he said. His face twisted a bit. He was soft in some ways. I suppose she had hit him where it hurt. Ego-stroking, and worse? Amy when she got going would stop at nothing.

"I want my wages."

"What wages? You want money? I'll give you money. Hell, you've got money in the bank. From your job," he sneered, desperate now, having to lean on the very resource he had campaigned against her having.

"You said I couldn't earn my way out of a paper bag."

"I did?" Block looked genuinely shocked.

"It was when she told you she was getting the job," I offered.

Block gave me a long look. He had always suspected I was trouble. Whatever he saw confirmed it. Regretfully he teamed himself with his remaining ally, the idiot.

"So is Brault telling me the truth, is this some kind of sociology project you've picked up on from the kids?" he said.

But Miss Amy would not be reduced. She stood over us all, tallest of the family when she wasn't slouching.

"No, Block. This is absolutely what it says it is. You don't think I worked all this time for nothing? The time has come for you to recognize my contribution." Her chin was firm and high, her expression calm. She was determined to get what she deserved, and now.

None of us moved.

The time had come for backpedalling, and Block knew it. "But Amy I do recognize —"

"Balls!" she barked.

We all jumped.

Block now walked around the bridge table holding his arms out to his wife. "Amy," he crooned.

Ace sniggered.

"Get out of here, you boys!" Block's neck snapped around. He showed us his teeth. "You've interfered with far too many things around here. I want to talk to my wife, alone."

We beat it for the kitchen but I heard Miss Amy.

"It's too late to talk," she was saying. "There's nothing to talk about. Just pay the bill."

I felt as if she needed me to stay. I hesitated.

"Get out of here!" roared Block.

I heard the paper being snatched up. "You've got three weeks," said my mother-in-law in a quavering voice. "Three weeks is normal, isn't it?"

Brault and Ace stood right at the kitchen door with their ears cocked trying to hear across the dining-room into the living-room. Their parents were yelling at each other. It had happened so many times before.

"I haven't got this kind of money! You're asking for more than three quarters of a million dollars!"

"It's no more than I'm worth."

"It's more than I'm worth, that's the point."

"Nonsense," said Amy calmly.

"What do you want me to do, liquidate?"

"Liquidate my share!" shouted Amy. "I want out of your stinking business affairs." She was getting herself worked up now; it was a bad sign. "I'm sorry I ever let you have that money my father left me, to get started."

"Amy, I told you when I die you'll be a wealthy woman," he pleaded.

"You needn't go that far. Just yet," she said dangerously.

Brault and Ace stood by the pass-through imagining terrible ruptures, I know, lawyers arriving with leather briefcases, voices rasping out deals behind the doors, suitcases being dragged over the flagstone. It was all breaking apart. It was all too possible. The moments all adding up to one final crisis, Divorce, and no more "boys." I wanted it to happen. I wanted it all to be over, and for us all to be on the outside like me.

"Amy," came the voice at last. A careful voice. "You know I'm very grateful to you for —"

He must have come up close to her and was perhaps stroking her arm. There was no sound from Amy.

"I realize I owe you a great deal."

Still no remark from the other side.

"But Amy, you'll see in my will that —"

This brought it out of her again. "I don't give a shit about your will. You can leave your money to whoever you want as long as you pay my wages first. I want my wages."

"But Amy! We never agreed on these rates."

There was a silence, as if she hadn't heard, and then Amy laughed in triumph.

"Aha! So you accept that I've got rates, and you're ready to negotiate them?"

Block grunted. "You would have made a very good businessman, Amy."

"Thank you," she said.

"Let's go back a step," he said, warmly. "When we were married, the understanding was that you would do all the normal things a wife did."

"There's normal and there's then some," she said. "Depends on who's doing the deciding, doesn't it?"

"Well Amy, I thought we both agreed that raising the children was normal."

"I'm not billing you for raising the children."

"You're not?"

Brault was leaning back and forth, back and forth, first toward his mother's voice, then toward his dad's, as if he could balance the two on their see-saw by adding or subtracting his weight. I felt for the guy. It's not his fault he's a creep.

"Oh," said Block in a matter-of-fact way. "I thought for a minute you were going back on your bargain."

She sucked in her breath. Her voice was haughty. "I would *not* go back on my bargain," she said. The paper rattled emphatically.

"All right, Amy, all right," said Block. "Do you want to talk seriously about this account? Do you want me to treat you like any contractor who's done work for me?"

"Well, yes," she said, slightly deflated.

"All right. Can I fill up your glass?"

We retreated to the kitchen. Ace opened the frig door. There was never any food in it any more. His parents almost always went out to restaurants. But he found some frozen white bread and in the cheese tray some old orange cheddar. There was a package of bacon with the fat gone a bit sticky.

"Wanna make pigs in blankets?" he said to Brault. Brault was standing by the can cupboard practising some bizarre karate chops on the door.

"Shhh!" he said. When Ace started banging the plates around he slid around the door to the dining-room to listen some more.

"Look," I heard Block say, "you haven't said anything here about your room and board. I've given you room and board for forty years — "

"Normal," said Amy. "Doesn't count "

"But this is five-star."

"Your choice. I never asked for five. I'd have taken — heck, I'd have taken anything."

"For the pleasure of my company?" he said.

"Out of my marital duty," she said.

He laughed. "Amy," he said, "I know you too well."

"A company car," Block was saying. "Really at your level you should have had one. You could add that to your claim. Mind, if you do, there will be taxes . . ." There was a moment of silence. "I've got you down now to a manageable $300,000. And we haven't even got to this . . . bedmate?" he said. "What's that?"

"Above and beyond," she said.

"You're complaining?"

She laughed and said something we couldn't hear.

"Look Brault, it's over," I said. "The fight's over. Turn on the radio, Ace, will you?"

While the pigs in blankets toasted we hung out on the balcony over the back yard, throwing snowballs down to pock the perfect surface. Brault kept giving nervous glances over his shoulder into the living room where his parents sat, bent over the card table.

"Do you think," he said, "do you think, they're having fun?"

"Yeah," I said. "They're having fun. I just hope he doesn't get her down too low." Then I smelled the bacon burning.

After the Fire

After the Fire

Ken put his head out of the window and looked down. Full shafts of Mediterranean sun fell past the sill, making white the pocked granite walls and cobblestones. Hot, hot, hot — and it was only ten o'clock in the morning. A vigorous wind flung itself around the corner of the house and at the hill behind. What was that? Smoke? He counted five separate trails rising.

He looked straight down. Below him, a blond couple who had found their way to the village from the main road took folding chairs and a thermos from the trunk of their car and set up just outside the front door. They poured themselves cups of morning coffee while looking at Ken's family's view. German, probably. The Germans were neat and quiet but managed to be obtrusive all over France. In Vegno the locals would have spied them at once from behind unpainted shutters.

The tourists annoyed Ken. His friends, who owned this retreat, and Ken himself, made an effort to get close to village life; then people like these barged in and ruined all their spadework. Vegno was a small village in the hills, a few miles from the sea on a road more than normally precarious even by Corsican standards. So far a mere trickle of the onrush of tourists visiting the island in August had discovered it. Most of those who did thought it deserted. Up the narrow steps between stone houses, open doorways were blocked with curtains of wooden beads; more than once a snooping visitor pushed aside the curtain and stepped into the neighbour's kitchen just as she was setting out the charcuterie and goat's cheese.

"Lock the front door," Madame Pianelli had said, when they arrived. "These tourists, they'll get in anywhere." With this benediction Ken and Althea were set apart.

Abruptly the German couple stood, folded their chairs and prepared to leave. After looking at the rising smoke one more time — what was it? spontaneous combustion in the extreme heat and dryness? or shepherds' signals? — Ken pulled his head in the window. He was not exactly bored, but he had begun to see that even exotic places became routine when you travelled with children.

Every day until today for two weeks they'd had breakfast, packed up and driven down the mountain to the beach. They parked the car and set out past the crowds along the soft white sand. Loaded with rubber dinghy, paddles, mask, flippers, floaters, pails, shovels, umbrella, towels and reading materials, they made their way to a favourite spot in the centre of the half-mile curve. There not a single rock marred the smoothness of the bottom, the water was shallow, the bottom dropping over gently. If the water was calm, Kate and Oliver might play by themselves, allowing up to an hour of peace. Ken would read the *Herald Tribune* while Althea dug into her book on local attractions from which she would occasionally raise her head to relay a notable fact:

"Did you know there's a town up the mountain where women had the vote in the sixteenth century?"

But before long the kids would want a castle built, and then they'd be thirsty, and then hungry. Lunch was a niçoise salad and frites at Le Snack with popsicles which melted faster than they could be eaten, making orange rivulets down little arms to which, soon, sand would cling. By three they'd always had enough sun. Yesterday they'd come home even earlier; this *tourbillon*, a whirlwind, had come up, whipping sand into their faces. When they returned to this third-storey flat at the top of the village, the gentle breeze that had thus far cooled them turned wild. Unfastened shutters slammed and fastened ones rattled as the wind raced through the rooms, lifting papers from the table and tossing them over lampshades, spreading the playing-cards in a path along the floor.

It was just too much trouble to try to get the kids to wait until 8:30, when the local pension served dinner. They had an omelette at home. Drained, he and Althea went to bed not long after the children. Ken was ready to leave the island; he began to plan their return. They would take the ferry from Ajaccio to Nice. Then they would drive through France. Sitting up in bed with the map spread on his knee, he showed Althea a route. He thought they could do it in three days.

"Oh, no," said Althea. "To do it that fast would be hell on the kids. A few hundred kilometres a day is the maximum."

Irked by this challenge to his planning, Ken pointed out potential places to stop for the night: Avignon, Beaune, then Calais, and across. Althea flew into a temper and bashed her fist into the map so that it crumpled.

"You need to control everything!" she said. "You've got all the money in travellers' cheques in your name and you never cash it. What am I supposed to do if something happens to you? You have this trip in your mind like some kind of military campaign! You won't let me decide anything!'' She flounced out of bed. ''You even do all the talking when we meet people.''

''That's because I speak French,'' said Ken with an air of great reasonableness. He struggled to straighten out the map and refold it on the original lines. He could not bear a misfolded road map.

She stood by the window looking down the mountain. ''You boss us all around and I never get my way,'' she said as if she wasn't sure she deserved her way.

''So get your way,'' he said harshly, turning out the light and lying down with his back to her. ''Don't paint yourself as such a victim. Take charge!'' Then, reckless, lapsing into sarcasm, ''You've got the vote, don't you?''

That pushed resolution beyond the realm of the possible for the evening. He went to sleep and this morning they hadn't spoken. But by silent agreement the routine had been varied; it was too windy for the beach anyway. And Ken was damned if he was going to make any suggestions about what they should do. He could hear Althea now, in the children's room.

''Well then, *find* it, Oliver. You're the one who hid it. I'm not going to spend my whole life looking for your . . .''

He poured himself another cup of coffee and lurked by the kitchen door. They appeared to be heading down to the garden. He took another look out the window. That crazy wind had not let up, and smoke was still rising on the hillside. A clump of villagers had gathered at the turn-off. Silently, he followed his wife and children down the stairs. There was a too-hot, stirred-up feeling out there. Something was going to happen. He had instincts for this kind of thing.

In the walled gardens at the back of the building were the ruins of a well and the old stalls where the nuns had kept their donkeys. It was prickly, dry and unwelcoming; only the fig-tree and some potted geraniums, faithfully watered by Madame Pianelli, thrived. For a while Ken kicked around a soccer ball with the kids, but after a few minutes they found a better game of their own, playing war with the ruined figs that littered the ground. Oliver threw them at Kate and Kate collected them.

When the children weren't looking, Ken climbed a few stones to look over the wall. The smoke fluttered away unabated up the hill and now there was a little pyre at the foot of the Vegno turn-off. Sparks must be travelling on the wind. As he watched, an old-fashioned truck with hoses pulled up. Suddenly he remembered the words of his host: "Once in a while you'll see fires on the hills. It's the rebels or something. Don't worry, they never go near the tourist areas."

"Come on kids," said Ken. "Let's go see the firemen."

Alone, Althea went upstairs and sat down at the kitchen table to write a letter. The wind lifted the edge of her paper.

"I should have come here when I was twenty," she wrote. "I should have done Europe with a knapsack. Now here I am with a husband and kids! But —" She heard a siren but did not stop. "— we find we can get them to go along with most things, if we try hard enough. We drink in the square in Ille Russe and they play *boules* —"

Reminded of how wonderful the trip was, Althea got up and went to the window. Vegno was built on the very top of a hill which itself was near the top of a rounded mountain covered with trees. Theirs was the highest house in the village, and on the top storey they had windows looking in three directions. She could see down to the sea, up to the next village, south, and higher, and back up the mountain-side.

Was that smoke rising from the thorny low *maquis* across the road? She remembered the siren. But there was no firetruck in sight. She pushed her head further out so that she could see to the cobblestones below. Ken was talking to Roger. Roger was not a friend, he was simply the only other English-speaking person in the village, an American. Roger's four-year-old son Sammy had shown up at their door early one morning wanting breakfast. Right now Sammy was playing in front of the church with Kate and Oliver, their piping calls obscuring the words of the adult conversation. But Ken's face was animated, the sullen look of withdrawal gone. Althea capped her pen. Her sandals slapped on the stone stairs as she went down.

Roger saw her approaching before Ken did.

"We're concerned about Georges's sheep," he said. "If the fires spread." Roger took everything so seriously you had to respond in kind, or laugh.

"Those little fires?" said Althea, smiling as she pointed up the hill.

"They're burning downwind too, where the sheep are. I'm going out to help Georges round them up."

"Why don't you go too?" said Althea instantly to Ken. She didn't know why she said it. They hardly knew Georges, the shepherd who lived in the village. Surely, as visitors, they did not have neighbourly responsibilities in Vegno. Perhaps it was a form of apology for last night: *go, enjoy yourself, be a man with other men.* A little of that, and a little trying to hurt him: *we don't need you, we'll manage on our own.*

They all walked together to Roger's little yellow car.

"I'm coming too, I'm coming too," said Sammy, clambering to get into the back seat.

"I don't think this is for kids," said Roger.

"Come on Sammy, you stay with us," said Althea. Roger hauled him out by one leg. She put her hand on the boy's shoulder. His mother must be around somewhere. Roger started the car. "We'll just wait for Renate. She's changing."

Now Renate ran up the square, dressed in khaki shorts and hiking boots with socks rolled at the ankle: *Vogue* magazine's designated fire-fighting outfit.

"You're keeping Sammy?" said Renate. "It's no difference, three, if you already have two?" She too jumped into the car.

So it was that at eleven o'clock in the morning Althea was running a nursery. She put Sharon, Lois and Bram on the tape deck and the children bounced to the music on the sofa. After forty-five minutes of Mother Goose songs Althea put eggs on to boil and made sandwiches on the crusty white bread they bought in the market. Every few minutes she went to the window.

The fires on the hillside above were no bigger. But it seemed to her the others, below, had trebled in size. Smoke appeared over the lower slopes of the mountain to the south in dark, voluptuous billows, and new columns of paler smoke rose from the brush between Vegno and the beach directly downhill. The wind ripped across the open spaces, shaking out the olive trees that spotted the hillsides, and leaping over the dry ridges of bush. The smoke rode high and ahead of the flames. Althea looked at the angle of its movement away from the source and extrapolated. If the wind kept blowing in the same direction the fires would travel uphill, missing Vegno but hitting the next village, which was just visible at the crest of the hill to the north.

Moving automatically, Althea removed the children's crusts and put a plate of grapes on the table. Within a few minutes Sammy had invented a game, squishing the purple centre out and spitting the skins and seeds around the table. Oliver and Kate joined in. Althea took advantage of their

being engrossed to go all around the flat looking out one
window after another. The larger fires were those travelling
horizontally across the mountainside between Vegno and
the sea. But they were down the hill, and not heading their
way. The closer, smaller fires would surely be put out by
local firefighters.

By the time she got back to the kitchen Sammy and Oliver
were under the table throwing grape skins at each other.
Kate sat stoically eating the slippery centres.

"I'm hungry too," said Althea to her daughter, and got
herself an apple and some cheese. She poured a glass of
mineral water and sat down. The boys ran out of the room,
and an unnatural quiet arose. There were no more sirens,
and no voices from the village. Was this, or was this not an
emergency? She began to get angry at Ken for going off and
leaving them. She had the car at least, but no money (damn
him and those travellers' cheques) and only a little French.
She hated feeling helpless. You've got the vote! he said to
her. But the Corsicans were still here. Surely if there was
danger, they'd help. Surely airplanes and tank trucks and
police cars would appear, as in normal life.

"I want to go down to the square," said Sammy, appear-
ing in the doorway.

"Yes," said Oliver, "we want to go outside."

"It's very hot outside. We never go out at noon."

"Pleeee-ase?"

"Why do you want to?" You weren't supposed to reason
with children, you just told them what to do. But Althea
couldn't help it. Their begging reminded her of how surrounded by prohibitions children were, how subject to other
people's decisions. She had hated it when she was a child,
she hated it now. She wanted to make her children's lives
fresher, more direct.

"Play water guns!" shouted Sammy.

Roger and Renate didn't allow guns, and Sammy had fallen on Oliver and Kate's water pistols with glee. You couldn't play water pistols inside.

"Please, Mummy."

"Wait one minute," she said, "and then we'll go."

Before going down Althea circled again from window to window. The shadow cast by the smoke cloud on the barren ground below them had shifted slightly closer to Vegno. Half an hour ago it had fallen over the gas station on the road below; now it fell on the clump of olive trees higher up. If she drew a vector from the flames on the ground through the dark patch of earth under the cloud which travelled ahead of them, and extended it in the same direction, the arrow still missed Vegno. But it missed by less than it had before.

"Outside! Outside! Outside!" chanted Sammy and Oliver.

"OK. We'll go down in the square and see what everyone is doing. Give me those water pistols and I'll fill them."

The square was no more empty and silent than it had been every day at noon. The madwoman with her rolling eye still sat on her stoop and cackled what must be obscenities in Corsican. But today this bit of local colour became hostility. Whatever the villagers are going to do about these fires they aren't telling me, thought Althea. Despite the fact that Ken and Roger and Renate are down there chasing up their damn sheep.

"Psssst!" Oliver jumped out from behind a wall, aiming the water pistol at her face. She screamed; the stream fell short. He dodged in front of her and ran ahead, up the narrow path between houses, toward the top end of the village. Kate was left behind, tripping on the uneven rocks. It *was* harder with three than with two, no matter what Renate said. Althea took her daughter's hand and they followed the boys, slowly. At the last turn before the wall two of the pension guests appeared, hurrying with duffle bags and snorkelling gear under their arms.

"Are you leaving?" Althea said to the tall young man, although it was obvious.

"Si, si," he said, gesturing toward the smoke visible above the wall. He said more in Italian, but she didn't understand.

By the time Althea reached the boys they were leaning over the wall, throwing rocks down to the scrubby earth below. She lifted Kate up and together they looked over the sheep's path, the solitary olive trees and thorny bushes, the sand-coloured soil. Orange flames shot up to giant brown stooks of smoke not a mile away down the hill. And right here, tucked against the wall, was something Althea had not seen before. A large blue holding tank for gas. It must contain fuel for their village cookers.

A surge went through her. She straightened her back; her eyes and ears became fine-tuned instruments of detection; her sluggish mind jumped ahead. This was real. There was fire out there, out of control. If it reached the tank, they'd blow up. What was she thinking to gain, hanging around, measuring the angle of its approach?

"OK, kids, OK. Up! Now!" she shouted. The boys ran off again. "Back upstairs. We're going to pack a suitcase."

"We want to throw stones."

But Althea was dragging Kate by the hand down the path. "Come on, come on!"

It took an age, that climb back to the flat. The boys hid in corners, and fought, and Kate hung back whining. Their voices rang in the empty stone streets and returned from the shuttered windows. They counted steps: eleven between each pair of landings, twenty-two on each flight, three flights

altogether: sixty-six stairs. Once inside the flat Althea ran
around putting passports, the little money she had (one hundred francs), warm sweaters and some fruit in a suitcase.
She scooped up Ken's media pass from the bureau — who
knew what she would need? — and then she stopped. Was
she being melodramatic?

Once more she went to the window. The flames were
taller. The black shadow of the smoke cloud was now just
beneath Vegno on the hillside, moving toward the propane
tank. The town appeared to be deserted, the road was empty.
Everyone was gone or in hiding. Would the firemen return?
She was not going to wait.

Hardly knowing if she was acting too soon or too late,
Althea took the car keys in her hand. Then she remembered
Sammy. There was no one to leave him with. She'd just
have to take him too.

Ken laid down the olive branch he was using to beat out
ground fire. There were clumps of burning bushes on three
sides and the smoke was so thick his eyes ran. The fire
brigade had run out of water an hour ago and now the
ragtag assortment of men, and Renate, were working hit
and miss. They weren't gaining anywhere.

He wiped his eyes with a sooty hand and reached for
Roger's shoulder.

"See that wind?" said Ken. "We ought to worry about
the big fires from Calvi. These little patches will burn
themselves out. We should get a strategy —"

"There's no time, no time!" shouted Roger. Short and
stocky with a thick head of hair, he looked like the Mad Hat-
ter. Ken had seen his type performing self-conscious heroics
in postings all over the world. A State Department official
who had worked in Africa, now he was teaching the Corsicans how to do what they'd done for centuries. And

probably already composing the dispatches home. He cursed himself for getting carried along when the sheep-hunting expedition turned into fire-fighting.

He picked up his branch again, and whacked down a clump of burning maquis, trampling on it. Beside him another blossomed into flame. He looked up and couldn't see the sky. He had no idea where he was. They had driven him here through a crazy web of little tracks. He was so used to covering disasters that he had only just begun to realize he was *in* one, that he had no crew with him, no helicopter waiting to take him away. He wasn't standing on the sideline taking notes, he was stuck in the middle. He wanted to get back to Althea and the kids.

"I think we're fighting on the back end of this thing now," he said, following Roger to a new patch of burn. "It's got ahead of us. Probably heading straight for Vegno."

"Well, we've got to do something," said Roger.

"I think I should get back to Althea. The kids," he said. He was conscious of letting down some male side.

Roger didn't look up. "We're staying," he said.

"Right," said Ken. "Well, show me how I can get back."

One of the firemen grunted. He was taking the truck back to fill up the tank and he'd drop Ken at the turnoff.

At the convent Ken ran up the three flights of stairs and in the door. He expected Althea to be angry. He did not expect her to have the kids lined up at the door.

"We're going for a car ride, Daddy," said Kate.

He hugged Althea. She was stiff with tension. "It's time to leave," she said. "I've watched the wind change. It's coming directly for us now. If it doesn't speed up we've got about half an hour."

It was the first time she'd looked him in the eye since the night before. Her look was flat and defiant. *I have made my decision.*

"All right," he said. "I want to water down the garden first."

Althea and the kids stood waiting as he dragged out the hose and shot water up the sides of the convent, over the trees, down the back wall. He felt this much obligation to the property, to their friends. About fifteen minutes' worth. He soaked the stone and then turned off the hose. What with the heat and wind it would probably dry off in as much time again. He ran back through the dark cellar to the front door. Midway, he stepped in a hole; a stone edge gashed his shin, and he swore.

Carrying the suitcase, they walked down to the square in front of the church where the car was parked. No one seemed to be watching from the shuttered houses, but it felt like a public defection. The fly-ridden dog which always limped forward wagging its tail when they passed did not move this time.

"What are they all going to do?" whispered Althea, meaning the inhabitants.

"Wait for the firemen, I guess. Trouble is, I've seen the firemen."

Ken put the car in gear. Althea couldn't get the kids' seatbelts done up; even that delay seemed as if it might be crucial. When they reached the turn onto the main road she let out a breath. "It was that propane tank," she said.

He gave a short laugh. "I thought I was the only one who knew about that."

"Oh you did, did you?" she said coolly, letting him know the issue was unresolved.

A white van with *Urgence/Secours* printed on its side and two white sawhorses with black stripes painted on them

blocked the road going left, down to the beach. Fire must
have crossed it further down. They could only go right,
southward, toward the port of Calvi, along the narrow two-
lane highway that traversed the mountain a few miles above
the sea.

There was no traffic on the road. The fire blew along
below them, in the opposite direction: in two minutes Vegno
had disappeared behind them. They went over a rise and
around a bend and came to another village. There was a café
with a terrace by the road. They'd stopped here on their first
night in Corsica; the owners were friendly.

"You want to stop? They might know something," said
Ken. He parked the car and got his camera out of the trunk.

On the terrace you could see over the square-topped
houses and palm trees of this village to banks of smoke blocking out the sea. The dark-haired waitress looked sad.

"*Deux bières, trois pollos,*" said Althea. And because Ken
had gone to the railing with his camera, chanced a few words
of French. "*C'est tragique,*" gesturing to the smoke.

"*C'est toujours comme ça, chaque année c'est la même chose.*"

"*Mais comment les feux sont commencés?*"

"*Ce sont les criminaux qui les mettent,*" said the woman
shortly. "*Et toujours quand il fait beaucoup de vent.*"

Criminals. But what sort of criminals, and to what purpose? Althea hadn't the subtlety in French to attack the
question, and something set and frightened in the woman's
face would have stopped her anyway.

"*Cette village-ci,*" said Althea, pointing to the houses
below, "*est-ce que la vôtre? N'avez-vous pas peur?*"

And the woman said no, that the fires never burned the
villages, only the countryside. "*Jamais les villages, jamais,*"
she said. People are not killed, only trees. Perhaps *les maisons
isolées* but nothing more. Why don't they stop it? said
Althea. The woman shrugged. They used to try to put out
the fires. But now they don't. *Ils prennent les photos,* she said.

Althea looked at Ken. His camera was down now, under his arm. Oliver, Sammy and Kate finished their popsicles and ran down off the terrace to the flat place below, where they found the heavy *boules* the men played with. As Althea drank her beer she watched them devise their own game: they picked up one ball and dropped it on the others, causing them to shoot out in several directions. She could hear Ken and the barman talking about the Canadairs, the airplanes that collect water from the sea and drop it on forest fires. There were Canadairs in the south of France, but they had not arrived yet, said the barman. Even when they did, it would be too windy, the waves too large, for them to work.

Sitting on the terrace, in conversation with people, there was a sense of being out of danger. "It's a great story," said Ken, coming to sit down with her. "Even a Canadian angle."

"Too bad you're on holiday."

But even as they finished their beer, they saw that the smoke was taking up more and more of the sky. Now the flames seemed to be just beyond the village walls.

Sammy dropped a *boule* near Kate and it banged her foot. She began to cry, and in a minute the children were clustered around Kate. Sammy put up a dirty hand and turned her face to his

"I want my Mummy and Daddy. You were very *bad* to take me here."

"Your Mummy and Daddy asked me to," said Althea, although in fact they had done nothing of the kind. According to Ken they had said nothing about Sammy when they opted to stay with the fire-fighters.

"Maybe your Mummy and Daddy are dead already," said Oliver. "Maybe they are burned in the fire."

"Yes. Maybe," said Kate importantly. She was still sniffing from her hurt foot.

"Of course they're not!" declared Althea. "They just

decided to try to put the fire out, and we decided to take you
out of danger. Look,'' she said, pointing back in the direction of Vegno, ''it's too smoky there.'' The entire north and
west were now blocked from view.

Surreptitiously, and with tension in his neck, the barman
began to take the bottles off the countertop. In a few minutes
the waitress came to Althea.

''We are going to close now,'' she said. ''We have to go
and see about my brother's cows.''

''Yes,'' said Althea, standing up. ''The fire is very
close.'' She felt heavy. It had only now occurred to her that
once out of their village they had nowhere to go. They were
tourists. They knew nobody here. The island was crammed
with tourists in August: there would be no chance of getting
a hotel. And now the road back to Vegno was blocked.
Another white *secours* van and two more striped sawhorses
had appeared.

''You may stay here,'' said the waitress. ''On the
terrace.''

''Thank you,'' said Althea. But it was smoky there now
too. ''I think we may go up the mountain further.''

The hot wind was still blowing hard. Althea's hair was
dry and hard, sticky with salt. She was thirsty again,
although she'd just had a large beer and mineral water.
They bought the kids juice in boxes with straws, to drink in
the back seat. They climbed into the car again. Althea put
on the Sesame Street tape. They knew all the songs by heart
now, it was how they had got through Germany, Italy and
France. Momentarily, a feeling of hilarious release attended
them. Althea wanted to laugh. Was this how to reduce social
inhibitions in the modern urban family? Cause them to drive
through a burning island without understanding or direction, with a carload of children. It's that holiday feeling.

''Let's go riding in an automobile,'' they sang, along with

Bert and Ernie, "let's take a ride in a car. Listen to the engine go vroom vroom vrooom as we travel near and far!"

Ken drew up at a fork in the road. "Which way?" he said to Althea, politely, making the point. *We plan together.*

She stopped singing. "Where are we going?"

He drew out the road map of Corsica. It floated between them in the space over the gear-shift, a different map from last night's, an apology for the fight. They leaned over it. If they took the left fork up and across they would come to a junction at Belgodere; from there they could go either over the mountain range to the other side of the island, or back up to Ille Russe, north of their village, making a circle. If the fire had passed, the beach road might be open allowing them to get home. The right fork would take them back down toward Calvi, the port, and airports.

"What do you think?"

"Up," said Althea. She had some idea that fire moved sideways faster than it climbed. Or maybe that was bears. Still. "Up," she repeated.

"We don't have a lot of gas."

"Up," she said.

They took the left fork. Soon they faced an unbroken line of cars coming down.

"They must be hoping to get off the island," said Ken. "Maybe the other coast is burning as well."

"But they won't get off."

"No way. The ferry's been booked for months."

"And the planes." Even if the road was open all the way to Calvi, which seemed unlikely given the direction of the fires.

Alone against the traffic they set off up the mountains. Kate fell asleep in her corner. Sammy and Oliver pushed each other. "You're it." "No, you are!" Their game created a little island of privacy in the front seat.

"I can't believe this," Ken said. "It's medieval. There's no radio coverage, there's no television, there's no army. I haven't seen a helicopter . . . you're right in the middle of a disaster and you can't get an overview."

But an overview was something imported to this place from the twentieth century, a modern luxury. You have to be above it to get an overview, you have to have an angle. The Corsicans went in, not up; they dug down inside their walls for protection.

They drove on, passing cars with dinghies strapped to the roof, windsurfs, paddles and kites sticking out of windows, trailers pulling campers, all heading down to the port. The tourists had been flushed out of their tents. The Corsicans were hidden. Now each gas station was closed, each café deserted. The smoke and fire made time a sieve; the fine-grained old fell through, but the new was coarse with paraphernalia, and became caught in the mesh.

After half an hour's drive Belgodere became visible on their left, a stubble of stone houses protruding from a fist of rock on the side of the mountain. There was no smoke visible. All three children slept.

The central square of the town faced converging roads. A long line of cars coming over the mountain from the other side was stalled at the top end of the village waiting to turn onto the road down to Calvi. A few cars like their own had collected, attempting the journey at cross purposes, presumably from opposite convictions about where safety lay. A silent seated chorus of local men nodded and squinted from café chairs at this great cross-up of foreign cars and people in sun-glasses. When Ken and Althea reached the road they wanted, leading back down to Ille Russe, they found it blocked by the now familiar striped sawhorses.

There was only one thing to do: stop the car. The children woke.

"Want a popsicle?" said Ken.

They crossed blinking to the café.

"Deux bières, trois pollos," said Oliver to the waitress. Ken and Althea laughed. They stretched their legs waiting for the drinks to come. Just like people on holiday in Europe. "We sit in cafés, and they play . . ." thought Althea, remembering her unfinished letter.

It was now four o'clock in the afternoon. An overhead drone signalled action. Gendarmes spilled from a truck to the road, waving their arms as drivers poked their heads out car windows asking what to do, where to go. Two of the soldiers picked up the sawhorses and carried them off the road.

"It's open."

"Shall we try it?"

Althea looked dubiously down the road, which would lead them in a circle, home.

"Home, home!" said Kate. The boys picked up the chant. When the popsicles came they licked them without enthusiasm.

"Do you think the fire's out?"

"Or passed?"

A line was forming to take the reopened road. In front of them was a black BMW and in front of that a yellow Volkswagen, behind them a small red car with Italian plates. The yellowish hillside descended abruptly at the edge of town. The first mile or two of road was fine. The boys looked out the window, acknowledging the fire now; it seemed no longer dangerous, and they were going home.

But before long Ken saw smoke on the downhill side of the car. They drove over the next hillock, and saw a line of fire moving rapidly between patches of tree and bush several hundred feet below them. On the exposed slope the wind was stronger than ever. At the next turn great black swatches showed where the fire had been, and orange scallops showed its leading edge, parallel to the road and below it. Ken took one more turn and saw the fire leap the road in front of them and begin to consume a dry olive tree fifteen feet from them. It burst like a firecracker.

"We're driving right into it!" said Althea.

"We're in it." He curled over the wheel, peering into the smoke. The fire was not a solid wall, not like forest fires he'd covered in British Columbia, incontrovertible, thick. It was quick, this fire, and devious, and darted catlike along a dry line of grass to take a tree in one grab. It swung from that tree-top to another, skirting down its side and pausing over a bush. It was a dancing, fighting animal.

All three children began to cry.

"The fire is going to get us! It's going to burn the car!"

Althea could feel the heat now. She leaned into the back to roll up the children's windows. Looking behind the car for a second she saw the fire surround the road, making it a tunnel, shutting off retreat.

A lump of burning wood dropped onto the hood. She wanted to scream but didn't dare. She wanted to open the windows, leap out, take the road at a run. But she couldn't. Not with three toddlers. She was slowed, muffled, weighed down by them. The whole trip she'd had this nightmare sense of not being able to move. Now it was real.

They couldn't even run for it. Not really, they'd be hopeless, scrambling on the mountainside with little hands and little bodies, at forty pounds each too heavy to carry, too weak to run. Even if they both carried a child that left one. Sammy. If they all burned up there'd be an extra body. They'd left the walled village in fear, taken the boy without asking, taken this road when they didn't have to, they'd driven straight into the fire.

"How could those jerks have opened the road?" Ken swore. The children were wailing. The yellow Volkswagen at the head of the line slowed almost to a stop. The black BMW honked. Move fast, move faster, the driver gestured out his window.

"Go!" said Althea. She had a vision of the closed fire-tunnel behind them.

"How can I?"

Ken honked. But the cars in front were stopped, and he had to stop. He turned and looked into her eyes, throwing off the last shred of the fight of the night before. *We must do this together. We must do it right. There must be no opportunity for blame.*

The traffic did not move. We could just as easily have gone to Greece, Althea thought. Or I could have said, let's not go to Corsica until the tourist season is over. Then we wouldn't be here now. Or I could have insisted on staying at Vegno, propane tank or no. And then would we be safe? She saw a map of their day, a red line showing how they had deliberately left the village, chosen this turn and that branch, broaching this one after it reopened as if deliberately seeking confrontation with the fire. As if they had travelled this way to find it.

"Well," she said quietly. "How are we going to do this?"

The red car behind them began to honk. The yellow VW in front had jerked ahead and then halted. The driver leaned out his window and shouted at Ken, "*Reculas!* Go back!"

"I can't!" The other cars were piling up behind.

Oliver stood up to look out the window. He saw the fire down the mountain, ahead of them. "Daddy, turn around!" he cried. "The fire's coming!"

The piping voice stung Althea. He was so young. And he had chosen. Daddy didn't know what to do, so Oliver would help.

"What do you think?" said Ken quietly, to her. "Which way is it?"

"Back," she said.

"To Belgodere?" He looked at her, remembering the tunnel of fire.

"We hardly have any gas."

"It's going to get worse."

"We know what's behind us."

"Let's go back."

But the real reason she wanted to go back was that Belgodere felt lucky. Belgodere was a talisman from the good times, yesterday, was it? It was the place where women got the vote in the sixteenth century. She had read it to him from her book. "Oh yeah?" Ken had said, looking up from the *Herald Tribune*. "And then what happened? What did they do with it?"

"Not much, someone took it away from them a few years later," she had said, and they laughed, lying on the hot sand. The children were sitting a few feet away with their legs poking into the lapping water.

"Back," she repeated, "and if we make it we aren't going to budge from that café until this whole fire is out. I swear I don't care if I sit there for days. I will not go on the roads again."

The black BMW swung left to try to pass the van, but was blocked by the burning limb of a tree. The VW began to chivvy on the narrow road to turn back on itself. The flames were so near anyone could open a window and touch them. The van and the BMW met head on. The wind and the flames were roaring, men yelled in diverse languages and shook their fists. The children were silent in terror. Althea began to understand about dying. This would be how it was. You thought you were getting away. You drove straight in. It had been there all the time waiting for you.

Her stomach began to feel hot. Her bowels especially. It

was like in war novels; people felt fear in their bowels. She was unable to move for fear. She seemed to be turning liquid.

Ken wrenched the wheel and backed up into the hillside. The yellow and black cars blocked the way ahead. Behind them the van sat crosswise on the road; the couple inside were arguing furiously. Ken inched his way back, forward, near the downhill edge now, turning around. Behind them the BMW got around the van and sped ahead, straight into the fire.

"He's running for it," said Ken with awe.

Kate and Sammy merely absorbed terror from the air in the car. But Oliver understood. His face was stretched, his tan yellow. Mummy and Daddy had driven them into the fire, and now they were going to be burned up. The knowledge drove his childishness down; he stood there on the back seat, stark as a fact. "You should have gone back."

"It's all right," she said. "We are going back to town. We are not going to be caught. We'll get a drink and another popsicle. You'll see." She did not believe herself.

"I hate popsicles," cried Oliver.

"Are you a little boy?" she said.

They entered the tunnel with flames on both sides without seeing the end. When they got to the worst part the heat touched the car again. Althea wondered how combustible cars were. Did the frames crack open like chestnuts, spewing their fluffy white insides?

"That was the worst of it," said Ken.

The fire was below them but it was fifty feet away now, a hundred. No cars approached them from Belgodere.

"They must have closed the road again."

"Barn door after the horse," said Althea. The fire had

scourged this hillside since they had passed; its traces were toppled trunks and smoking roots. Althea remembered a line from a novel: "Fire doesn't burn clean."

"Deux bières, trois pollos," said Ken.

"Oui, Messieursdames," said the waiter as if it were an ordinary day.

Along the roadway the local men had watched their return without expression. An Englishman had leaned from his car in front of the blockade.

"Can we drive down there?"

"No, no, it's all in flames!"

But the Corsicans standing at the side of the road had laughed. "It's not so bad," one said in English. "Go on, drive through." And the Englishman drove through.

All this had happened and was still happening in front of them. It made no sense. Althea and Ken sipped Kronenberg. The children giggled. They had found a steep path behind the square; they climbed it and ran down to the café and Althea's arms. Their faces were streaked with tears and dirt and popsicle. Now Althea thought it was lucky they had Sammy after all; he distracted Kate and Oliver.

The sunlight began to fade and the heat to lessen. The sound of airplanes came and went overhead, and the gendarmes held up walkie-talkies, spraying their distorted voices. It was time to eat, and the restaurant served no food. Ken engaged the waitress in conversation. The fire had hit Belgodere badly last year, but this time they had nothing to fear.

"It's worse this year," he said, "out of control."

"No, no," she said. "It's always the same."

"Then don't the fires discourage the tourists?" he said.

"Mais non, Monsieur. Ce n'est pas les mêmes touristes."

Althea was still shaking. She heard one man describe

them as Germans. She kept her face to the road, her back to the people. She concentrated on the image of Belgodere as she had first seen it, high on that outcropping of rock. The idea of the rock calmed her. The fire could not reach over it. Not in the villages, *jamais les villages*. They might survive after all. But only if they stayed here. Belgodere had become safety. They must not go on.

They ordered more beer.

Ken grew restless. He thought of telephoning Madame Pianelli, who had the only phone in Vegno. It was something to do. In five minutes he returned. Wonder of wonders, in France, where the telephones never worked, with acres of burning bush and trees and the island in an uproar, his call had gone through. But the message was not so reassuring. The fire had surrounded the village, the women and the children were in the church and the men fighting the fire. No help had come. He told her they had Sammy. She said not to try to come back.

They sat watching the children play.

"We must make a friend," said Althea.

A new waitress came. Ken smiled at her. He was a good-looking man, charming. He spoke excellent French. "Is there any place we can stay in this town?" he said. "We can't go home. Our village is surrounded by fire."

She looked blank.

"Any hotel? A pension?"

"*Non,*" she said.

"Does anyone rent rooms? Just one room?"

"*Non,*" she repeated, clearing the beer glasses.

The children began to stray from the square to the other side of the road. Ken followed them. The cars were still streaming down to Calvi. But what would they meet on the road? Who was to say if the fires were there? Danger was on the roads, safety was staying in one place. Althea examined

the inside room of the café. They served no food at all. Even
if they had no dinner and slept in the car, she would stay in
Belgodere.

Ken struck up a conversation with a group of local
women. He described clouds of smoke with his hands. He
gestured to the children, three of them, and no place to go.
He pointed out Sammy. Not even our child. Good old Ken,
pulling out all the stops. The women looked unaffected.
After trying the third, Ken crossed back to Althea.

"You've gotta come over," he said. "I think one of them
is weakening. There's something different about her."

On the other side of the road she picked up Kate and held
her in her arms. It steadied them both. Three of the women
folded their arms in front of their breasts. The fourth in-
spected Althea closely.

"Here is my wife," said Ken in French.

"You should not have left your village, that was your
mistake," said the woman who watched so closely. She was
stern, and strong. But she was not unkind.

"I telephoned. They said don't come back. It is surrounded by fire. There are no *pompiers.*"

The woman considered.

"We have an empty top floor in our house," she said
carefully. "But the house is not mine. It belongs to my
father." She assessed them another long moment. Her eyes
lingered on the three little children. "I will go and ask him."

Again the other women began to complain loudly. But the
kinder one, who had some status in the village, Althea decided, who seemed even to come from a century closer to their
own than to the village's, climbed up a curving set of stairs
leading into the narrow rows of houses, and disappeared.

Althea turned to the boys. They had invented a dangerous
game, jumping from the wall. She rounded them up, and

crouched down on the dry grass. She picked up a thistle. "Find me one that looks like this," she said. Their hands dug into the spiked blades. The dirt on their faces was streaked over a blank, as if the hours before had made no impression but rather had removed memory.

"Are we going home?" said Oliver.

"We can't go home. The fire is all around our village."

Sammy began to cry again. This time he hit her shoulder. "You took me away from my Mummy and Daddy. Now they're all burned up."

The woman returned.

"It will be fine," she said, in her measured way. "Come now and follow me." And there before the eyes of the sceptical men in the cafe and the disapproving women on the steps Ken, Althea, Kate, Oliver and Sammy mounted the steps into the heart of the ancient stone town.

The old man was short and thick and erect. The woman, his wife, stood opposite him in a formal way inside the door of their home. It was like the others, patched and grey outside, but the sitting-room was modern; a television sat on a shelf between silky cushions. In the kitchen were blue tiles and a row of books, gleaming bowls and a stainless-steel coffee-pot.

They entered dazed. It was as if they'd been under a spell of the past, and woke to find all objects amazing, comforts once available but lost, retrieved now for a new present. The woman offered food and drink. A younger woman, her daughter, came from rooms behind, and everyone began to speak. Identities were brought out, like fresh clothes.

Was Ken a reporter? What were the ages, the names of the children? Someone washed the black smudges from their hands and faces. Althea was filled with wonder. There was Ken across the table, ruddy, his glass of cold water in a circle of his hands, and the three little ones solemn as eggs, quite safe and whole. That which had been ordinary, even oppressive in the morning was, as dusk fell, brilliant.

And Althea, did she work? It was a strange, deliberate question, rarely asked that directly.

"I raise money," she said, finding a few stray French words in her mind. "For women's groups."

"*Mais vous êtes bien tombée!*" pronounced the younger woman. She herself worked with battered women. Had Althea too done something for this cause?

Yes, there was a hostel. Once Althea helped organize a benefit . . .

A hostel? But she worked in such a hostel, in Paris. There was very good research being done in Canada, did Althea know this? By a woman sociologist?

Yes, Althea did know. The sociologist was her friend, yes, Althea knew who was meant. How strange, how marvellous, the same name should now be on both their lips.

Althea shook her head, and blinked, and bit into the glass. It would have been the expected thing to say that she could not believe their luck at the end of this terrible day, etcetera. But she could believe it. More than that, she expected it. It was what she always expected, the recognition of people, their kindness. To find herself at home in the world. The hard thing to believe was that the rest of the day they had been strangers and lost. She wondered if the women knew that in Belgodere in the sixteenth century women had the vote. What had they done with it? How had they lost it? But it was too difficult to find the words.

The top floor had a little balcony looking over the rooftops and down the mountainside. It was not quite dark. The wind had at last dropped. In the air was the drone of airplanes, the Canadairs, presumably, carrying water from the sea. Ken was on the staircase, talking to a brother of the family. The brother had been out fighting the fires. He said the "criminals" were what you called a mafia, and that the *pompiers* had not gone to Vegno because the mayor of Vegno had not paid the protection money. The brother said it was madness, and it happened every year.

From the tiny railed balcony at the top of the old house the three children looked down the mountain. There were places where the fire still glowed, marking the slopes with rings like the scars of a hidden disease. See? And see? they said to each other. Oliver stood between the other two. They were dark, silhouetted against the lucent sky. They would inherit a wasted landscape. With their thin bare legs and frail arms they looked like three tiny old people, but they were barely on their way to being grown up. Althea felt as if she herself were the agent of time, she had aged them with the terrible fires of her middle years. But this was absurd, it was a case of inflated responsibility, like Oliver's.

Ken sat on the edge of the bed. Inspecting his leg, he found a gash on his shin. It was a two-inch gash, purple, caked with blood. "I stepped in a hole," he said, "running through the cellar." He regarded it with wonder, something he got a long time ago. Althea went to him.

"Have you hurt yourself?" she said, putting out her hand to touch the place.